THE THINGS WE NEVER KNEW

MEGAN MAYFAIR

Copyright © 2020 by Megan Mayfair

All rights reserved.

No part of this book may be reproduced in any form or by any electronic or mechanical means, including information storage and retrieval systems, without written permission from the author, except for the use of brief quotations in a book review. This is a work of fiction. Names, characters, and incidents are used fictitiously.

For Michael

THE THINGS WE NEVER KNEW

CHAPTER 1

*G*lancing up at the crest of the university, sitting smugly against the brick wall of the office, Michelle's stomach turned over.

She knew what was coming. It shouldn't be a surprise after the last few years, but even so, today felt like a foregone conclusion.

Maybe there was a small glimmer of hope that one day she would have a nice piece of paper with the university's logo on it, but that seemed like a distant possibility now, especially after everything that had happened.

Did she care?

Her brother Pete lined up his iPad and phone on the table in front of him with perfect precision. His attention turned to her, a worried look on his face. "Have you gone over the transcript? And the notes we made?" He was always one for notes, records, and paperwork.

She shrugged, but as his eyes narrowed in a concerned, overprotective brotherly way, she nodded and rummaged in her bag, producing the crumpled papers. She placed them on the table in front of her and smoothed them with the palm of her hand. She wasn't sure how much they would help.

Her transcript was not exactly pleasant reading.

"Michelle Fitzgerald?" A man with greying temples and a dull suit entered the room, a file perched under his arm.

"Yes," she said.

Her brother hissed, "Stand up." He was already on his feet.

Following his lead, she scrambled to stand. "Do you want me to curtsy, too?" she whispered back. "Doff my cap, gov?"

He scowled. "Don't be ridiculous."

"This whole process is ridiculous," she muttered.

"And you are?" the man asked Pete.

"I'm Dr Pete Fitzgerald. I'm Michelle's brother, and I'm here to be her advocate."

She watched as her brother and the dull-suited man leaned over and shook hands. Advocate? She didn't need an advocate—it made her sound helpless—but the family had insisted, so Pete had taken annual leave to be there to support her so she'd gone along with it. And with a PhD to his name, nobody in the family knew academic-speak like Pete did.

"Yes, that's fine. We'll wait for my colleagues and we'll begin the process." The man nodded to Michelle and sat down. He unbuttoned his jacket, the colour of which reminded her of the colour of water that was left in the bucket after washing the car.

Michelle and Pete also sat, and she tilted her head to the roof. She wanted this over with. She knew what the outcome was. Why couldn't they have just sent her a text message or an email about this? Maybe a gif. *'Hey girl, you stuffed up!'* sort of thing. That would tell her what she needed to know and would save her from this overly formal 'hearing' in the university's offices.

The door flew open, and in shuffled an older man who nodded at her and took a seat next to the man in the dull suit. On closer inspection, both their suits almost seemed the same colour. Coincidence, or standard issue?

A woman walked in next with a severe bob haircut and a black knitted dress. It was chunky, and far too big for her. She was all hair and scarves and wild earrings, and her over-rouged red cheeks added to her overall flustered appearance. She also took her place on the panel, letting a pile of papers fall onto the table in front of her.

This was the panel of people that was going to determine Michelle's fate? It seemed depressing that this was what her life had come to. She was being judged by a woman with a smear of lipstick on her teeth, and two men in ill-fitting suits?

There was no glamour, that was for sure. Michelle picked up her transcript and fanned herself with it. The room was stuffy and oppressive in a physical sense, but also in a less tangible way.

The sound of shuffling pages and the clearing of throats cut through the air as the proceedings begun. She listened as the woman recited her academic transcript, which consisted of the odd pass (that would be the highlights) but mostly fails and withdrawn units.

Pete had a copy of the transcript in front of him on his iPad and was ticking off each unit with his finger as the woman spoke to ensure no passes had been left out.

He was a good advocate. Michelle couldn't fault him for his dedication, and she felt guilty for being such a rubbish case for him to defend.

The discussion commenced. It was sort of surreal, having three complete strangers pick over her academic performance and commitment to study. But it was real.

Painfully real as the failures were noted and discussed with vigour.

"And the exchange program in Canada, Michelle?" the woman asked, the fire-engine red lipstick still spotted on her front teeth.

"Err, yes?" Michelle scrambled to sit up straight.

The woman tapped a pen on the table. "A disappointing year in terms of academic performance. You didn't pass one unit while you were there." She narrowed her eyes.

"No, I didn't. I tried really hard, but I couldn't concentrate." On study, at least. She shifted uncomfortably as she thought of Ashton. She'd not had any trouble focusing on him.

"Since she's returned, she's refocused on her studies," Pete said. "Michelle has committed to a regular study pattern and has worked very hard to bring up her GPA with subjects over the summer."

Oh yes. The subjects she'd done over summer, which she was unlikely to pass.

And her GPA? It was low. Seriously low. Oh, Pete. His eternal optimism usually grated on her, but now she harboured a pang of sympathy for him. He was so diligently fighting a lost cause, like an inspirational football captain rallying their team when they were ten goals down with six minutes to go and the supporters were starting to pack up and leave.

"Is this true?" The tone of the woman was sharp and matched her eyebrows, which were now fiercely arched. "Your marks for ACC20002 are very low. We're still awaiting the exam results, but it doesn't look like you'll pass without an excellent mark in the test."

"I've tried," she admitted. It was so hard to concentrate when Ashton kept popping into her head and turning the words on her computer screen to mush.

But she hadn't tried hard enough. Her grades were still awful. Assignments were still not handed in. Tutorials not attended. And that exam they were waiting on? She'd be lucky to string together twenty marks out of one hundred. She'd sat in that test and for a good ten minutes, she'd wondered if she'd accidentally wandered into the wrong exam, as nothing on the page made any sense to her at all.

"Hmmm." The woman ran a finger down a page as she made her doubtful noises. Her lips pursed, as no doubt she noted the scores dwindling. "I feel we have enough information to make a decision. We will take a moment to confer," the woman said, looking up.

"Of course," Pete said, and gestured for Michelle to stand.

They walked outside and Michelle leaned against a wall. She could use a drink now, a lovely, crisp, refreshing Canadian beer like Ashton used to order for her when they'd settle in front of the fire in the ski lodges after a day on the slopes.

"I'm not sure how long they'll take." Her brother inspected his watch.

"Why are you so good at school and I'm so rubbish?" she asked.

He rubbed his chin as if perplexed by the idea. "I don't know. I guess I found my passion."

Chemistry and medical sciences certainly weren't a passion for her. Too many calculations and things to remember. "Lucky you," she sighed. What was her passion? It certainly hadn't been the business degree she'd been studying.

Skiing? Clothes? Men she shouldn't have been dating? She could hardly make a career out of that.

"You'll be right. You're smart."

"Not smart enough." She rubbed her temples. "They're going to throw me out."

"You don't know that, but if they do, you'll figure something out."

The optimism now was not only annoying it also felt misplaced, as if he was lying to her.

She really had no idea what she'd do if she weren't studying. Not that she spent a lot of time actually studying, but being a student was her job. What could she do if she didn't have that?

"Mum and Dad will kill me," she told him with a groan.

"I'll make sure they don't."

They'd invested money in her. She chewed her lip before pausing. She didn't want to end up with lipstick over her teeth like the woman inside had. Yet, the thoughts remained. All that money she'd wasted while she was in Canada … and for what point? A broken heart and a ruined future. Her parents worked hard, very hard to finance her trip, and she'd just partied through it.

"Michelle?"

She looked up as her name was called, and they filed back into the room, and as quickly as they sat down, it was over. She couldn't follow everything that was said, but awful-sounding words and phrases peppered the dialogue. *'Disappointing'*, *'unfulfilled potential'* and *'failed'* stuck with her. But they were enough. She knew it wasn't good.

Suddenly, there were no distractions. No inner commentary on the clothing of those judging her. No thoughts of anything but a whistling noise that ran through her brain as they told her it was better for her to seek "opportunities elsewhere."

Unable to speak clearly, she mumbled something as the room emptied, leaving her alone with her brother.

"I'm sorry." Pete placed a hand on her shoulder. "You'll have other options."

She nodded glumly, but she knew it was her brother's extreme positivity at work. She had no other options. Besides, the only option she wanted was Ashton.

And that simply wasn't going to happen.

CHAPTER 2

Bebe walked into the National Gallery of Victoria, perched her sunglasses on the top of her head and scanned the foyer for an attendant.

Finding a woman in a grey uniform, she asked if Petra Baranov was available.

The woman gave her the once over, her gaze lingering on Bebe's vintage, purple Doc Marten shoes tied with polka dot laces. She looked up. "And you are?"

"I'm her daughter."

The woman brought a hand to her chest. "What a talent your mother is. We are so lucky she was available to curate the Picasso exhibition. There are few people who understand his work like your mother does."

"Yes. She's an expert." Bebe hesitated. She wasn't in the mood for a long conversation about her mother's curation skills. "May I see her, please?"

"This way." The woman beckoned, and walked towards a door.

Bebe followed, taking in the gallery space, and paused to

run her hand along a glass panel that encased a stunning water feature.

She'd been born in Melbourne, yet had never been to this gallery. She'd not been many places at all in her hometown, and had spent the morning exploring various monuments and buildings in an attempt to immerse herself in her own history.

The attendant cleared her throat as they walked through to an exhibition space.

Bebe caught her mother's eye, who blew her a kiss and immediately turned back to a pair of black-clad assistants, who were supervising the unpacking of a painting.

Ouch. Bebe rubbed her temple to dull her headache. She was still jet-lagged after her flight from London a week earlier. She'd swallowed a couple of aspirin tablets on the tram on the way to the gallery, and was looking forward to sitting down and resting.

"A little to the right." Her mother's voice echoed against the empty walls as she directed two men who were attempting to hang a painting in the exact spot she wished.

They placed it where she had requested and looked back at her.

"Well?" one asked.

Petra exhaled and placed her hands on her narrow hips. "I'm not sure."

"Me neither," said one of the black-clad assistants.

"Or me." The other assistant clearly didn't want to be outdone.

Bebe removed her phone from her bag. This could take a while.

Her mother clasped her hands in a prayer-like position against her lips and stared at the painting.

Yes. This could definitely take a while.

There was a familiar look in her mother's eyes—a laser-like focus that meant her mind was on her art and her art alone. Not that it was *her* art. She hadn't painted or drawn the works in the frames, yet she treated her arrangement of them as if she had created them. She could pull paintings and art together in a way that told a story of its own. Sometimes a bold narrative to make a point, sometimes a subtle story to allow the viewer to immerse themselves in the art, but it was always an arrangement that would take a lot of time and concentration to perfect.

Best to leave her to it.

Bebe checked her email and bit her lip as she opened up a new message from the Director of the L'Or Master Class in New York, reminding her of her upcoming enrolment and course information.

A shiver of anticipation hurtled through her body. She'd applied three times for this class and finally, it would be happening in two months, three days and…she checked her watch…four hours.

She traced a finger over the flourish of L'Or logo with pure joy. Just about every graduate of the Master Class found themselves a place at one of the world's cutting-edge fashion houses. All that hard work was finally going to pay off.

Moving from her email, she opened her Instagram feed. She hit search and found an account she dared not follow, but regularly looked at.

Michelle Fitzgerald. Otherwise known as Shell_Fitz27.

There wasn't much new to see. Michelle was back in Australia too after spending time in Canada. It appeared she had been on some sort of student exchange at a university. There'd been lots of photos of Michelle on ski fields and in bars holding Canadian beer bottles, one of a university campus, but mostly of parties and gatherings.

Michelle was a party girl and perhaps not the best

student, but Bebe couldn't help but like her. She had since the moment she'd started searching for the Fitzgeralds.

Bebe was closer in age to Lauren, the fourth child in the large Fitzgerald clan, yet Lauren was a closed book—all her accounts were set to private and she gave precious little detail. Her profile picture was a cartoon drawing of a cupcake.

Michelle, on the other hand, she hid nothing. No matter how embarrassing or private, she shared what she had for breakfast, her outfit of the day and arguments with her phone company.

In the series of endless photos, posts, shares, and videos, she had, unwittingly, shared her entire life with Bebe.

"To the left!" Her mother's voice boomed around the room.

Bebe flinched and looked up.

She wasn't the only one startled. The two men rushed towards the painting and lifted it.

"No, no, no! More!" The directions rattled around the deserted gallery, echoing against the parquetry flooring and largely empty walls.

Bebe glanced around her surroundings. As much as she enjoyed the final exhibition, she loved to see the space before it was filled with paintings, sculptures, textiles and etchings. The space had to be blank enough for the pieces to shine but still have character and charm to make the visitor feel welcome.

This space achieved that, she decided, before returning to her phone—specifically to Michelle's feed. The girl-next-door with the chestnut hair and wicked grin hadn't posted much since she'd been back in Australia, but it didn't appear she'd been back for that long. Maybe a few months?

Photos from late the year before had shown Michelle hanging out in bars in Canada with a dark-haired, good-looking guy that Bebe had discovered to be Ashton James, the playboy, hard-partying son of a wealthy family who dabbled in business and politics. The 'Canadian Kennedy' as he'd been dubbed by the press had been a firm fixture on Michelle's feed until any new photos of him dried up a few months earlier.

Did the departure of Ashton from her photos have anything to do with her returning home to Australia?

Whatever had caused her to come back, it had strangely seemed right.

After all, it had been the reason Bebe had started to check into her account. Never following her. That would be weird. But just checking. Looking. Watching. Gaining a sense of what her life was like.

A life Bebe could have had? Perhaps.

Not that it was a life she pined over, but Michelle's life was so completely different from her own that it had been strange and exotic in a steady, stable, structured sort of way.

She hovered over the photo of Michelle and her parents. She focused on it, meditated on it, as she often did, trying to imagine everything about them. Social media was so brilliant for stalking, and it certainly made it easy when people were as open and shared as much as Michelle did. Sometimes she posted two or three times a day, and over the last few years, Bebe had watched the photos carefully, piecing together so much of the Fitzgeralds' lives—birthdays, holidays, family events…

She brought the phone closer to her nose. They looked so happy, and as usual, it set off a deep sense of longing in the pit of her stomach. She hated that feeling. Why did she have these strange pangs of jealousy when she had such an enviable life?

"Bebe?" Her mother's crisp tone caused her to fumble her phone.

"Yes?"

Her mother gestured at the painting and folded her arms. She raised an eyebrow as if seeking her daughter's guidance.

Bebe was lost in the whirl of cool, blue tones and Pablo Picasso's angular brush strokes. She turned her attention to the weary men in overalls, one of whom was wiping his brow with a handkerchief and the other one had his hands on his hips.

She disliked adding to their workload, yet it didn't look quite right. Squinting her eyes, she assessed it and finally knew what was wrong. "It's too high."

Her mother was tall, as was she, but sometimes forgot the more vertically challenged of art patrons. To appreciate the painting, it needed to be at the perfect level, and a millimetre could ruin the entire viewing experience.

It was much like fashion. Get a measurement wrong, even by a few inches, and a gown could go from red-carpet to potato sack in the blink of an eye.

Her mother frowned and glanced back at the painting, nodding. "Agree. Move it lower."

One workman sighed, and the other stuffed his handkerchief back into his pocket before starting the task again.

Bebe flicked some strands of her blonde hair from her face and turned back to her phone and Michelle's feed.

Was it cosmic that Michelle should be back in Melbourne at the same time she was here, awaiting her visa to be finalised and L'Or to commence?

She placed the phone back in her bag and looked again at the painting as her mother carefully supervised the repositioning.

If it was fate that both be here now, perhaps it was time to finally answer those burning questions that had haunted her for most of her life.

CHAPTER 3

The worst part of the day hadn't even started. Michelle closed Pete's car door behind her and followed him up the garden path. Her stomach churned, causing a wave of nausea to rise into her throat. Could she take ill?

There was little point. It would only extend the misery.

Pete gave her a hopeful look as they approached and stood on the stoop. "You'll be right," he said as he unlocked the door.

"What will they say? I'll never hear the end of it from Mum."

"They'll understand."

Was he talking about someone else's parents? Calm, reassuring parents who never interfered or offered unwanted opinions? Perhaps those parents could also do her laundry for her.

There was no way *their* mum and dad would understand.

The Fitzgeralds were all about hard work and solid foundations—the exact opposite of what she'd been building the past few years.

"Please say nice things at my funeral," she begged her brother. "Ask Clare to do my eulogy. She'll put a positive spin on my life." Her sister-in-law had a lovely Pollyanna quality to her that was perfect for glossing over any sort of dodgy moments of Michelle's life.

He scoffed and opened the door. "It'll be fine."

Mum was in the hallway, arms crossed, a red and white chequered tea towel flung over her shoulder. "Well?"

Michelle looked to her brother. He placed his hand on Michelle's shoulder. "The academic board decided it was best for Michelle to start somewhere new."

"She got kicked out?" Lauren appeared and bit into a shiny, red apple.

Michelle stared at her sister. What was she doing here, casually eating fruit? She was certain she'd be on shift today at the hospital.

"Kicked out?" Another voice echoed from the hallway. Luke? Why was everyone here? Didn't they have anything better to do with their lives than hang out in their childhood home? "You're kidding me. I thought they just wanted to scare you with all that academic woo-woo stuff," he added, with a low, incredulous whistle.

"Yes. Kicked out," Michelle muttered and walked through to the living room, leaving Pete, her mother, and Lauren whispering, punctuated by the crunching of Lauren's apple.

"I can HEAR you!" she called back to the hallway.

Marching into the kitchen, she flung open the fridge and started looking for a block of cheese. That was what she needed now, along with an enormous, novelty-glass-size serving of wine that might render her unconscious and in sweet oblivion regarding how pathetic her life was right now.

Removing the cheddar and closing the door behind her, she found her Mum standing in the kitchen. She looked down at the block of cheese in her hand. "I'm sorry," she whispered, her eyes meeting her mother's.

Mum sighed, took the cheddar and placed it on a chopping board on the bench. She expertly cut a couple of perfectly even slices, retrieved a barrel of crackers from the pantry, and laid some on a plate.

She handed it to Michelle.

"What do you think Dad will say?" Michelle looked at the snack. It was her go-to comfort snack ever since she'd been a small child.

"We'll talk about it at dinner." And with that, her mother swept from the kitchen, the red and white tea towel flying behind her.

Michelle chewed glumly. If she'd been judged today by the dull brigade, now it was time to be sentenced by the Fitzgeralds.

It was like having dinner in a parallel universe or watching a play about her life. A really bad play where it was clear the characters were in for a bumpy ride, but there was nothing that could be done other than keep watching the inevitable train wreck that was about to follow in the second act.

"She could help with the business," her brother Steve suggested through a mouthful of chicken.

She? She was right here, crammed around the wooden family dining table with her parents, siblings and their partners and kids. Why were they talking about her like she was the cat or still in another country?

She picked at her meal, shuffling peas from one edge of the plate to another, and then back again.

"Doing what?" Mum demanded. "She's not a qualified plumber."

Exactly. Excellent point. The problem was she wasn't qualified to do anything. She did have some sort of certificate that meant she could teach skiing to rich children whose parents sent them to ski school in Canada, but that was hardly going to be in demand at the start of autumn in Australia. There would be some snowfall come winter, but ski slopes were small and offered fewer employment opportunities than in Canada.

"She could be an apprentice," Steve's wife Heather suggested, draining her glass of wine. "Help Steve out a bit during the busy times and learn a trade. That would be good for her future."

A plumbing apprentice was definitely not high on *her* list. Unclogging toilets and bathplug holes filled with other people's hair? No, thank you.

"Yeah, it'd be great." Steve leaned back, his hands resting on his stomach. He looked pleased with himself, like he'd solved a complex problem.

"Would you like to work with your brother, Michelle?" Mum asked, as if this was the most exciting and tempting opportunity, like being cast in a James Bond movie, or being whisked away on a private jet to inspect five-star properties in the Maldives.

It was as far from any of that as humanly possible. The offer was essentially to embark on a long and exhausting apprenticeship in an area she had no interest in, and in the meantime, be her brother's cheap labour so he could take on more clients and make more cash for his wife to spend on manicures and expensive trinkets like charm bracelets and designer sunglasses.

"It's just not me." Michelle examined Heather's charm bracelet, already heaving under gold love hearts and four-leaf clovers.

"Well, what *is* you? Clearly, your business degree wasn't

you." Mum gritted her teeth and took a deep breath, as if she were trying to stay calm.

"I don't know. I think I need some time to figure that out."

"How much time? You left school years ago," Luke said.

Oh, Luke: subtle as a sledgehammer.

"I can put in a good word and see if I can get you some hours at the hospital," Lauren suggested, leaning forward.

"Oh!" Mum said. "That's a good idea. Reception, perhaps?"

"No. You need to be a medical secretary for that, and she doesn't have any qualifications." Her sister shook her head. "I was thinking maybe in the canteen or the car park or something like that."

"That's nice of you," Dad said to Lauren before turning back to Michelle. "Would going into some sort of medical administration be of interest to you? I'm sure you could do a TAFE course for that. You're very organised."

That was a blatant and ridiculous lie. She was always losing her keys and forgetting dentist appointments, and she missed the cut-off date to lodge her taxes regularly. Imagine if she lost someone's medical records, or, heaven forbid, got them mixed up with another patient's files? She shouldn't be allowed anywhere near such sensitive materials. Especially not when it came to people's health and surgical procedures.

"She should get an apprenticeship," Heather said loudly while pouring another glass of wine, her bracelet clanging against the bottle. She was clearly unwilling to let the idea of the cheap plumbing labour for her husband's business go. Must have been all that daydreaming about some new car with the heated seats and tinted windows to show off to all the yuppie school mums at drop off. "It'd be better for her long-term options." She turned back to her meal, as if aware of how self-serving her suggestion truly was.

"But a medical secretary"—Luke rubbed his chin—"that's a good, solid option. People are always going to need to go to hospital. You remove the risk if the economy flattens out."

"People are always going to need drains and showers, too, no matter their financial situation," Heather countered.

Michelle didn't really think either of them knew anything about economics, and certainly nowhere near enough for her to base her next move on their flimsy advice.

"I know people need plumbing, but look at her! She's not very strong." Luke crinkled his nose. "You have to be fit for that sort of manual labour."

"She'd get fit," Steve said, helping himself to the last piece of roast chicken from the platter in the middle of the table. "All that lifting and moving stuff about. She'd be in great shape in a few weeks."

Michelle buried her head in her hands as everyone squabbled over her future, the economy, and her fitness levels.

Clare cleared her throat, and everyone, including Michelle, turned to look at her.

"Perhaps Michelle's right. Maybe she does need some time to think about her options," Clare said quietly, before turning red. "This only happened today. These things take time to sink in."

"That's true." Pete bounced his baby, Timothy on his knee. "Things tend to work themselves out. We're not going to sort it out over dinner. On another note, Mum, any chance of dessert?"

"Oh! I did make a trifle." Mum stood and hurried into the kitchen to retrieve a sweet reward for the son with excellent qualifications, long-term career prospects, a stable marriage, and an adorable, cherub-like grandbaby.

Michelle had never liked trifle with the strange

combination of fruit, custard, cake and cream, but right now, she was delighted to hear her mother had constructed one. *"Thanks,"* she mouthed at her brother—the golden child. At least he used his powers for good in helping her out—the screw-up of the family.

She leaned over and held Timothy's chubby little hand as he gave her a gummy, wet smile. He was a cute baby—all cheeks and big eyes and tufts of dark hair. He let out a sudden shriek of delight, and Michelle couldn't help but smile at him.

His pure childhood innocence was a nice reprieve from the reality of her terrible 'adulting'.

Following the trifle, and a minor squabble about fantasy football teams that further took the focus from her woes, Michelle escaped to the kitchen with Clare.

"I'm sorry," Clare said as they loaded the dishwasher.

"It's okay." Michelle gave a weak smile. "I brought it on myself. I've not paid any attention and Canada was …" She couldn't find a good way to end that sentence. A disaster? That didn't really capture it.

Clare nodded knowingly. "I know that none of those jobs that everyone mentioned tonight were a good fit for you." She paused and furrowed her brow, as if trying to think of the right words. "I meant what I said. Now isn't the time to rush into anything."

"Like a plumbing apprenticeship?"

Clare gave a small smile. "Perhaps not, and I don't want to confuse you any further, but I do have an idea if you're interested."

Michelle nodded. It couldn't be any worse than any of the other ideas, and this sister-in-law wasn't as self-serving as Heather. "Why not?"

"I was talking to Tessa yesterday, and she's looking for

some help at Espresso Walk. You know her café that's not far from that big apartment complex Steve is working on."

"Yeah." Michelle remembered Clare's friend Tessa. Her café, Espresso Walk, was cool. Michelle had been there with Pete and Clare. Not only was it situated in a trendy street nestled amongst funky converted warehouses that were now airy studio apartments and eclectic design spaces, but the coffee was awesome and the food was always on point.

"You've done some waitressing, right?"

"A little." Taking orders wasn't necessarily her best attribute, but her customer service skills were passable. At a pinch.

"I thought it might be a good place to work for a little while and take some time to figure out what you'd like to do next. I'd be happy to put in a good word for you." Clare smiled.

"That would be awesome." It would get her family off her back, it would be cash in her bank account, which could fund further trips, and it would be a pretty cool place to hang out in the meantime.

And it was certainly more appealing than unclogging toilets or directing cars at the hospital.

"Thank you. It's a wonderful idea. I really appreciate it."

"Clare!" Pete hollered from the living room. "Timothy's thrown up."

"I'd better go and help sort that out. I'll speak to Tessa for you," Clare promised and left, calling out to Pete that she was on her way.

Michelle slipped back to her room. She usually didn't mind the noise and chaos of her family. After all, being the youngest, she'd lived with it her entire life. Tonight, however, she wanted to be by herself to mope about and flick through fashion magazines while snuggled in the pink, fluffy blanket that lay on top of her bed.

She gazed at the collage on her wall of all the cut-out pictures and maps of places she wanted to visit one day. Miami. New York. Buenos Aires. Madrid. Stockholm.

It used to inspire her. Now it depressed her. She didn't have the cash to get to Brisbane, let alone Beijing.

She picked up her phone to message Pete and Clare to thank them for their support. She opened her messenger app, but as she did, she found herself searching for Ashton. She hadn't intended to, but it was a bit like muscle memory. Her fingers typed his name without her brain even realising it until she was at the 't'.

He was there. Online. A little dot next to his name indicated he was using the app. It was early in Vancouver. What was he doing online at this hour? He usually slept in until at least eleven if he could.

Maybe he was doing something for his father's business, or his mother's campaign. It surely wasn't too far away until their election now—not that she paid much attention to elections she was required to vote in, let alone in Canada.

No wonder he'd dumped her. She wasn't exactly the brightest spark in the room, and especially not in the rooms he circulated in.

Hovering her finger over his photo, her heart ached as she considered sending him a message. But it was no good. It was over. The messages she'd sent him had fallen on deaf ears. He'd made it very clear that he didn't want her, and who could blame him?

She closed the app, stuffed her phone under her pillow, and picked up a magazine from her bedside table to keep herself busy. Tomorrow would be better. She'd get over Ashton, she'd put her failures behind her and ignore the numbness that overtook her body and zapped all of her energy.

Tomorrow would be the day.

Michelle turned the page of the glossy magazine. Of course, it would be—she'd been telling herself that for months.

But, maybe tomorrow, it would finally be the truth.

CHAPTER 4

Bebe's eyes fluttered open. Blinking several times as she adjusted to the light streaming in through the gaps in the blinds, she looked around the room she had taken within the furnished apartment her mother had leased for the length of the exhibition.

The room, like the rest of the apartment, was elegant with gilded mirrors, highly polished floors and heavy wooden furniture. It might have been a little old-fashioned for Bebe's taste, but the bed was soft and the shower powerful.

They were her main two requirements to create a comfortable house.

She stretched her arms out and reached for her phone. Swiping a manicured finger across the screen, she entered her password and immediately began scrolling Instagram.

Given the fact she was upside down in the world, she was out of sync with her friends in Europe and the United States. While she slept it was daytime in the northern hemisphere, and her friends were getting on with their lives at the small studio where she used to work.

A knock sounded at her door.

"Come in," she called, placing her phone down on the bedside table.

"Bebe." Her mother's face appeared at the door. Her impeccable make-up and chic bob gave her an Anna Wintour-like appearance, and she was just as fiercely talented and creative as the legendary *Vogue* editor.

"Morning." Bebe sat up.

"Good morning, my darling. I need to leave early this morning, and I won't be home until late. I have a dinner tonight with sponsors ahead of the opening of the exhibition. My assistant is organising a grocery delivery today with some meals, so simply help yourself."

"Thanks. That would be great."

Her mother didn't eat very much. She only drank champagne and black coffee, and ate strawberries and almonds. Yet she had always provided Bebe with the most nutrient-laden, square meals over her entire life, cooked on the little stove of the apartment they'd lived in during their time in London, or fresh bread rolls crammed with the most succulent tomatoes and cheese purchased from the markets in Paris.

"My assistant will email you with all the upcoming events: the gala dinner, the opening night, the charity high tea." She waved a hand to indicate the large number of events. "You come to whatever you would like, but feel no obligation to attend. If you'd like to bring a friend, that would be fine."

Bebe didn't have any friends in Melbourne. Or in Australia, for that matter.

Cole at work was as close to a friend she had in town. Maybe she could see if he would like tickets. "I'll think about it," she said. "Good luck with today."

"Thank you, my darling."

"Mum?" Bebe hesitated.

"Yes?"

"While I'm in Melbourne, I'd like to visit Dad's grave." She swallowed. "I think it's important."

Her mother paused. "You would?"

"Yes, I would. Where is it?"

"He doesn't have one. He was cremated."

Bebe's heart sunk. She'd never known this. "What?"

"I said he was cremated."

"I heard you," she snapped, before taking a breath. "I'm sorry. I'm surprised you never mentioned this before."

Her mother blinked. "You never asked."

A little rush of anger rose up in Bebe's chest. She'd asked so many things about her father over the years—about his family, about his job, about his personality—and received little information in return. Did she have to ask about everything? Couldn't her mother ever volunteer some information? She pinched the bridge of her nose. "What happened to his ashes?"

Her mother paused. "I had them spread along the Great Ocean Road. That's where he liked to ride his motorbike, so I thought that's what he would like."

"Maybe we could go down that way one weekend. I hear it's beautiful there."

"I don't think I will have a weekend free before we leave for New York, but we'll see. I better go. Have a nice day." Her mother blew her a kiss, and closed the door behind her.

Bebe rolled back onto her side and snuggled into the soft linen sheets.

She was surprised she'd never known about the cremation, but she wasn't surprised at her mother's response. It had been the same whenever she'd asked about her father in the past. And she didn't hold out much hope for 'we'll see'—that usually meant no.

Bebe turned back to her Instagram feed. Amongst the

photos from her friends and influencers overseas, there was one of Michelle. A new photo. She brought the camera to her nose to inspect the picture only posted a minute earlier.

Michelle's long chestnut hair was tied into a messy bun and her bright hazel eyes sparkled with mischief, as they usually did. She was wearing a three-quarter-length black and white striped top with black trousers. There was a black apron over her shirt with a little logo embroidered on the top corner that Bebe couldn't make out. She was holding a large coffee cup and leaning against an aqua and chrome coffee machine.

I'm back to work, baby. If you want the best coffee in town, stop by Espresso Walk and I'll fuel your caffeine addictions xx.

Bebe glanced at the time. Most cafés opened early given they were catering to commuters and office workers. She clicked on the location tag. The streets weren't that familiar to her, yet she noted a main road that was near the studio she was freelancing at until she went to New York.

She stared at the ceiling. It was all too weird—Michelle being back at almost the exact same time, and now working in a café so close to the studio.

It really didn't look that far, she decided, as she re-examined the map. Certainly somewhere she could easily visit while at work, either via a walk or public transport, or even an Uber.

The word rang in her mind. Visit? Was she really thinking that she would go and see Michelle?

It was ridiculous. She flung back the covers to get ready to go to work. It was one thing to scroll through Michelle's social media and ponder her life, but another thing to move her stalking beyond the realm of cyberspace.

She wasn't sure of the exact lines in these situations, but that was definitely crossing one.

Material was strewn over her desk when Bebe walked into Earth & Fire's airy design studios.

Cole looked up, his arms full of fabric. "Sorry. It's a shambles, isn't it?" He grimaced.

"I didn't say that." She looked around the converted warehouse space at the polished concrete floors and beams and industrial lighting.

"Maybe not with your words."

"Not even with my thoughts. This place is impeccable."

While it was a popular studio, it certainly was nothing like the mayhem and chaos of the studio she'd worked at in London where she'd been one of dozens of designers working on hundreds of projects.

Despite only having worked here for two weeks, she'd already eased into a peaceful and collaborative working arrangement with Cole, who was in charge of the studio. He was such a calming force that his idea of a 'shambles' were a few rolls of fabric not put away and a couple of unwashed coffee cups in the sink in the small kitchenette at the back of the studio.

She needed Cole's order and Zen-like attitude today. Her mind had gone back and forth on the decision to go to Espresso Walk to sight Michelle in person to the point where it felt like a jumbled mess. It was hard to remember which decision she'd arrived at last.

As she'd walked to the studio from the tram, she'd decided a little visit wouldn't hurt. It wouldn't be like she'd talk to Michelle or anything. She just wanted to see this girl in person, this girl who had led a life so different from her own but one that could have been hers.

"Great news! Zoe was delighted with the gown!"

Zoe Diaz was the partner of a football player and had

needed a last-minute gown for some *very important* event. Bebe had worked overtime on it, drawing inspiration from a 1960s style she'd seen on exhibition in London to create the perfect fit for the glamourous Zoe. "That's wonderful."

"That dress will be all over Instagram and the papers. Everyone follows Zoe around here."

"Do they?" Bebe rubbed her temple. Another headache? It must still be the jet lag. She paused at her desk. That didn't seem possible. Jet lag didn't last weeks. But then again, she had pulled an all-nighter working on Zoe's gown earlier that week. Maybe she just needed more sleep.

She sat down and heaved a sigh.

"Do you need some tea?" Cole had teas for everything. He kept them in small silver tins in the kitchen, neatly labelled with their alleged powers written on the side. 'Energy!' one would say. 'Clarity!' another. And they all had exclamation points as if to reinforce, or perhaps warn, of their potency.

"I'm fine." She forced a smile. "I can't seem to shake this jet lag."

"You've been here for weeks. How are you sleeping?" He leaned against her desk.

"Not as well as I should." She didn't want to be prescribed tea. "I need a coffee." She stretched her arms. "A real caffeine hit. There's a place I saw on Instagram that looks good," she said, casually. "Espresso Walk?"

"That place is good. Jordan and I did brunch there last week. The waffles are amazing. I know I shouldn't be eating carbs, but the calories were worth it," he added, ruefully. "But it's a bit far for this morning."

Bebe's face fell. It had appeared quite close to the office on the map, but she'd clearly misjudged. "How far is it?"

"It's a twenty-minute walk at least." He inspected a silver wristwatch. "We have a meeting with Claudette in fifteen. Go over the road. They do a good espresso."

They did make delicious coffee at the café across the road, but it wasn't about the lattes.

She'd have to wait a little longer to see Michelle, or maybe it would give her time to come to her senses.

No good could come from this, surely, yet the need to sight her was becoming almost overwhelming.

CHAPTER 5

Michelle glanced at her phone and gave a fist pump as the comments and likes appeared on her post about working at Espresso Walk.

She'd made her manager, Harry take the photo at least ten times, and he'd rolled his eyes on the final three shots, but it had been worth it.

There was no way she couldn't chronicle the moment. She left so few gaps on her social media that not mentioning a new job would be considered weird.

So, she'd taken the cutest photo she could and put a positive spin on it. And no one in her circle needed to know anything other than she was back in Melbourne, loving life, wearing a chic little apron and making coffee in a trendy café. It was so random! Super fun! Heart emoji! #worklife

Oh, the mask of social media. How perfect everything could look when cropped to a cute square and a filter applied to it. She even had an app to make her face look thinner and remove any annoying blemishes that popped up when she indulged in too much fast food.

It was amazing the life she could curate and present to the world. And if the comments were anything to go by, her followers thought she looked adorable and the job sounded awesome.

Brilliant.

She pushed the phone back into her bag. Her break was over and there was certainly no time to worry about social media when she was working. The lunch rush had arrived and the light and airy café was crammed full of professionals with slick laptops knocking back espressos, and toned, fit-looking people in Lycra coming in from nearby group exercise classes to order protein-laden superfood snacks and smoothies.

Fixing her apron and washing her hands, she found Harry at the coffee machine.

"What do you want me to do?" She put her hands on her hips and looked around.

"Could you take the register again?" he asked.

"Of course." She walked to the register as a willowy girl with long, swinging blonde hair streaked with violet approached the counter and ordered a coffee.

"I like your scarf." Michelle loved everything about this girl's outfit, but the scarf was divine. It was black with lots of little icons embroidered onto it. Birds and bows and leaves. The shades of mauve on the scarf electrified the purple highlights in the woman's hair.

"Thank you."

Michelle couldn't place her accent. It was posh, clipped and elegant. Maybe a little British, but there was a tinge of German to it. Or was it Swiss? Whatever it was, she sounded glamorous, like a citizen of the world.

"Can I ask you where you got it from?" She deserved to splash out on some sort of trinket to congratulate herself on her new job. Though it was day one. She should perhaps make sure she could make it to a full fortnight before she started spending money she didn't have.

"Oh." The girl touched her neck. "I made it."

Michelle could sew a button on a shirt. Her mother had insisted all the kids knew the basics of self-survival, but making accessories and clothing far exceeded her abilities with a needle and thread.

"Did you want to have the coffee here or take it away?" Harry looked up from the coffee machine.

"I'll sit down."

"Great. Anywhere you like. I'll bring it out to you," Michelle said.

"Thanks." The girl walked to a table and sat down, removing a glittery sketchbook and a pencil from her handbag. The pencil flicked back and forth.

It was hard for her not to be in awe of people who could do creative things. Michelle couldn't draw or sing or act or play an instrument. She'd been sent off to old Mrs Hayes who'd lived on the next block for piano lessons, but she'd been so fidgety and badly behaved that she'd been sent home with Mrs Hayes telling her mother that Michelle was by far the 'worst' of the Fitzgerald kids. She still wasn't sure if being the 'worst' was a reflection of her behaviour, or a general lack of talent. Perhaps both.

She took the coffee Harry had made and slipped it onto the table where the girl was still sketching. "You're a lefty too."

"What?" the girl fumbled her pencil.

"You draw left-handed. So do I. Well, I can't draw well, but I write left-handed."

"Oh." The girl stared at the pencil in her hand, almost in confusion. "Yes, I'm left-handed."

"It can be a bit of a pain when you are writing in ink. I have to be careful not to smudge up birthday cards and things."

"That's true." She cleared her throat, and looked back to her sketching.

Michelle's eyes lingered on the scarf. "Do you sell those scarves online or at markets? It's gorgeous."

"I work in a studio nearby. We do sell some things in there, but we mainly do couture work."

"Really? Like wedding gowns?"

The girl took a small sip of her drink, leaving a smear of mauve lipstick on the glass. "Sometimes, but all sorts of gowns. You should come and have a look. It's called Earth and Fire."

"It sounds fancy. I doubt there will be much I can afford." She eyed the girl's perfectly tailored, black lace dress and cropped velvet blazer. The fabric, styling and stitching seemed far outside Michelle's usual price bracket. She'd bet Ashton could afford it. *Stop thinking about him!*

"I'm sure I can get you a staff discount."

"Really?" Michelle tilted her head, surprised at the girl's generosity. "That's so nice of you. I'm sorry, I don't even know your name."

The girl's cheeks flushed. "Bebe."

"Hi, Bebe. I'm Michelle."

Bebe coughed, and took another sip of her coffee.

"Are you okay?"

She cleared her throat. "Yes, thank you. I…I drank too quickly."

"That happens sometimes. Is your studio near here?"

"It's about a twenty-minute walk."

"I'll come down." Since Bebe offered, she should take a look. Besides, she did love beautiful clothes, even if she was unable to afford them.

It would be nice to have a little sneak peek and a touchpoint back to the glamorous life she'd briefly led in Canada before it abruptly ended, like she'd been living some sort of Cinderella story in reverse.

CHAPTER 6

Bebe drained the remaining coffee from the cup and escaped outside, leaving the money on the counter.

She hurried around the corner to a small, cobbled laneway, where she paused, taking in what had just happened.

Resting her head back against the graffiti-covered wall, she took a deep breath and rubbed her temple. Why had she done that? She'd gone to look at Michelle, see her in the flesh, and then what? She'd invited her to the studio and offered her discounts? No. That shouldn't have happened. This was insane. She had crossed the line.

What if her illusions about the Fitzgerald family were simply that, or even worse? What if they were true?

Did she think that somehow she'd be embraced into the fold of their family barbecues, Christmases and birthdays?

How foolish.

She took a deep breath. Hopefully, Michelle was simply being polite about the scarf and wouldn't bother to show up at the studio.

Bebe wouldn't come back here. She'd let the whole thing rest. It wasn't right. It could end up with a lot of people getting hurt, open up old wounds, or simply cause trouble.

Maybe it was time to accept her mother's version of events and call it a day.

"Are you okay?"

Bebe started at the sound of a man's voice. She looked up to find the blond barista from Espresso Walk. She'd noticed him when she'd been sitting in the café, with his wavy hair and dark-rimmed glasses. He was holding out a note and coins towards her. "You forgot your change."

"Keep it; that's fine."

He frowned. "You look a little pale. Can I get you a glass of water?"

She shook her head. "No, thank you, I'm fine. I'm a bit jet lagged, that's all."

"I'm Harry, by the way." He held out a hand.

"Yeah. I saw you inside the café." Despite being focussed on seeing Michelle, it hadn't been hard to notice her cute colleague and certainly up close, his broad shoulders, lean frame and defined jaw were even more attractive. "I'm Bebe." She shook his outstretched hand.

"That's a cool name. Where have you flown in from?"

"London."

"I love London. Are you here for work or a holiday?" he asked.

"I'm doing a short contract while I sort out a visa to go to New York. But I'm from here originally."

"Yeah?" He sounded confused. "I wouldn't have picked that with your accent."

"We moved when I was a baby. I've lived all over the world." Why was she telling him her life story?

"I've always wanted to go to New York," he said. "Bucket-list stuff for me."

"It's amazing. I'm attending a design Master Class there." For goodness sake. How many details did she need to tell him? Maybe she should just tell him about Michelle while she was at it.

"That's cool. I'd better get back inside. Lunch rush and all that." His feet remained firmly planted though, as if he were reluctant to move.

Perfect time to end the conversation before too much else tumbled out of her mouth. "Thanks for checking up on me."

"Anytime." He smiled and walked back towards the café. "Hope you get over the jet lag soon," he called back with another grin.

She rubbed the bridge of her nose. So did she. The lack of sleep was beginning to do strange things to her thoughts.

At her desk in the studio, she found herself staring down at the pencil in her left hand. A coincidence, or something more?

She stared at the empty page and took a deep breath.

Her headache hadn't eased up, despite the coffee, paracetamol, and a never-ending supply of Cole's fragrant tea collection.

Her lack of attentiveness was even wearing the usually patient Cole down, especially when she accidentally deleted a brief from the files and sent him the wrong sketches.

"Where is your mind today?" he asked, tapping at his laptop, trying to retrieve the deleted files.

After apologising profusely, she tried to buckle down and focus, yet her mind wandered back to the card. The card that had turned her life upside down.

She hadn't seen it since they'd arrived in Melbourne, but

she bet she knew where it was. It was always in the same place. Perhaps she needed to look at it again.

Twirling her pencil between her thumb and forefinger, she made a decision to look for it when she got home if her mother was still out.

After sketching an 'I'm sorry' note to Cole featuring a bulldog holding a rose in its mouth—that made him laugh—she caught the train back to the apartment, kicked off her ankle boots, and shrugged off her blazer.

Surveying the neatly stocked refrigerator, she chose a ready-made meal and put it in the microwave while she changed into a large T-shirt that she'd bought at a market outside of Milan. The original emerald green colour had faded and the seam was fraying at the edges, but slipping the soft fabric over her head always made her feel comfortable and relaxed. That was the thing about not having a permanent address. It was finding the little things to make any place home.

The microwave made a loud dinging noise that irritated her headache. Standing at the marble bench in the kitchen, she forked spoonfuls of paneer masala and saffron rice into her mouth as she listened to the trams trundle past outside the window. They sounded nice, quieter than a train, and the old-fashioned bell that *dinged* as they stopped had a nostalgic tone.

Pouring herself a glass of crisp white wine to relax her mind and help her sleep later, she sat on the balcony. She ran her hand over mint, which was growing in a small black pot. The smell lingered in the warm autumn evening and took her back to travels of Vietnam with her mother where each dish was generously drizzled with mint leaves, leaving everything tasting fresh and zesty.

And now their travels had brought them back to Melbourne. Back to where she was born and had lived the first three months of her life before her mother had taken them to London.

What could her life have been like if she'd been raised here with the backdrop of the trams, large parks, funny little alleyways and unpredictable weather?

How had it been for Michelle growing up here?

It had been strange to see her in person, and while the chain of events had left her on edge and unfocussed for the rest of the day, she couldn't help but come back to one point.

She'd liked Michelle. She'd been friendly and open. Perhaps not surprising, given the amount she shared on social media. Her Australian accent had seemed stronger than she'd ever imagined, and she was much shorter in person. Her face had been a little rounder and fuller, making her look younger. Sometimes on social media, her photos seemed heavily airbrushed and full of pouty lips and contoured cheeks. More glamorous, yes, but Bebe had liked the natural version she'd met today.

She ran her finger across the screen of her phone and flicked through Michelle's feed, hovering over a photo of Michelle with a number of people, all of whom Bebe had pieced together as Fitzgeralds.

Staring at the photo of Michelle's father, she locked the phone as her thoughts of earlier that day rushing back to her. She'd been right. Too many people could be hurt with what was little more than a hunch.

Yet, she still couldn't get the thought from her head. It was time to find the card. Maybe that would help. Perhaps it wasn't as strange as she'd remembered, or perhaps looking at it with fresh eyes would help unravel the mystery.

Re-entering the apartment and locking the balcony door behind her, she crept into her mother's bedroom. She opened the doors of the ornately carved wooden wardrobe and noted some of the few but outstanding pieces of clothing in her mother's collection. A beautifully tailored blazer, a black woollen coat, two pairs of slim-fitting cigarette trousers, two crisp white shirts, a French navy crepe dress with an elegant boat neck, and an evening gown made from a glittering fabric that Bebe loved to touch.

But she wasn't here to admire the craftsmanship and elegance of her mother's capsule collection tonight. What she wanted was behind these items, hidden way back on a shelf. That was where it always was, no matter where on the planet they had landed over the last twenty-something years.

She slipped her hand along the shelf, searching for a wooden box wrapped in a soft scarf. Sliding it out, she carefully unwound the vibrant fabric and flipped the lid of the box open to examine the items.

Her mother wasn't sentimental. She claimed she didn't need things to remind her of people or places—the memories and feelings were enough. Yet, there were a few things that were kept securely in this small box.

The box itself had come from Morocco when they'd visited there when Bebe was maybe five years old. Or was it six? Whenever it was, she vividly remembered the trip, and especially the weather. After living in London, the blinding, all-encompassing heat had wrapped her up.

Procured from a crowded street market her mother had taken her to, the box was wooden with a silver inlay. Despite being wood, it was light and the clasp was secure. Although, there were a few dints in it thanks to all the moves they'd made.

As if testament to her mother's view of the unimportance of mementoes in one's life, there were very few items inside.

Bebe sat cross-legged on the floor and pulled out the first piece of paper. Her mother's birth certificate, nestled along with her passport. Bebe's birth certificate was underneath it (she kept her own passport in her handbag). Unfolding it, she ran her finger over the key information and looked at the name of her father. Arne Andersson. She'd never known him —the name was that of a virtual stranger.

Her eyes moved to a thin, silver ring that sat inside the box, along with a piece of rose quartz and a gold St Christopher's medal on a short chain. Bebe had no idea why any of those items were in there, and, given she hadn't been shown them, she'd never asked her mother about them. She'd never seen her mother wear the ring, nor the chain, and they were separated from the jewellery she did wear on a regular basis. Were they hers, or had they belonged to someone else? Arne? Her parents? A trusted friend? Someone else?

The items were still as strange and seemingly unconnected to anything as they had been when she'd first stumbled upon the box while looking for a belt to borrow.

She picked up the photographs first. Some were of Bebe's late grandparents, and others a series of snaps charting Bebe's age across different places. Four years old in London, five years old in Milan, seven years old in, perhaps, Copenhagen? So much of her childhood was a blur of places. Some they spent a lot of time in, like London, or others had been for a few months, like St Petersburg or Helsinki, where her mother had fulfilled short contracts.

As Bebe flipped through the snapshots, she gazed at her mother, in awe of the strength and courage associated with raising a child on her own in foreign lands while studying and working. It hadn't seemed like a big deal as a kid. After all, she'd known nothing else, but as she'd grown, she'd realised it couldn't have been easy to juggle high-pressure work commitments, a young daughter, and the constant movement of schools and apartments.

She flicked through the photos until she found a faded and dog-eared photograph of a man on a motorcycle. Arne Andersson. Her father. He conjured up thoughts of Nordic homelands, and certainly explained the fair hair and pale eyes they seemed to share, but otherwise, they seemed nothing alike. She couldn't see her nose, or the shape of her face or her eyes in either of her parents.

Her mother told her Arne had been killed in an accident before she was born, but other than that, she knew next to nothing of the man and as she grew, she occasionally asked questions about him, but was met with changes of topic, or short answers that gave no further information.

"Did Dad have any family in Australia?" Bebe had asked one morning as they rode the Tube together on the way to her school in London. She'd been watching an older couple with a small child rugged up in a knitted hat and matching scarf. The child was sitting on the lap of the man, and had called him *"grandpa"* several times as part of an in-depth conversation about whether chickens could fly.

Her own grandparents had died when she was a small child, and without her father's parents, it seemed like she and her mother were very alone in this world.

"No." Her mother had been adamant and turned back to a book in a way that suggested the matter was over.

But it wasn't over for Bebe. *"No brothers or sisters?"*

"He was an only child."

"No cousins?"

Her mother had put the book in her lap and looked at Bebe. *"None of which I'm aware are in Australia. There may have been some in Sweden. His parents migrated from there when he was small. Now, I thought you were revising your notes for your literature assessment."*

Bebe had shrugged, removed her book from her bag, and continued her schoolwork while still watching the small child interact with his grandparents opposite, a warm, loving glow in the older couple's eyes as they entertained him. That sort of relationship with extended family had eluded her and, given her mother's responses, seemed like it always would.

Yet something didn't click.

Staring at the photograph now of her father, Bebe's questions were still unanswered. A name on a birth certificate and a photograph, and perhaps his fair colouring, were the only things she had of him.

She put her hand in the box and removed the last item: a card with a floral arrangement on the front. It looked old-fashioned and yellow with age.

She opened and read the note again.

Petra. I know you want the world, but if you ever need anything, I'm here.

And it was signed.

Greg Fitzgerald.

It was still there. Her mother had kept it for all these years.

She turned back to the photos and peered closely at the last one in the pile: her mother, young and dressed in a black turtleneck top and grey, A-line skirt, standing in front of a giant computer. Two men, one of whom was Arne, flanked her. He was looking at the camera and smiling. He had a nice smile, but in the photo, her mother was looking directly at the other man who, after many years of searching and piecing things together, Bebe had come to learn was Greg Fitzgerald. He was also looking at the camera, a grin on his face and his arm around her mother's shoulders.

Having seen Michelle in person, she could see her similarities to her father in clearer detail. They shared the same shape nose for sure, and there was a similarity around the eyes.

She gasped. Greg was gripping a pencil in his left hand. She'd never noticed that before. Michelle's words came rushing back at her and she shoved the contents back in the box, wound the scarf around it, and pushed it back on the shelf in her mother's room.

She climbed into bed and rolled onto her side, digging her head deeper into the cool linen pillowcase and shutting her eyes tightly to avoid any light from the outside street lamps filtering in and further aggravating her head.

And to keep the whirling of thoughts as grounded as possible as she contemplated exactly why Greg Fitzgerald had written that card, and why her unsentimental mother had kept it.

CHAPTER 7

"I know you!"

Michelle glanced up from stacking cups and locked eyes with a man. He was about her age, tanned and muscular. He had messy, dark blond hair and cornflower-blue eyes. Workman style overalls sat over a blue fitted T-shirt that appeared to have been chosen to highlight his eyes and show off toned, sun-kissed arms.

Or perhaps he'd thrown it on that morning and the combination magically worked. His hashtag on Instagram? #hottradesman.

As much as she could appreciate his physical attributes, she had no idea who he was. "I'm sorry …" Would he offer a name or some detail to help fill in the blanks?

"You're Michelle Fitzgerald!"

"I am."

Oh no. Her heart sank. Had one of her brothers gotten into a dispute with him over some money? Steve, in particular, could get a little argumentative with people on worksites.

He held out a hand to her over the counter, accompanied

by a grin far too friendly for someone seeking revenge or retribution. "Leon Marek."

She shook his hand. *Leon Marek*? Her jaw dropped, and she hurriedly clasped it shut again despite her stunned disbelief. It couldn't be.

Leon Marek had been a plump kid at her primary school who never seemed to say anything to anyone. Until grade three, she'd wondered if he could talk at all. By grade four, bigger kids would steal his order from the canteen, and she remembered sneaking him half of her doughnut as a gesture of goodwill. By grade six, Michelle hadn't really noticed him at all. She'd been too focussed on the boys playing footy at lunchtime and batting her eyelids at them. "I'm sorry, I didn't recognise you. How are you, Leon?"

"I'm good. You look exactly the same." His grin widened.

"You don't" was what she wanted to say, but she managed to hold her tongue to prevent herself asking how he'd gone from dorky kid to suburban Adonis. Talk about ugly duckling to gorgeous swan. She murmured a vague agreement.

"I heard you were in Canada." He furrowed his brow in confusion. "Studying or working or something?"

"I was, but I'm back now. I did a bit of uni and some ski instructing. How did you hear that?" How long could she gloss over her multiple failures before people started to see the cracks in her story? Or had one of her family members opened their big mouths? That was perhaps even more likely.

"I occasionally see Steve on some jobs. I'm a locksmith now."

"Really?" That would explain the overalls and how he knew about Canada. Steve possibly had the biggest mouth in the family. "And Steve is okay to work with?" she added, hesitantly.

"Yeah! He's a great guy. A bit of a perfectionist, but I get that. Do the job right or don't do it all, that's what I say."

Phew. "How long have you been a locksmith?"

"I started my apprenticeship as soon as I finished year twelve so what, five years?" He scratched his head.

"That's cool. Do you enjoy it?"

He nodded. "It's good. How long have you been working here? I swear I've been in here heaps of times, but I've never seen you."

"I only started a week ago. Would you like a coffee? Sorry, that's why you've come in, I imagine."

"It was," he said, rubbing his neck. "I got distracted. It's really good to see you again. How long has it been?"

A customer stood behind Leon and coughed, loudly, as if to gain Michelle's attention and indicate how much of an inconvenience their little school reunion was.

Leon turned around. "Sorry, mate. I don't know what I want so you order ahead of me. I don't want to hold you up."

The man gave a relieved nod, and Michelle took his order. While she was making his coffee, Leon moved to the side and continued to talk to her. "Do your parents still live near the school?"

"They do."

"I remember you lived the closest to the school and were always late."

Michelle gave a shrug. "That was just me, I think. I'm not great with keeping track of time. Are your parents still out that way?" She had a vague recollection of a cheery set of plump parents with the same fair hair as Leon's, and like the Fitzgeralds, a tribe of loud children chowing down on muesli bars and crammed into a people-mover.

"Yep. They are indeed. Surrounded by grandkids now."

She looked up. She'd not noticed a wedding ring. Was he married with kids? Surely not. They were too young for that, weren't they? "Your kids?" she asked, hesitantly.

"My sister's."

Michelle nodded. His sister had been in a grade between Pete and Lauren. That was the thing with a big family—usually, there was some overlap in year levels or football teams or dance lessons with other families.

She handed the customer his coffee. "Are you sure I can't make you one of these?" she asked Leon, pointing towards the silver travelling mug with a black rubber lid he was holding.

"Thanks. A latte would be good." He handed her the cup. "I'm due back on-site soon otherwise I'd stay and catch up."

She ground the coffee beans. "Are you working on the apartment building that Steve is?" This was perhaps the project Clare had mentioned.

"That's right. I'm doing some security locks now, and then I'll come back later when it's ready for handover."

After pouring the milk into the silver cup, she pushed the lid down and handed it to him, once again taking a second to appreciate his arms. He must work out regularly, or maybe his job kept him fit. Perhaps if she had become Steve's slave, she could have kept fit and been able to check out Leon at the same time.

Goodness. Was she really perving on *Leon?*

"Thanks." He placed the money on the counter. "Great to see you, Michelle."

"You too." It had been nice to wander down Memory Lane. She often thought that things around here didn't change, but perhaps they did. Leon was evidence of that. "Maybe I'll see you again."

"Absolutely." He grinned. "Good luck with the new job!"

He walked away, a strange reminder of her school days coming back to her in an unexpected, yet extremely pleasant way.

CHAPTER 8

Bebe looked around the café. Where was Michelle? Despite her initial hesitation and moment of sheer panic in the alleyway near Espresso Walk, she had made a return. After going through the box stashed in the back of her mother's wardrobe, it was even clearer that there were too many unanswered questions.

"Are you all right?" Cole asked. "What are you looking for?"

"Oh, nothing." Bebe slid her chair closer into the table. "Just taking it in. It's such a nice place."

"I agree," a cheerful voice said.

Bebe looked up to find Harry standing next to the table holding a jug of iced water and sliced lemon.

"You came back?" He poured glasses of water for her and Cole.

"The coffee was so good," she said. It had been, and she could hardly reveal the real reason she was there.

"Great to hear. What can I get you?"

After they placed their orders and Harry returned to the counter, Cole leaned forward. "Barista boy has a crush on you. He's been unable to take his eyes off you. He'll be lucky if he doesn't burn his hand on the machine he's so distracted."

Bebe waved her hand, dismissively. "I'm only here for a couple of months. There's not enough time for anything like that."

Cole raised his eyebrows. "Why not? Nothing wrong with a bit of a fling. He's cute."

She looked across the room at Harry. He smiled at her, which she returned.

"Ask him out," Cole urged.

She wasn't sure about that. She didn't want any complications. Bebe turned back to her colleague. "Hey, what are you doing on Friday night? Do you want to come to the opening night of the exhibition my mother has put together?"

"Walk me through it." He sat back in his chair. "By opening night, what do you mean? Canapés and wine, or just free tickets?"

"The first. Fancy food, lots of champagne, the odd celebrity sighting."

"I'm in."

"According to my mother's assistant, I have five tickets so bring Jordan, if he's free."

"Thanks. He'll like that." Cole nodded his head towards the counter. "You should ask coffee boy to join us."

"Maybe." She wasn't planning to, but hoped this would get Cole off her back.

Harry returned with their coffee orders. "Macchiato and the soy latte."

"Do you like art?"

Bebe kicked Cole under the table. What was he doing? She didn't need Cole going rogue and playing matchmaker for her.

Harry shrugged. "Depends on the art."

"Bebe's mother, Petra, is curating the new collection at the National Gallery of Victoria."

Harry turned to Bebe. "Really? That's cool. Is that the Picasso exhibit?"

"That's the one," Cole said.

Bebe kicked Cole again, but he just smiled at her sweetly. "Bebe, weren't you just saying you had some tickets? Seeing as … err … I'm sorry, what's your name?" He peered up at Harry.

"Harry."

"That's right. Seeing as Harry is such a fan of Pablo."

She glanced at Harry, whose eyes were on her and his smile crooked. "Err, yes. Actually, there's an official opening on Friday night if you'd like to come."

"With her, that is," Cole said. "I'm attached."

Bebe glared at him. Why had he said that? Now Harry would think it was some sort of a date. "There's a group of us going, and you'd be welcome to join us. They usually have nice food and champagne at the opening."

"That would be great. I am a bit of a fan, actually, and had meant to go and see it when it was open," Harry said.

"Great. I'll drop the ticket in here tomorrow, if that suits?" Bebe asked.

"I'll shout you lunch to say thanks."

As he walked back to the counter, Cole leaned in to her. "Told you. He's smitten."

"Cole," she warned. "That wasn't fair. You put him on the spot and you made it sound like it was a date."

He scoffed and took a sip from his coffee. "You get a date and a free lunch with the coffee boy out of this, and he gets a night out with a babe. Not a bad deal for anyone."

Bebe watched Harry speak with a customer. Cole was right. It wasn't a bad deal. Harry was attractive and seemed like fun. She wasn't here for long, but perhaps it would be nice to date a little.

Cole dropped a folder on Bebe's desk. "Here's the no-no list for Andrea."

She flinched. She'd been immersed in her work since they'd returned from their coffee break at Espresso Walk. "A what?"

"A no-no list. These are things that cannot go anywhere in her designs."

Bebe skimmed it and looked up at Cole. "Zippers?"

"No. Only buttons."

She continued to read. "Sequins?"

His eyes widened. "No! Absolutely not. Don't even mention the word sequin to her, or you'll see the biggest adult tantrum you can imagine."

"It's just a sequin. It's a plastic disc. What's the problem with it?" She hadn't planned on using sequins at all, but now she'd been told she couldn't, she wanted to.

"Try telling her that."

The door swung open. Bebe glanced up as Michelle stood in the doorway, waving and grinning madly.

She'd really shown up? Despite any hesitations, Michelle was so friendly and childlike, Bebe couldn't help but smile, and wave back.

"Who's that?" Cole asked.

"Michelle. She works with Harry at the cafe." Bebe walked over to Michelle. "You came!"

"I'm on the late shift at work and figured I'd stop by here first. This is gorgeous!" She ran her hand over a gown and gave a gasp. "This is so fancy!"

"Let me show you around."

She introduced Michelle to the team, and she gestured to a small retail section they offered.

"This is beautiful." Michelle sighed over a silk dress. "I have nowhere to wear it, but it's beautiful."

"Find an occasion."

"I really don't think I can afford much though. I returned home from studying in Canada totally broke." Michelle continued to flick through the dresses, murmuring in delight at each gown. "I like skiing, but it doesn't love my bank account."

"That is an expensive hobby."

"Tell me about it. Got in over my head, but I'm so desperate to go back. I loved Canada."

"Me too. We lived in Montreal for a little while."

Michelle gave a sheepish look. "I went a little bit mad on a college trip to Montreal." She pushed back her fringe to reveal a pink scar above her eyebrow. "Everyone in the family calls me Harry Potter now."

"Oh no!" Bebe's heart beat faster. She knew about this ill-fated trip to Montreal where Michelle had inexplicably fallen off a boat. A photo had appeared on Michelle's social media accounts of her in a hospital with a bandage around her head. The post, naturally, had received hundreds of comments from concerned family and friends. Lauren Fitzgerald (from behind her cupcake profile picture) had asked Michelle if she needed blood, and if so to remember she was Type O Negative, not O Positive as Michelle would always forget.

Bebe had been at home, scrolling through her feed, and that comment had floored her. That was *her* blood type, yet her mother was A Negative.

If she and Michelle had the same blood type … She pushed it from her mind. She needed to remain completely normal around Michelle or she'd begin to suspect something.

"Harry said you're from here originally, but you're going to do the L'Or Master Class in New York? Don't all the top designers do that class? He said you'd lived in London too. That's so cool!"

Bebe's heart raced. Was she a talking point at the café? Maybe she was getting in too deep.

"Bebe?"

"Sorry!" She blinked, and pulled a dress from the rack and held it up to Michelle. "Yes, but when I was a baby, my mother took me to London. After that, well, I've never been in one place for more than a few years at a time. London, Paris—"

"Paris?" Michelle's eyes shone. "How wonderful! Why did you go there?"

"Mum worked at a gallery for a while as a contractor. It was just the two of us."

You and me. Me and you. It was their mantra. It had always been their mantra.

"So? Where did you go after that?" Michelle looked at her.

"Milan, then Copenhagen. And then back to London for a while. I spent most of my teenage years there. Then St Petersburg, then back to London again."

"Wow." Michelle's eyes were wide. "That's so unbelievably cool."

Bebe shrugged. "Then we did other places for short-term projects and things. Or just travelled. We're sort of nomadic gypsies."

"My parents live in the same house they bought in the 1970s. Replacing the carpet was a huge change for them, and it took them three years to decide on the right colour."

"There's something nice about that though." Bebe pulled out a scarf and handed it to Michelle. "You know, someplace that's yours, that's your home. Nowhere has ever felt like that for me."

Michelle wound the scarf around her neck. The flecks of amber throughout it brought out her eyes and the soft highlights in her hair. "I guess, but it's boring though. That's why I had to get out, not that it worked very well, but you know. I'll do it again. I'll save up and then go."

"Go where?"

"I don't know. Someplace."

Surely Michelle had specific goals in where she wanted to travel. "What would you like to see?"

"Anything new and exciting. Maybe I could go to Argentina. Perhaps Morocco."

Bebe could understand wanderlust and travelling to find new experiences, but Michelle seemed more like she needed to tunnel out of a prison, desperate to get anywhere. "I'm sure you'll get to those places."

"Perhaps. I'll be making coffees for a long time to pay for it." Michelle touched the scarf. "This is beautiful. You're so talented. Harry said your mother is curating the Picasso exhibition that's about to open. That's impressive. Talent must run in your family."

"She's very clever." She paused. "I have some tickets to the opening night if you'd like to go. A group of us are going."

"I don't know much about art," Michelle warned, "but that sounds like fun, and I'm always up for a party. Thank you! I'd love to."

"Great. I'll drop in your ticket to Espresso Walk tomorrow," Bebe said even though a voice inside her head was telling her this wasn't good at all. Was it a terrible idea to invite Michelle to somewhere her mother would be?

"I'll take this." Michelle hugged the scarf to her chest. "I need something to celebrate my new job." Her face fell. "Oh, how much is it? I probably shouldn't blow all my pay on one scarf."

"It'll be fine once you apply my discount." Bebe walked

over to the counter, and laid it out to fold and wrap it for her.

"This is so nice of you." Michelle trailed behind, before stopping to examine another dress. "Oh wow. These sequins are amazing."

Bebe paused at the counter.

Michelle poked at the garment with such enthusiasm, Bebe could only hope Cole couldn't see what was happening to his precious merchandise.

There was something so naïve and lost about Michelle. Bebe bit her lip, doubt creeping over her. She'd thought she could find out the truth while she was here, but what could that do to Michelle? What would be the impact of one of the most stable parts of her life—her family—being blown apart?

Her hand shook as she wrapped the scarf. Had she opened a door to a world that she had no right to step through to without hurting innocent people?

CHAPTER 9

Michelle was tidying the counter at Espresso Walk when she looked up to find Leon. Once again he was wearing his overalls with his snug T-shirt underneath (this one was a khaki colour, which was nice, but not as attractive as the blue that highlighted his eyes). He was holding the same large, silver travelling coffee mug he'd used last time he'd been in.

"Hey," she said. "Good to see you again."

"It was great coffee." He handed her the cup and a five-dollar note. "Can I have a latte, please?"

"Of course."

"Michelle." He cleared his throat, and she looked up from the register. "Can I buy you a drink after work?"

Unlike the simple coffee order, that request had thrown her. Not because she wanted to say *no*, but she wasn't entirely sure she should be saying *yes* at this point. Was she sufficiently over Ashton?

He cleared his throat.

She was taking too long to answer and he'd noticed.

"Thanks. That would be nice." She didn't want to hurt his feelings and maybe it would be good to have a drink with him.

"Cool. What about we meet at Pacific Place later?"

She'd not been to Pacific Place in years. "Eight o'clock?" It was hardly the worst idea. He was cute and she was single. Perhaps she could message Ashton with all the worldly 'moving on' type vibes. He may have dumped her, but there she was, dating again. Check *that* out, Ashton!

Perhaps she could post something to Instagram with some thoughtful hashtags like #movingon or #learningtoloveagain or a cheeky #allthesingleladies.

Then again, Ashton's most recent photo he'd posted to social media had been taken on board his family's yacht with Gretchen, who had looked sickeningly gorgeous in a skimpy bikini.

Michelle couldn't compete. There was no way she'd be posing in next to nothing, and where on earth was she going to find a yacht?

Leon waved again as he left, holding the door open for an older couple. His cheeriness was so *nice*. Too nice for her. Would she just break his heart?

A bit like those bullies in the schoolyard who used to steal his meat pie and iced doughnut. Back then, she could offer him part of her lunch, but it was only a part. She'd never really made too much effort to spend any time with him, even though he used to lurk forlornly through the playground or hide out in the library at lunchtime while the other kids played downball against the brick wall of the canteen, or traded football cards on the park benches.

She didn't want to hurt Leon like the schoolyard bullies had, but was she ready to move on?

A little ripple of anger hurtled through her body at how

much the request for a simple date was throwing her so much.

Ashton had stolen everything from her, and she wasn't sure she'd ever get it back.

CHAPTER 10

$\mathcal{B}$ebe brought a pencil to her mouth and glanced up and down at Tessa De Luca.

She was beautiful. Too curvy for the catwalks of Paris; she was more 1950s pin-up with an hourglass figure and cascading long dark hair. She was a fashion designer's dream. So many styles could work on her.

"I'll finish these measurements and then we'll talk designs," Bebe told her.

"I'm so sorry for the rush," Tessa lamented. "I've been so busy with the businesses that time got away from me."

"It's perfectly fine. Can I offer you a tea?" Cole asked Tessa. "Let me guess?" He narrowed his eyes. "Peppermint?"

Tessa smiled. "Thank you. That would be nice."

"I saw you on that cooking show, by the way," he added, almost shyly.

There were plenty of local celebrities who came into the studio, but Bebe hadn't thought Tessa was one. She thought Tessa owned cafés, at least that's what Michelle had told her when she introduced them.

"Did you?" Tessa asked Cole. "Which one?"

"The one where the contestants are always yelling at each other."

Tessa sighed. "Ah, yes. That one."

Bebe ran her measuring tape around Tessa's tiny waist.

"Do they really yell at each other when the cameras aren't rolling?" Cole cocked his head. "If they do, where on earth do they find such angry people?"

Tessa laughed. "They're much calmer behind the scenes. They edit those things so everyone looks a little cray-cray."

"You didn't. You were gorgeous. Are you going to do more programmes? You'd be perfect as a judge."

Cole was always very polite and charming to their customers, but he genuinely seemed to fawn over Tessa.

"Thank you," Tessa said. "It's nice to do sometimes, but I try to focus on my businesses though."

He disappeared into the kitchen to organise the tea.

"I'm all done," Bebe said, making a few further notes. "Sit down and we can discuss a few ideas."

"Fantastic. Michelle said your designs were stunning so I'm sure whatever you come up with will be perfect." Tessa flicked back her chocolate-coloured hair as she sat and they discussed preferred colours and options.

Cole's hand shook when he handed Tessa the tea. Was he worried he would be judged?

"This is lovely, thank you. It smells gorgeous."

Cole gave a satisfied smile and asked for a selfie with Tessa, as Bebe made a few notes.

"I didn't know you were such a fan," Bebe said, after Tessa had finished her tea and left.

"She's brilliant. I love the way she will cut down those nasty contestants.

"And she loved your tea."

Cole waved his hand. "Who doesn't? Now, what are you

going to do for her? She's given you free rein. She's so sexy you could really vamp it up."

She could. "It's her engagement party. She'll look back on photos forever. I'm thinking more of a classic."

Cole brought his fingers to his lips. "Not boring though."

Bebe agreed. The balance was difficult. Tessa could pull off anything, but she also wanted to respect the timelessness of the occasion.

"Better get on it." Cole removed the empty teacup from the coffee table. "The party isn't far away, and I don't want you up all night on this one."

She stretched out her arms. Neither did she. She needed her sleep at the moment. "First thing tomorrow, I'll be on it. I'm off for the day."

Cole clasped his hands together. "Want to get a drink?"

"I hope to do something with my mother tonight. I've barely seen her since we've arrived."

"Sounds good."

Good. Yes, it would be good but it would also allow her more opportunity to find out more information about Arne, and maybe once and for all put this notion about her family to rest.

CHAPTER 11

When Michelle had gone on dates with Ashton, she'd carefully considered everything. What perfume to spray on her wrists. What clothes to wear. What lipstick shade to choose. Everything had been tailored to make an impression. Little wonder she didn't have the cash for her university textbooks—everything her parents sent or she made from working on the slopes or in the bar had been carefully funnelled towards impressing him.

She entered the bathroom at home, flung her work clothes on the floor, and stepped into the shower. It had been fun dating someone like Ashton, but it had been exhausting. The parties. The eyeing off other girls, jealously in case one of them tried to steal him. The fear he was 'slumming it' with her and would come to his senses and dump her.

And then, of course, he did.

She let the water cascade over her, familiar feelings of pain and rejection coursing through her body. Tears rolled down her face, mixing with the water, she slammed the taps off and dried herself.

How many tears was she going to cry over him?

Her hair blow-dried and carefully straightened, she threw on a pair of jeans, ankle boots, and a black top. She looked down. She'd put no effort into her outfit. But upon winding the cute scarf from Bebe around her neck, she was impressed with how it had all come together. She added the last touches to her make-up and the jangly bracelet she'd bought in Canada, and moved out into the kitchen where Mum was making a cup of tea.

"Where's Dad? I need to ask him about the windscreen wiper on my car." She looked around. Usually, at this time of night, he'd settled in to watch television or read. She stretched her head around the corner to his chair, which contained a Dad-shaped imprint, yet no father. "I thought you two liked to watch that home renovation show together?"

"I'm recording it for us to watch tomorrow night. He's the footy club tonight. It's the first home game of the season so they are doing some sponsor night or something."

"You didn't want to go?" The football club had been a big part of the Fitzgerald social scene for many years for both her parents.

"Goodness no." She scoffed. "I'm relieved no one plays there anymore. Do you know how many football jumpers I washed over the years for that club?"

"Thousands?" Michelle had heard this lament before.

"Thousands." Her mother echoed. She brought her cup of tea to her lips. "I like your scarf." She peered at it with interest. "That's very nice actually." She sounded surprised, as if she wasn't used to Michelle looking so presentable. "Are you going out?"

"I'm meeting someone for a drink."

"Anyone I know?"

"Actually, you might do." Michelle paused.

"Really?" The excited tone in her mother's voice meant she needed to provide some details at least.

"Leon Marek."

Wide eyes stared back at her. "Little Leon Marek? From primary school?"

"Yes, though he's not so little anymore."

"Oh." Her mother's voice softened. "Poor little Leon. I hope you were nice to him. He had a rough time, I think."

"I'm always nice." Did her mother think she lacked social skills or basic decency?

"What does he look like now?" Curiosity filled her mother's voice.

Hot. "Good."

"Well, there we go. You know, I see his mother sometimes at the fruit shop. Not the one I go to—the other one that sells the fruit that's always mushy. I don't know how they get away with it. Remember that time I bought those raspberries and they—"

"Fell apart when you were washing them under the tap," Michelle finished.

"You'll never catch me buying anything from there."

"Okay. I'll see you later," Michelle said, scooping up her handbag and escaping to the back door before she heard about the time her mother purchased the disappointing mangoes and tasteless watermelon from the same establishment, and then threatened to call Consumer Affairs.

While she wasn't sure if she was ready to start dating again, at least Leon had thrown a lifeline to her social life and a chance to escape the confines of the Fitzgerald compound.

CHAPTER 12

Bebe arrived home from work to find her mother slipping on a jacket in the hall. "Where are you going? I thought maybe we could have something to eat together."

"I'm sorry, I have plans." Her mother peered into her small, silver compact.

"Plans?"

"Dinner with an old friend."

"Here?" Bebe didn't know her mother had any friends living nearby. She let her handbag fall to the floor.

"A former assistant of mine. Henrietta."

Bebe couldn't remember Henrietta. The name sounded familiar, but her mother, as a freelancer, had worked with so many people. Names were a blur. "When was she your assistant?"

"When you were little and we were in London. She operates a private gallery now in Melbourne, and I thought it would be nice to have a drink with her." She frowned. "I'm sorry. We can do something another night."

"That would be nice, or ... maybe I could come with you?"

Her mother froze, before snapping her compact closed. "Another time, my darling, perhaps after the opening. I'll see you later." She kissed Bebe on the cheek, twice. Tucking her bag under her arm, she closed the apartment door behind her.

Bebe stood, open-mouthed as her mind raced. Before she could talk herself out of her snap decision, she picked up her bag and threw it back over her shoulder and followed her mother out, carefully locking the door behind her and taking each step lightly as not to make a sound.

She watched from the stairwell as her mother crossed the lobby floor of the building and went outside, where she stood and hailed a taxi.

Bebe flagged down the next cab she saw and instructed the driver to follow the car containing her mother. Something didn't sit right with the abruptness of her mother's departure, and her unwillingness to allow her to tag along.

As a child, Bebe had often been dragged along to catch-ups with her mother's friends. It had rarely been a problem. When she was smaller, she'd read or sketch in a little notepad. When she was older, she'd join in the conversation or just listen to her witty and informed mother discuss art or current events, or literature with her equally as intelligent and worldly friends.

Bebe tapped her foot against the floor as the cab in front drove towards the city, her driver faithfully following his instructions.

Rain splashed against the windscreen, and the brake lights from the car containing her mother blurred through the watery glass. After a couple of turns, the cab pulled up in front of a large hotel, the driveway flanked by large marble statues and heavy pot plants overflowing with white orchids.

A uniformed attendant opened the taxi door and held an

umbrella over her mother's head as she stepped out and walked into the foyer. Bebe pushed some cash over to the driver and opened the door as the attendant appeared again with his umbrella.

"Thank you," she told him. "The woman who got out of the cab in front of me—did you see where she went?"

"Through to the bar."

Bebe thanked him, and paused in the doorway, surveying the room. She felt wrongly dressed, as if she needed a trench coat, dark glasses and a scarf like a spy in a cold war drama.

But she didn't have anything like that, so she needed to sight her mother without being spotted herself. There was no way she could explain following her.

The bar was crowded with people after work, and it appeared some sort of conference was taking place, as many patrons wore lanyards with their names and departments printed boldly on a name-tag.

The noisy crowd made it easier to blend in behind Dave from Accounting and Emma from Marketing as they drained company-paid house red wine, but harder to spot her mother, and her mother's companion.

She moved closer to the bar, where she hoped she could get a better view of the seating on the other side while still maintaining a discreet distance. Her eyes skimmed through the crowds.

Zach from Human Resources offered to buy her a drink. She politely declined and continued to scan the room until she spotted her mother's shiny, silky bob and her elegant black jacket with a trademark Chanel brooch glistening in the light of the elegant chandeliers that spotted the bar.

A man stood in front of her, his back to Bebe, but he appeared to be talking to her mother. She could see her mother nodding and talking happily in return.

Bebe swallowed. Who was the man? Was it Greg? It

certainly wasn't Henrietta. While she felt somewhat vindicated of her suspicions, the confirmation that her mother could have lied to her was confronting.

Craning her neck to the side, she tried to see the man's face, but as he moved, she saw it wasn't Greg and that her eyes had been playing tricks with the distance. The stranger wasn't speaking to her mother but to another person: a shorter woman who had been obscured by the crowd. As they both walked away, she saw her mother talking to a woman, a woman familiar to Bebe.

Henrietta.

She did remember her now. A tall, elegant woman with long hair wound around her head in small plaits. Even though twenty years must have passed, she looked exactly the same as she had the last time Bebe had seen her.

Realising now that being spotted would be even more difficult to explain, Bebe rushed back to the foyer and into a waiting taxi. This was ridiculous. Her mother hadn't been meeting Michelle's father or anyone other than simply her former assistant—as she'd said.

A wave of nausea hit Bebe's stomach. If she'd been telling the truth about her father? Was it possible the coincidences and mementos that had caused her so many sleepless nights were simply nothing?

CHAPTER 13

Fairy lights wound around trees and awnings of restaurants greeted Michelle as she looked for Leon at Pacific Place. A noisy sports bar was located at the far end with a raucous crowd gathered to watch a football match in the beer garden.

She spotted him and waved, her stomach flipped when she saw him. He looked good in a pair of jeans and a white shirt.

"You really haven't changed," he told her as they sat down in an Italian restaurant and ordered a large pizza to share and two glasses of wine.

"Not at all?" She remembered the home haircuts her mum used to give her—wonky fringes and blunt edges that gave her head a triangular appearance. A couple of dodgy teeth had also since been capped and securely held in by slim braces in her teens giving her a less rabbit-like look, or so her brothers had teased.

"Well, maybe a little," he conceded.

Little had changed at Pacific Place since she was a kid. It

was like being in a time warp, yet something of that teenage fizz of being on a date with someone cute hadn't changed.

"You said you were studying in Canada. Are you still studying?" he asked.

It wasn't the time to go into all that now. He'd think she was a loser. She placed her glass carefully on the table. "No, I'm not studying at the moment. I'm working at the café full-time."

"It's a great café. How did you find the job there?"

She nodded. "My sister-in-law, Clare—"

He frowned. "Hang on, which one is she married to?"

"Pete."

"Aha." He nodded. "I sometimes get confused."

Easy to do. "Let me know if you need a chart to keep my family straight. We're pretty confusing. Granny Fitzgerald used to refer to me as 'the baby' until I was about eight. I think she used to have trouble keeping track of us."

He smiled. "My family's big too."

"Anyway, Clare does some public relations work for Tessa, who owns that café and another one. She's looking to start a third venue. I got the job through them."

"It worked out well then."

"How do you like being a locksmith?"

"It's okay. I'm working for another bloke at the moment. He's a great boss, but in the long-term, I want to start my own business. I've been taking some accounting and finance courses so I can do it properly. I know the trade and have a general sense of the business, but if I'm going to make the leap, I want to be prepared."

"That's wise." That was exactly what Steve had done with his plumbing business. It was all *so* sensible.

Just like Lauren and her nursing, or Pete and his PhD, or Luke and his engineering degree. Sensible, grounded, hardworking. And there she was, the black sheep of the

Fitzgerald family. Party-girl Michelle. Fell-asleep-in-the-back-of-a-taxi-and-ended-up-on-the-wrong-side-of-Melbourne Michelle. Got-on-the-wrong-train-and-missed-her-VCE-Literature-exam Michelle. Left-her-wallet-on-a-ski-lift Michelle. Fell-off-a-boat Michelle. Screw-up Michelle.

"You've got more of a plan than I do," she said. "I'm not sure what I want to do in the long-term."

"I'm sure you have plenty of options."

He was too kind. Too nice. Far too nice.

After the pizza, shared memories and a few laughs, they stepped into a video arcade where they found coins in their pockets and her purse. They played a couple of games she'd not seen since she was at school, and took a photo in the photo booth.

"I didn't think these things existed anymore," she mused as a strip of three black and white photographs tumbled out. She held it up, examining them. The pair of them looked adorable, all smiles and bright eyes. In the last photo, Leon's head was tilted towards her, his eyes fixed on her face. "I can take a photo of it for Instagram," she said, holding it out and taking a shot of the images.

"It's like retro Instagram. Can you send me a copy, please?" he asked.

She handed it to him. "Keep the original."

"Thanks." He looked at it for a moment and then slipped it into his wallet.

"Come on, let's play Skee-Ball!" She grabbed his arm and led him over to the throwing game that had been a firm favourite of hers in arcade games growing up. She placed some coins into the slot; the balls were released and she picked one up.

"I'm pretty good at this," she said, raising an eyebrow. She wasn't the most athletic in the family, but in arcade games, she excelled. Perhaps it was the music and bright lights—others found them distracting, but she thrived on chaos.

"Yeah? Okay, bring it on."

With a best-of-three games tournament almost complete, Michelle declared herself the winner. She'd well and truly bested his score.

He rubbed his neck. "You are good at that."

She tossed the ball up in the air and caught it before throwing it down the alley. The ball bounced and slotted into the ring marked 20,000. "I played a lot of backyard cricket." She grinned.

Tickets spilled out and she redeemed them for a fluffy teddy bear at the counter.

"I had fun." She hugged the bear. "Thanks for asking me." Her cheeks warmed and she dipped her head.

"Thanks for meeting me. Err..." He put his hands in his pockets, and then removed them again. "I was wondering if you'd like to do something on the weekend?"

"I'd like that." She paused. That had come out of her mouth before she even had time to think about it.

"What about a game?"

"A game?"

"Footy. New season and all that. You go for the Kangaroos, yeah?" He narrowed his eyes as if trying to remember.

All the Fitzgeralds went for the Kangaroos. It was just what happened in their family. It was like a baptismal right—a blue and white jersey and a club membership.

"I do. How do you remember that?"

"Err...Steve has the club song on his phone, and when it rang yesterday on-site it brought back a few memories of you wearing a Kangaroos scarf in the week before the grand final."

She tilted her head. She only had vague recollections of

him at school, but he appeared to have noticed everything. Perhaps being a little on the outside had given him an expert view in the dynamics of the classroom.

Her heart lurched. She should have spent more time with him as a kid, especially as she'd seen he'd been struggling. "Leon. I hope I wasn't mean to you at school. If I didn't include you as much as I should have, I'm sorry."

"No. You were always nice to me. I had a hard time fitting in. Once I got to secondary school, things clicked a bit more. I got into sports and found some good mates. I had a better time there."

Thank goodness. "I'm glad you did. And, yes, I'd love to go to the footy if there's a game happening. I'm rostered on Saturday morning, but I'm free after that."

He removed his phone and brought up some sort of sporting app, which he tapped and finally held up at her. "Well, that's a bit of luck. Saturday afternoon at the MCG. Tigers versus Kangaroos. Will that give you time to get to finish up work?"

That did seem exceptionally lucky that the Kangaroos were playing locally this weekend. Had his suggestion and subsequent checking been as innocent and casual as it appeared?

Serendipity, or whatever it was, her smile widened. It had been a while since she'd been to a game, and going with Leon seemed like a nice way to spend an afternoon.

Not to mention the fact that she'd barely thought about Ashton in hours.

She hugged the bear tightly to her chest. Arcade games, photo booths and a childhood friend, perhaps a trip back in time was going to help her move towards her future faster than she could have anticipated.

CHAPTER 14

*W*as this a huge mistake? Bebe sipped from a glass of champagne in the foyer of the gallery surrounded by her posse: Cole, his partner, Jordan, and Harry and Michelle.

The crowds mingled, talked, and laughed while taking in the pieces as waiters swirled around the room, balancing polished silver trays filled with delicious champagne and canapés on their hands.

Harry looked, well … sexy, was the only word for it. He had on a well-cut skinny suit and a thin tie. His hair was slicked back, and his dark-framed glasses popped. It was such a pleasure to see a man in a suit that was perfect for their frame, but also for their personality. He had a sense of style that was timeless and unique.

"How many of these type of openings have you been to?" he asked her.

She exhaled and fidgeted with an empty champagne flute. "More than I can remember."

"Can I get you another?" He gestured towards her glass.

"Yes, please."

"Told you. He's obsessed with you," Cole whispered in her ear as Harry walked towards a bar.

"Hardly." She brushed off his words with a scoff, before she noticed Michelle dissect some sort of hors d'oeuvres, removing some green garnish and stuffing it in a napkin.

Harry returned with two glasses of champagne and handed one to Bebe. He paused and watched Michelle's ritual. "What are you doing?" he asked her.

"This looks amazing, but I'm allergic to parsley."

Bebe nearly spat out her mouthful. Parsley?

"Does removing it help?" Cole scooped up a canapé from the tray of a passing waiter. "Shouldn't you stay away from the whole thing if that's the case?"

"I'm not missing out on that beef." Michelle scrunched up her nose. "It's not super serious if I do have a little parsley; it's eating a lot makes my mouth itchy. Besides, it's a tasteless weed. I don't understand why people smother food in it."

"Hang on, is it an allergy, or just something you don't like? That's quite different." Harry raised an eyebrow.

"I get an itchy mouth," Michelle insisted. "I mean, I've never been tested for an allergy or anything, but I'm sure that's what it is."

Bebe fanned herself with the program. Had someone cranked the heating up?

"Are you okay?" Harry whispered.

"I'm fine." She smiled at him. "Why don't we go through to the exhibit?" She needed to escape discussions of parsley, and the possible implications of their shared issues with the herb.

Harry smiled. "Perfect." He took her glass from her, and set them aside on a table. "Is your mother around?" he asked as they walked into the gallery space. "I'd like to thank her for the tickets."

Bebe glanced over at her mother, surrounded by people.

She didn't know who they were specifically, but she was certain they would be wealthy donors to the gallery: politicians, business people, journalists and anyone who was anyone in Melbourne. She probably wouldn't be interested in Bebe or her friends. Thankfully. What would happen if she recognised Michelle? The thought had made Bebe nervous after extending the invitation to include Michelle, but they'd all be beneath her mother's notice tonight.

"She's over there." Bebe gestured. "But she's always so busy at these things."

"I can imagine." Harry looked over, and then glanced back at Bebe. "You look a little like her."

"A little."

"If there's a chance, I would like to say thank you, but if not, could you pass on my thanks for the ticket?" Harry asked.

Bebe smiled. "Of course. Thank you for coming. It's nice to have some company."

"What's your favourite piece here tonight?" he asked.

She looked around, unable to choose but remembering that was how her mother liked to stage her exhibits. So not one piece stood out. They all worked in harmony to present a story.

"I like the whole lot, but …that's my favourite." She pointed towards a painting, largely red. It was chaotic and angular, but whenever she saw the piece, it calmed her. Was it strange to find peace in chaos?

Harry nodded. "It's beautiful. It's busy and the colour is bold, but it's not aggressive, is it?"

She tilted her head, appreciating his summary of it. He had a good eye.

When they finished the circuit and arrived back in the foyer where drinks and food continued to be served, and Michelle, Cole and Jordan were hanging out at the bar, Harry turned to her. "Thanks for tonight. I really enjoyed it. I love going to galleries, but I've never been to an opening of such a big exhibition."

"It was nice of you to come with me. Mum is always so busy working at these events, it can be lonely, but tonight was fun with everyone."

He jabbed a finger towards the rest of their party. "Cole seems like a good guy to work with."

"He's great."

"The people always make the job," Harry said, thoughtfully. "That's what's always sad about leaving a workplace. Not leaving the work, but the people. Probably why I've been where I have for a while now."

"How long have you been at Espresso Walk?"

"Since it opened, but before then I worked at Double Shot —that's Tessa's first café. She's an awesome boss and Espresso Walk is in such a good location." He put his hands in his pockets. "Hey, I don't know if you are into films, but there's a great little cinema not far from Espresso Walk, and they show a lot of classics. Noir-type stuff."

"I love old movies." She loved the fashion, especially in 1940s films.

"Cool. If you'd like to grab a movie, that would be nice. There's a bistro near it if you wanted to get something to eat first."

"I'd love that."

He grinned, and a pleasant feeling pooled in her stomach. Cole was right. A few dates and a little innocent flirtation wouldn't hurt her.

"I wonder if anyone else wants a coffee?" she asked.

"There's a good café near here. It'll be open for a bit."

"Perfect. Let's go." She glanced back where her mother appeared to be in an in-depth conversation with a couple.

There was no need to tell her mother she was leaving, or

how brilliant the exhibit had been. There would be plenty of people tonight to tell her that.

CHAPTER 15

Who knew going to the opening of an art exhibition could give her such a hangover? After the opening, Bebe and Harry had wanted to go to a café, but Michelle had convinced the group to go on to a bar instead. She wasn't sure what time she'd eventually stumbled home, but whatever time it had been she'd not had enough sleep.

She yawned as she put on her apron and washed her hands ahead of her shift, but straightened when she saw Tessa in the café.

Tessa looked up and waved her over. "How are you finding things?" she asked.

"It's great. Thanks again for the opportunity."

"My pleasure. Harry says you're learning the ropes very quickly and the customers love you." She removed an envelope and handed it to her. "This is for you."

The cream paper was heavy and expensive-looking. Michelle opened it to reveal an invitation to Tessa and her fiancé, Matthew's, engagement party. She looked back at her boss. "That's so nice of you."

She hadn't known Tessa that long, and she didn't know her very well, but it was nice to be involved in such a lovely event—a cocktail party at a very glamorous rooftop bar in the City.

"My pleasure. Clare and Pete are invited too, of course. And people from here, and Double Shot. I thought it might be nice to hang out with everyone outside of work and let your hair down."

"And celebrate your engagement."

Tessa laughed. "Have I tried to turn my engagement party into some sort of team-building exercise? Poor Matthew."

"I don't think he'd mind." Michelle had only met Matthew once when he'd come into the café, and aside from being absolutely gorgeous, he'd clearly been enamoured with Tessa. "How did you get on with Bebe for your dress?"

"Brilliant. I can't wait to see what she comes up with."

"Neither can I. She's so talented. Thanks again for the invite. I'd better get to work."

She tucked the embossed cardstock into the pocket in her apron and walked past the kitchen where Gabriel was glazing a tray of doughnuts. Michelle looked longingly at them and remembered how her work trousers had been a bit snug that morning.

There was a drawback to working here—the food was far too good. And that was mostly Gabriel's fault. He was the chef at Espresso Walk, and also Tessa's father. According to Clare (officially the world's worst gossip as she never liked to say anything bad about anyone), there had been some 'bad blood' between Tessa and Gabriel. She'd said this slowly and wisely, but hadn't elaborated, which of course made it even more interesting in Michelle's mind.

She'd made a mental note to ask Pete when Clare wasn't around. He was more of a gossip than his wife.

Whatever the situation had been, it didn't appear to be an

issue anymore. They worked well together and were in some sort of discussion to open up a third café that would also be a gourmet deli. It sounded pretty cool to Michelle.

She paused as her own father walked into the café, a newspaper under his arm. The collar of his knitted navy jumper was sticking up on one side and it was missing a button on the front. He'd never been a snappy dresser and kept clothes until they disintegrated.

"Hi, Dad," she called out.

"Your father is tall," Harry said to her.

"Most of my family is, aside from me." Her lack of height had disappointed endless netball and basketball coaches who'd been originally excited about the prospect of another Fitzgerald athlete to slot into a team, only to discover the youngest member of the family was scrappy and somewhat clumsy.

"Pocket rocket."

Not really. She was a much slower-moving vehicle than that, and one that had terrible navigation skills and was likely to end up in a ditch.

She grabbed a menu, a bottle of water, and a glass, and approached the table where her father sat.

"What are you doing here?" she asked as she poured him a glass of water.

He unfolded a newspaper. "I thought I'd see you and have a coffee. I need to go by the office to grab a couple of files."

She reached over and straightened the collar of his jumper. "On a Saturday? Aren't you going to the football match later?"

"I want to get it done before Monday." He looked at his watch. "Plenty of time before we need to go to the game."

Her father worked too hard. He'd always spent far too long at the office when she was a kid, or spreading out files on their kitchen table on Sunday evening to prepare himself for the week ahead.

"I'll get you a coffee," she said. "I think you're missing a button. That jumper has seen better days."

"Ah." He shrugged. "Your mother bought this for me for my birthday a few years back. It's my favourite."

"Well, if you find the button, I'll sew it on."

"Thanks, honey." He smiled and slipped his glasses on and fanned out the newspaper, instantly immersed in the sports pages.

As she made his coffee, she glanced up at the clock. It wasn't too long until home time and she could look forward to her date with Leon to the football. She paused. Clock-watching had always been her favourite activity at any job she'd held. It was probably one of the greatest skills she brought to the table as an employee.

No wonder nothing worked out for her. Her siblings with their jobs and businesses had inherited the Fitzgerald work ethic, but clearly, like the family's height, she'd missed out on that attribute too.

CHAPTER 16

$\mathcal{B}$ebe placed her phone on the table. She'd been reading the reviews after the opening. The critics were calling her mother's exhibition a *"triumph"*. She was so proud of her, but within there was a little ache. Would her designs ever be called a triumph?

She closed her eyes and allowed herself to dream a little movie in her head where she'd slowly but surely achieve dizzying heights of success. Working at a leading fashion house? Her designs on a catwalk in Paris? On the pages of *Vogue*?

Footsteps sounded along the hall and into the kitchen. She opened her eyes and looked at her mother. "Congratulations! The critics love it."

"Thank you. I'm very pleased with how it came together. What do you have planned for today?" Her mother fastened a Chanel brooch to the lapel of her hand-stitched blazer.

As usual, she was effortlessly stunning.

"I have a date later."

Her mother arched a finely plucked eyebrow. "A date? With whom?"

"Someone I met at a café near my work. He was at the opening last night." Bebe said this last part quietly. "He really liked the exhibit."

"Well, have fun. I'm off to a fundraising lunch the gallery is hosting and then I'm going to dinner."

"Mum?"

"Yes?" Her mother looked up from securing the clasp on her handbag.

Bebe smoothed her skirt. "When you and Dad dated, what sort of places did he take you?"

Her mother shrugged. "Nothing particularly of interest. Just here and there."

"You must have gone somewhere."

"Life was a little simpler back then. Perhaps a movie, or we'd listen to music."

It sounded like they'd dated in wartime. It hadn't been that long ago.

"You worked together. What was that like?"

"I was only in on Fridays, and we didn't have that much to do with each other. I reported to someone else." Her mother glanced at her watch. "Now, I must go. Have fun on your date, and I'll see you later."

The sound of heels against the floorboards grew farther away and the door closed.

She slumped into a chair at the kitchen table. Disappointment settled over her. There seemed so few opportunities to get to know anything about Arne. She'd hoped that maybe back here, there would be more glimpses of their life together, but once again, few details and a swift departure.

Once her mother finished this contract, she was taking up a role in a gallery in New York while Bebe did the L'Or Master Class.

Would they ever get back to Melbourne again? It had

taken years to get here and who knew where in the world she would end up after she completed her studies at L'Or.

Goodness knew there would be precious little information about her father to find in New York. Or anywhere else for that matter.

Many years before, she'd been able to piece together where her mother and Arne had worked—a small engineering firm in Melbourne's eastern suburbs.

She located it on a map on her phone. Given the nature of the businesses around it, it seemed a good day to go when it was quiet. She wasn't exactly sure what she was looking for, but something compelled her to go to the scene where that photo was taken—the one of Greg, her mother, and Arne safely stowed amongst her mother's most precious and secretive possessions.

Swinging her bag over her shoulder, she locked the door of the apartment, and walked down to the train station.

Slipping her air-pods into her ears and playing her current playlist, she boarded the first train, quickly switched to another line, and settled in as she watched the inner suburbs of Melbourne become the outer suburbs as the train made its way to the industrial park.

Following her map, she paused in front of a grey, concrete building, shaped like a giant box. The only colour visible was coming from limp, brownish-green plants nestled in grey pots near the doorway.

Dull.

That was the only word for it. So dull, in fact, that it almost didn't look real. Like it was part of a movie set during the Cold War. A gust of wind hurtled towards her, faintly whistling against the concrete. She glanced along the row of small, neat factories, offices and warehouses. As she'd predicted, it was deserted, given it was the weekend.

She pulled her arms around her. This was where her mother had worked. Where she had met Arne, but also Greg.

Was it the story of a sweet, workplace romance between her and Arne, or an illicit affair with Greg?

As she stood, she heard a car drive past behind her, and up the driveway of the office building. It startled her. It was so quiet she hadn't expected to see anyone.

Glancing towards the car, her eyes widened as she recognised the driver.

Greg Fitzgerald.

She swallowed and looked around. She didn't have a car she could dive into. Where could she hide?

Would he recognise her? Even if he didn't, he might ask what she was doing here or if she was lost. The streets were empty, and it would be unusual to find a girl standing in the car park on the weekend.

The car door slammed, and she sprinted towards the next office building where she took refuge on the doorstep and peered out from behind an electricity pole.

Greg unlocked the door and walked into the office.

She exhaled. In person, he wasn't much different to how he'd appeared in Michelle's photos. Maybe a little softer and rounder in the belly, and a little greyer around the temples, but he had that same 'dad' look.

Chewing at the edge of her fingernail, a heavy feeling set over her.

Was it him? She'd once overheard her mother tell a friend about a man she loved who 'wouldn't leave his family'.

Bebe had only been small, and it hadn't made much sense to her at the time, but as she'd learned more about Greg, it did make sense. In fact, it made a lot of sense.

She looked at the office building: a suburban-based, probably fairly small, workplace. Everyone would know everyone, and everyone else's business.

A scandalous affair would certainly have caused a ripple of problems, especially Greg, who remained married to this day.

Had her mother protected Greg's marriage, and reputation, by pretending Arne was Bebe's father?

She paused as she heard the office door squeak open.

Greg walked from the building, manila folders stuffed with papers under his arm. A piece of paper flew out, catching the wind and he turned, awkwardly chased it down and shoved it back inside the folder. He piled them onto the front seat, climbed in and drove off again.

There were still too many questions. And she wouldn't get any answers standing in front of this building, yet she knew whatever happened here all those years ago was critical.

She needed to learn more about the puzzle to make it all fit, and the more she looked at the building, it was clear the biggest missing piece was Arne.

CHAPTER 17

Michelle hadn't been to the Melbourne Cricket Ground since she'd returned home. The season for Australian Rules Football was only starting, and the excitement had been palpable in the Fitzgerald household with great discussions over fixtures, player injuries, chances of playing finals, and coaching tactics.

"This is our year!" Pete had exclaimed over their weekly family dinner. But he said that every year. She didn't get her hopes up.

She showered and threw on a pair of jeans, white sneakers and a white long-sleeved top. She slipped her footy jumper on and wound her worn, blue and white Kangaroos scarf around her neck. The white parts were nearly grey and the scarf was pilling, but she'd had it since she was a child. It was her lucky scarf, crammed with badges of players, some of whom had retired when she was a kid but were still favourites.

Walking out into the living room, a sea of blue-and-white-clad people were watching Timothy attempt to crawl, or so it appeared.

THE THINGS WE NEVER KNEW

He was perched on all four of his chubby hands and knees with a broad, watery grin plastered over his little round face as he rocked back and forth, as if willing himself to move.

Mum and Dad were on the couch, Lauren on a nearby chair, while Clare and Pete were lying on the floor on their stomachs next to Timothy, Pete holding out his iPhone.

"Is he crawling?" Michelle asked with interest.

"Shh," Lauren hissed, waving a hand at her.

"Why do I need to be quiet?" Michelle whispered, but received no answer.

"Look how strong he is!" Dad's tone was low. "This is amazing!" He sounded astounded like he was witnessing something he'd never seen before. Did he have no recollections of any of his own *five* children performing the exact same feat?

The commentary continued in hushed voices as the family watched Timothy who, despite continuing to rock, still hadn't edged forward.

"Maybe it's the carpet," Pete suggested. "Would it be easier if he were on the tiles? He might be able to slide his knees across to get some momentum."

Mum shook her head. "No. The carpet provides a good grip. All you kids crawled beautifully on carpet."

Whatever the optimal surface for crawling was, it appeared Timothy was making them wait, and it seemed everyone was prepared to camp out until it happened.

"Are you going to the game this afternoon?" Michelle whispered.

"The game?" Lauren didn't take her eyes of Timothy.

"Of course." Pete scoffed as if his status as a lifelong member was being challenged. "We'll go soon. Coming with us, Shell?"

"No, I'm meeting someone first."

"Oh!" Clare grabbed Pete's arm. "Did he just move that leg?"

"I don't know. Did he?" Her brother groaned. "My phone battery is running low!"

"I'll see you later," Michelle whispered and headed out the front door, closing it carefully behind her so as to not disturb the Timothy-watch.

∽

Leon was already at the stadium when she arrived, wearing a St Kilda scarf. She giggled. St Kilda wasn't playing today.

"Can I get you a better scarf?" she asked, waving the edge of her scarf at him.

"No. I'm right, thanks. This is all I need."

"They're not even playing today!" She waved her arms around at the crowds of people clad in Richmond or North Melbourne scarfs, jumpers and beanies.

"I'm always happy to fly the flag."

"There's no shame in trading teams." She ducked to avoid a giant Kangaroos flag a man was waving.

"Oh, really?" Leon took her arm to lead her away from the man who was now shaking the flag more vigorously. "I can't convince you to become a Saint?"

"Not in any sense of the word."

He chuckled, and they walked to the MCG where crowds of people were starting to enter through the gates before buying pies, doughnuts and coffees from the food trucks situated around the entrance. Some people even purchased a copy of the game day Record magazine. Little kids raced around, kicking footballs back and forth, each draped in their team's colours.

Going through the turnstiles, she breathed in the sights and sounds. The emerald-coloured, manicured grass, the sound of the crowd, the smell of hot chips and beer, and the sight of the players warming up on the ground.

With beers in hand, they found their seats.

"I'm sure my family are here somewhere." She took a sip from her cup. "This place is probably crawling with Fitzgeralds." Those who could or couldn't crawl, for that matter.

It had been the first game she'd been to since she'd arrived back, and she'd forgotten how much she enjoyed it as she chatted happily with Leon, shared a bucket of hot chips smothered in tomato sauce, lamenting the umpiring together and swapped stories about their favourite matches and players.

As the final siren sounded, and the winning team song played, she sang it until she was hoarse, and then they went to a nearby pub, and found an empty booth in the corner of the room.

The pub was bursting with the football crowd and the highlights were showing on a nearby big screen with the over-excited commentary blaring from massive speakers.

Leon leaned forward. "Tell me more about Canada. I hear it's beautiful."

"It is." She looked down at the table and moved around a series of cardboard coasters that had been left there. What exactly was there to say about Canada? Though, he'd started with the scenery, so she could continue on that topic. "The cities are lovely and the snow is amazing. I love skiing, so I really enjoyed that."

"And you taught skiing?"

"To little kids who were always falling over in their giant skis and poles. They were so funny, but the parents want the kids to learn young so they can get more out of family ski trips."

"That would have been fun. Those ski places always have good bars and things, yeah?"

She nodded. "Expensive, but it was fun. I got to know a lot of the staff there." *And Ashton.* She pushed the thought from her mind.

"And then other times you were at university?"

"I did an exchange. I'm not sure how I got into the program to start with, as my grades were pretty average, but I scraped through."

"Did you like studying there?"

She took a sip from her glass. "About as much as I liked studying here."

He raised an eyebrow.

"I recently was kicked out—that's why I'm working at Espresso Walk until I figure out my next move."

He frowned. "I'm sorry."

"Don't be. I'm fine. And it was my own fault. I was okay at school when I had teachers constantly reminding me and following up about assignments, but the freedom of university? I probably enjoyed it all a bit too much and my natural disorganisation took over." She plaited the blue and white fringe on her footy scarf.

"Do you like the cafe?"

"I do."

"Perfect. Maybe it worked out for the best then."

The other patrons cheered as the highlights continued to play on the big screen.

Their heads snapped towards the television where the Captain had just kicked, arguably, the goal of the year.

"Actually . . ." She paused as he turned back to face her, "Tessa recently got engaged, and she's having a big party to celebrate. She invited me, and a guest. Would you like to come?"

"I'd love to go. Thanks."

"Great."

"Drink?" he asked. "Should I get a menu as well?"

She nodded and once he'd moved to the bar, she sneaked her phone from her pocket and brought up her messenger app. Ashton was showing up as online. Her finger hovered over the icon revealing his face with his glistening, white teeth and perfectly combed hair. She longed to tell him that despite how he'd ended things and having to return to Australia with her tail between her legs, that the joke was on him.

Leon returned, two glasses in hand and a menu sticking out from under his arm. He sat next to her in the booth.

She slipped her phone back into her bag. "Next to me?" she asked, taking a sip of her wine. "This is a bit cosy, isn't it?"

"I could say it was so we could both look at the menu."

She smiled.

"Or was it that obvious I wanted to do this?" He put his arm around her shoulder.

His body was warm against hers and his arm felt strong and secure—not surprising given how muscular it had looked in his work t-shirts when he'd come into the café.

She tilted her head up. "Totally obvious. But I approve."

"That's good news."

Their eyes met, and she was overtaken by an aching sensation of wanting to be held and kissed. Properly kissed. Passionately. Uncontrollably. Desperately.

The noise from the pub disappeared as she moved her eyes to his lips.

He cupped her chin and butterflies hurtled through her stomach as she cuddled further into the crook of his arm, bringing their faces closer.

As their lips met, a loud cheer sounded through the pub, and while she knew it was in response to some of the game's highlights on the big screen, it was almost like the universe was sending her a message that it was okay to move on.

In fact, it was the best play she could make.

CHAPTER 18

Bebe pulled on a pair of ankle boots, a floral dress and her biker jacket. She wound a long set of amber beads she'd found at a flea market outside of Paris around her neck and flicked her hair.

The events of the morning remained with her. Had Greg seen her? Or had he been too wrapped up in his files and papers that he'd simply never noticed a girl peering at him from behind a pole.

She wasn't sure, but either way, her visit reconfirmed that she needed to find out more about Arne. And with no family to ask, and all the relevant documents she had been able to find in her possession, she'd need to undertake some research.

That, however, would have to wait. Tonight, she had a date with Harry, and was looking forward to the distraction.

Stepping outside, rain sprinkled the umbrella over her head and the pavement around her as she walked to the tram stop. The crisp, drizzly weather was invigorating and romantic. It was the season of crackling fires, full glasses of red wine and snuggling under chunky, knitted blankets.

She sniffed the air—the smell of rain demanded being cosy, and when she was cosy? That was as close as it got to home for her.

Folding her umbrella, she boarded the tram and tapped her hand against the rail as they trundled towards the cinema Harry had suggested for their date.

Her stomach flipped when she saw him standing under the black and white awning of a restaurant next to the cinema.

He was wearing a black velvet blazer over jeans and a white shirt. A red-spotted handkerchief popped out of the pocket. Oh, his style!

The tram stopped and as the doors sprung open, their eyes met and they exchanged a smile.

"Hello," she said, kissing him on the cheek. "This is perfect weather for a movie."

"Couldn't agree more. Do you want to get something to eat first? This place is fantastic." He gestured at the bistro behind him.

She wasn't hungry. Her appetite certainly was down at the moment, but as she glanced through the window of the candlelit bistro, complete with white tablecloths and vases of red flowers on the tables, she changed her mind about getting a bite to eat. The restaurant was inviting and the idea of being tucked up inside with Harry and a glass of pinot noir was very tempting.

"I could have a little something to eat," she told him. "And a glass of wine?"

"Sounds like a deal. After you." He held open the door and they walked through.

Seated at a table near the glow of a fireplace, they ordered a cassoulet.

"Is there any parsley in that?" she asked the waiter.

"As a garnish, yes."

"That's fine," she said, handing him her menu. She could remove it.

Harry tilted his head. "You don't like parsley either? Michelle thinks she's allergic to it."

Bebe's cheeks flushed. "It sometimes tickles my throat."

"There we go. I better remember not to give either of you any parsley at Espresso Walk."

She re-arranged the napkin across her lap and smiled. "So, tell me a little more about working at Espresso Walk."

"There's not that much to tell. Your job is much more interesting."

She leaned back as the waiter poured them each a glass of wine. "I don't think it's more interesting than yours, but I do love it. I can't imagine doing anything else."

"When does your class start in New York?" he asked, taking a sip of wine.

"In about six weeks. I'm waiting for my visa and then I'll book tickets."

He leaned forward. "What does it involve?"

"It's intense, but you learn from the best in the business, and just about everyone who successfully completes it ends up at a big fashion house. It's widely respected in the industry." She became lost in their conversation about L'Or, and started when the waiter placed the cassoulet between them, accompanied by rustic, crunchy bread and creamy butter.

They washed it down with a glass of fruity pinot noir and talked about their favourite movies, art and travel destinations, the conversation flowing across the flicker of candlelight.

After the meal and coffee, they walked into the art-deco style cinema, where they took their seats and, within moments of the opening credits, she found herself lost in the gorgeous 1940s fashion, especially the beautiful cuts of the suits. They were so impeccably tailored. She actually let out a sigh at times when she saw Cary Grant. What a stylish man.

The stylish man who she was on a date with rested his hand on the armrest between them. She looked at it out of the corner of her eye before placing her hand next to his. They weren't quite touching, but their hands were so close, a coin could have barely slipped between them.

Her heartbeat accelerated as she moved a fingertip to his hand. He glanced sideways, and pushed his fingertip against hers so they were almost playing a game of footsies but with their pinkie fingers.

A shiver of excitement hurtled through her body; far greater than what she would have expected from such a seemingly innocent move.

The movement, so small, yet so intimate and romantic, continued for the rest of the movie.

The film ended and the lights slowly rose, her heart gave a little jolt when he took her hand and they walked from the cinema slowly.

"Cab?"

She nodded, and he flagged down a waiting taxi. Light from the streetlamps flashed by the window, and once again, she reached out so their hands were touching as they discussed the movie.

Disappointed the trip wasn't longer, she pulled the key from her bag as the cab pulled up in front of her apartment complex. Harry got out and moved around to the other side of the car, and held the door open for her.

"Thank you," she said as she slid out. "And for the movie and dinner. I had a really nice time."

Harry took her hand, and she stepped towards him. "I did too," he said.

Her lips parted as he leaned into her and kissed her. Like

the subtle, spine-tingling sensation of their hands meeting in the movie theatre, his kiss was soft and tender.

She started when he pulled back, wishing it could have gone on for longer, like every other part of the night.

"Can I call you tomorrow?" he asked.

"Of course." She smiled.

They said their goodbyes and she walked up the steps of the building and watched as the taxi departed.

Unlocking the door, she realised the hall lamp was still on. Her mother didn't appear to have arrived home, despite the late hour.

As she lay down in her bed, she reached for the packet of aspirin she kept in her bedside table. She paused and brought a hand to her temple. Her head felt clear. This was the first day in so long she'd not had a headache. The jet lag was over and perhaps she was beginning to feel more settled, or maybe the date had relaxed her.

Was Melbourne starting to feel like home? She may have been born here, but like everywhere else she'd lived, home was a vague concept rather than a reality, but thanks to a warm quilt, a romantic evening and a tender kiss with Harry, it was the closest to home she'd felt in a very long time.

CHAPTER 19

Leon juggled his reusable coffee cup while whistling a tune and holding the door open for a woman with a pram.

"He's drinking a lot of coffee," Harry teased Michelle. "He'll be bouncing off the walls of his worksite."

She blushed. She was getting used to seeing Leon's face when he dropped by to have a coffee made, and ask her on another date before disappearing back to work. "You should be happy. I'm bringing in more customers."

"Yes. You never stop working." Harry pulled cups from the dishwasher and handed them to her to stack back on the coffee machine. "But he's a nice guy."

She sighed. "Yeah. Maybe too nice."

"What's wrong with that?"

"I'm not really used to it."

Harry frowned. "Your other boyfriends haven't been nice?"

She stared at the coffee cup in her hand. Nice wasn't the word for Ashton, that was for sure. Her boyfriend before him—one she'd tried to keep a long-distance relationship going with—had been okay. "Not as friendly as Leon."

"Friendliness is an underrated quality." Harry wiped his hands on a tea towel.

"Maybe so." Leon wouldn't treat her like Ashton had, yet there was something a little dangerous about Ashton that, despite their brutal break-up, still had a hold on her. Maybe it was that sleek, cool attitude that made everything a little exciting.

Leon was good-looking and sweet, but *exciting*? When they kissed, she would feel excitement pool in her stomach, but that was different—that was her body's reaction to a guy as attractive as Leon.

Exciting? That was more—it was attitude, spontaneity, creativity.

"Are those women waving at you?" Harry pointed towards the door. "Are they familiar to you, or just strange?"

Michelle looked up to find Mum and Lauren taking up a position at a table near the front window. "They are strange, but also familiar. That's my mum and sister."

Harry nodded. "Ah yes, Clare told me a few stories about them when we worked together at Double Shot."

"They're all true."

"But, you don't know what she said."

She raised an eyebrow. "I can guess." She collected two menus and approached their table. "Are you here for lunch?"

"We are." Lauren leaned forward. "But we also want to know if you're ready for the competition?"

"What competition?" Michelle handed them the menus and put her hands on her hips.

"The competition," Lauren repeated.

Michelle shook her head. "You can't keep on saying the same word over and over again and expect me to understand. I need more information!"

"Is she serious?" her sister asked their mother, before turning back to Michelle. "It's the Fitzgerald Family Master Chef Trophy Challenge." Lauren said this slowly and carefully as if Michelle were a dim-witted fool.

"Oh. Sorry, I forgot." She had forgotten. On purpose perhaps?

Mum's mouth hardened into a firm line. "We have to beat Pete this year. I'm getting sick of his smug face."

"Smug face? I thought he was your favourite child?" Everyone knew Pete was the golden boy of the family. He had the most photos on the wall in the house.

"When he beats me in the competition he most certainly isn't." Mum folded her arms.

Lauren sniffed. "I really thought I might have won last year with my chocolate tart, until someone sabotaged me."

"Don't be ridiculous." Mum looked away, seemingly intrigued by a saltshaker on the table. "That pastry was far too flaky."

"You should see what I have planned for this year," Lauren said. "You don't need to worry about Pete; I'll be the one to beat."

"Do you want to know what I'm making?" Michelle asked.

Her sister scoffed. "Not really. It's not like you're a threat or anything. I thought you might have the inside word on what Pete's doing."

"Well, that's nice, isn't it? I might just have a secret recipe. I'd be cautious, if I were you." Michelle folded her arms.

"Maybe. But if you know what Pete is cooking, let us know. Clare was cagey the other night, and I thought maybe Tessa had been slipping them some extra-special family recipes."

"Remember when Clare brought home Tessa's gnocchi?" Lauren asked.

They appeared to contemplate the gnocchi in silence.

"It was like eating clouds of potato," Her sister whispered. "I've been unable to order gnocchi again at any restaurant. It's ruined me."

"Okay. I have other customers to look after. Have a look at the menu and let me know what you want."

Hurrying back to the kitchen, Michelle slipped inside and stood beside Gabriel. "I need your help with something."

"What can I do?"

"I have a family cooking competition coming up."

He raised an eyebrow. "A what?"

"It's a long story, but basically, we all cook a dish and then my dad blind-tastes them. There's a trophy, but it gets really nasty. People try to cheat and sabotage each other's dishes."

He blinked—perhaps at the sheer ludicrousness of it—but nodded. "Okay."

"And because I'm basically the family screw-up—"

Gabriel tilted his head. "You are?"

"I was thrown out of university," she told him. "I'm always making stupid decisions."

"I'm sorry. I wasn't thrown out of uni. I didn't even get into university, but I know something of being the black sheep in the family." He paused, before nodding. "What can I do to help?"

"Thank you!" This was her secret weapon. "I need to blow them away. They think I can't cook anything worthwhile, but if you can show me something amazing, maybe I can win."

"Okay. Do you want to come in early when I'm doing preparation—"

"Early? How early?"

He smiled. "Early."

She paused. She wasn't exactly a morning person, but it was worth giving up sleep to gain a competitive advantage over her family. It certainly would be nice, for once, not to be the black sheep of the Fitzgerald clan.

CHAPTER 20

Bebe sat with Harry on a park bench near Espresso Walk. It was a beautiful autumn day where the light had a warming amber glow. The breeze was gentle and the colours of the trees were golden, red and brown. Autumn was a comforting time. A slowing time. A time to change. A time to start over.

He broke apart a chocolate and cherry muffin and handed her half. "These are our signature at the café."

She bit into the fluffy cake and let out a small moan of delight as the taste of chocolate, sour cherry and vanilla hit her tongue.

"Good?" He raised an eyebrow.

"So good." She took a second bite, revelling in the sweetness. The simplicity of it was a masterstroke, but the ingredients all came together in a way that was homey and comforting, yet with a tiny bite of sourness.

Maybe she needed some inspiration for her design of Tessa's dress from Tessa's own cooking—a classic combination, but with an unexpected twist.

"What are you doing tonight?" Harry asked.

She brushed the crumbs from her dress. "Nothing."

"You want to go to a club with me?" He handed her what she had thought was his half of the muffin. He was as sweet as the cakey treat.

"A nightclub?"

"In like an old-school way, yes. I play at a jazz club every month."

She paused. "Play?"

He mimicked holding drumsticks and tapping on an imaginary drum kit.

"In a band?"

He nodded. "We used to play more gigs, but our saxophonist became a corporate sell-out and we couldn't quite juggle that many gigs."

"Oh." She smiled. "Creative differences."

He laughed. "Tell me about it, but we do play sometimes at a little place in town."

"That's cool." She'd always been drawn to music. She couldn't play an instrument, and her singing voice could best be described as 'nails against a chalkboard' in pitch, but she loved the way she could get carried away by the rhythm and lyrics of a song. "I'd love to go with you."

He stood up. "Great. I have to get back for the rest of my shift, but what about I pick you up around eight?"

"Sounds good. I'll come with you. I quite like working in Espresso Walk."

It really was a nice place to draw, Bebe decided, sitting in a corner booth. She smiled at Harry as she caught his eyes on her. His admission about his band had been unexpected but also rather intriguing. She was looking forward to that date.

She drained more of her coffee, hoping it would give her a buzz. It certainly didn't help her creativity when she felt so tired and foggy at the moment. She stretched out her arms.

"How are you going?" Michelle slipped onto the chair opposite.

"I'm struggling."

"I think it looks good. I like that one with the flowers."

"It's just mucking around." Bebe started sketching Michelle. She drew her cheekbones first. They were rather striking and gave her face a nice shape. She followed with the lips, nose and eyes.

"Is that me?" Michelle asked.

"Yep." Bebe finished with the hair, glancing up to make sure she had the nose right—*the Fitzgerald nose*—and pushed the sketch towards her.

Michelle beamed. "That's so cool! You have to sign that. You'll be famous one day."

"I don't think so." Even once she graduated from the L'Or Master Class, she'd have to work hard to be noticed in such a competitive field.

She turned a sheet over in her notebook, where she continued her sketches for Tessa's gown, though none of them seemed right.

"How do you come up with stuff?" Michelle asked, curiously.

"What do you mean?"

"How do you think of a dress to design?"

Bebe shrugged. "Sometimes I sort of dream stuff. It sounds weird, I know, but you know when you're about to fall asleep? That's when I get my best ideas."

"Do you remember them the next day?"

Bebe pointed her pencil at Michelle. "That's the only problem in the plan. Sometimes I don't. Sometimes if I'm aware enough, I'll get up and write things down."

"And if not?"

"I guess they aren't meant to be. Perhaps another designer will dream them."

"You think it works like that?" Michelle's tone was curious.

"I don't know. I've stood in so many art galleries and design studios, and I wish I knew where inspiration came from exactly."

Michelle narrowed her eyes. "I think you're born with it. Look how talented you are. It's probably genetic."

Bebe shifted in her chair. "Genetic?"

"I mean, your mother is so good with art and things, it makes sense that you would have a good eye."

"Oh. I guess so." She rested her chin on her hands, allowing her heartbeat to return to normal.

"Wherever it comes from, I'm sure it will strike you soon." Michelle glanced at her watch. "Oh! I'd better get a move on, I'm seeing Leon for lunch."

"Have fun!"

She stood and slipped the drawing into the pocket of her apron. "Thanks again for the sketch. Mum and Dad will get a kick out of that."

"My pleasure."

Bebe stared at her notebook. She hadn't thought that Michelle might show her father the sketch. What if she mentioned her to him? Would he put two and two together if he recognised her surname?

She drained her coffee.

Getting to know Michelle had been dangerous. She glanced over to the counter where Michelle was telling Harry some sort of story, using her hands and some sort of exaggerated expressions as Harry laughed. Bebe smiled. It had been risky getting to know Michelle, but she was fond of her.

She paid for her coffee and waved goodbye to Michelle and Harry. With the afternoon to herself and no further inspiration manifesting for Tessa's gown, she caught the train to Melbourne Central Station. It was the perfect opportunity to continue her research.

Upon alighting, she carefully consulted the map on her phone and followed the directions until she arrived at her destination: The State Library of Victoria.

Her visit to the office where Greg, Arne and her mother had worked hadn't provided her with any answers. She needed to know more about Arne, and with no luck with various Google searches, she needed to look in places other than the internet.

Arne's motorcycle accident may have been in the newspaper at the time. Such old newspapers weren't online, but after speaking to someone at the State Library of Victoria earlier that week, they were able to confirm they had newspapers on microfilm from that time.

Entering the library, she momentarily stopped and admired the great old building. University students scuttled past her as she found someone to ask for help with the newspapers.

She entered a small, dimly lit room at the back, filled with desks and large machines, the likes of which she'd really only ever seen in old movies. She'd certainly not used microfilm before, but quickly grew confident with the machine as the attendant demonstrated how to perform a search.

Crouched on her ankle boots, she flicked through the archives, located the film for dates she needed and settled in at a machine.

She knew when Arne had passed away, but she wasn't certain if there would be any record in the newspaper, or what date it might feature on. It may not have been reported until days after the event.

She pushed a button and the pages of the old newspapers whirled by. She paused and inspected an advertisement for clothing, taking in the cut of the 1990s floral dresses. There was simplicity in the cut that she liked. But this wasn't the time for that, so she continued to flick through, yawning as the papers sped up in front of her eyes, whizzing past her in a blur.

She had to pause a couple of times to allow her eyes to settle down as the movement became dizzying, but, finally, she stopped.

There it was. A newspaper article dated a few months before she was born.

It spoke of a road accident that had occurred in the morning and Arne Andersson, aged twenty-five, had been killed when his motorcycle had been clipped by another vehicle.

Her heartbeat sped up. She read the article again. There wasn't much detail other than a quote from a police officer urging witnesses to come forward, and that the driver was 'assisting police with their inquiries'.

There was no mention of her mother, or anything about having a baby on the way. The final quote in the article was from a Greg Fitzgerald, saying he was in shock and Arne had been a friendly and talented co-worker.

She leaned back in her chair in the darkened room as she looked at Greg's name. How come whenever she looked up her father, she kept coming back to Greg Fitzgerald?

The truth was that memories and blood types and left-handedness and parsley and quotes in the newspaper were all very well and good, but they weren't definitive proof of anything.

It could take years trying to sew all these little pieces of information together. She didn't have years. She had weeks until she would be in New York on the next chapter of her life, and career.

It was time. She needed to take drastic action to find out who her father was once and for all.

CHAPTER 21

"What's that?" Leon stabbed a finger at the menu.

"What's what?" She raised her voice over the noise of the bustling Vietnamese restaurant they were seated in.

"I can't pronounce it." He turned the menu to face her.

"Oh, Phở. You say it like 'fuh'."

"However you say it, it sounds pretty good."

"It's delicious." Her stomach rumbled as a waiter brought out a crispy Banh Mi and placed it at the table next to them.

Michelle gave him a smile, and placed their orders.

"Thank goodness you're here," Leon said. "Otherwise I'd look a complete idiot to the waiter."

She smiled. There wasn't anything idiotic about him.

"What are you doing later?"

"Nothing." She shrugged. "I have the rest of the day off. Did you want to do something? See a movie or go for a drink?"

He ran a hand through his hair. "I've already committed to something, but you're welcome to come. It's not glamorous and it'll be hard work."

"Sounds like my life."

He smiled. "My niece's preschool is having a working bee. I said I'd do some repairs on a cubby house for them and check their window locks."

Okay. Even though he'd warned her, it wasn't what she'd been expecting. She glanced down at her jeans, boots and silky shirt she'd purchased in Canada. She wasn't really dressed for constructing play equipment, despite having a pair of sneakers in the car.

"I might need to change my clothes. I'm not really dressed for yard work."

"I can loan you a work shirt," he offered. "It'll be fun, but if you would prefer to do something else, that's fine."

She did want to spend the day with him. "That would be great, and you did promise them."

"I did. It would mean a lot to my sister if I helped."

"Then we'll go."

The waiter brought out their dishes and Leon picked up a pair of chopsticks.

"Hang on, wait!" She removed the phone from her handbag. "I need to take a photo."

"But it will go cold." He looked at the noodles and tapped the chopsticks together.

"I'll be quick." She stood up and angled her phone above the table. "Move your arm."

"Like this?"

"Yes. That's good. Also, can you shift the chilli." She gestured towards the right side of his bowl.

"What?"

She reached over the table and picked up a chopstick and directed slices of red chilli to the middle of the dish. "That's better." She snapped a few photos and leaned back in her chair.

"Am I allowed to eat now?" he asked. "Or do I need to move the beef a little to the right?"

She nodded, flicking through the shots, satisfied with the effect. "All good."

"Great news, as I'm starving," he said with a grin, before twisting noodles around his chopsticks and lifting them to his mouth. "But if you want to photograph more stuff, I wouldn't mind one of those rice paper rolls."

With Michelle changed into her sneakers and one of Leon's work shirts rolled up at the sleeves and tied in a knot at the edge, sitting jauntily over her jeans, she looked casual and cute, but still practical for an afternoon's work.

She wasn't bad at fixing things or doing odd chores. She used to follow her father around their yard and shed as a child, 'helping' him as he'd repaint window fittings, or change light bulbs, or fix cupboard doors.

As they walked into the grounds of the preschool, she felt a sense of nostalgia. Even though she hadn't attended this preschool, it was similar to the one she had gone to—a small red-brick building, lots of trees, a playing area with a sandpit, and lots of paintings hanging in the classroom, vividly displayed as they passed.

As they turned the corner, Michelle paused. "Are your parents here?" she whispered, grabbing his arm. Leon's mother distributed cups of milky tea to other parents, and his father examined a fence pane.

This wasn't the time to meet his family. She was wearing one of his shirts, for goodness sake, and her hair was scraped up into a bun. It looked mildly inappropriate and completely out of place in a preschool, like they'd been up to no good and she'd flung on his shirt after being unable to find her own.

"Yeah. You know them."

"From when I was a kid, not as your girlfriend." Her stomach knotted.

He tilted his head. "Are you my girlfriend?"

They looked at each other.

"Guess so?" She hesitated. She was, wasn't she? They'd been seeing each other a few weeks now and spoke just about every day. They'd not discussed any sort of official terms, but it seemed like a good description of their relationship.

"Brilliant." He gave a broad grin. "The day gets better and better."

Did it? She looked down at the shirt and did up another button to be on the safe side. Her past track record in impressing parents was pretty woeful. She needed to be on her best behaviour and minimise the amount of skin on display.

"Michelle Fitzgerald!" Leon's mother pulled her into a hug so tight that, despite a split-second panic that a rib might be crushed, she found herself surrendering. "You look exactly the same!"

"Thanks." The family looked largely the same to her too. Older. But that wasn't polite to say.

"Look, Bruno, look! Michelle Fitzgerald! You remember Jennifer and Greg, right?"

Bruno, Leon's father came over, who reminisced about the football club before they all got to work on the various chores the efficient preschool president had arranged. Michelle trimmed a hedge and washed thirty toddler-sized chairs, and then it was onto the cubby house to help Leon.

"Screwdriver, please." He held out his hand.

Michelle leaned over and handed him a screwdriver from

a toolbox. He turned it a few times and handed her the screws.

"That one doesn't look right," she said, looking at them in her hand. She jiggled them and held up one that was longer. "No wonder it was loose."

He gave a low whistle. "You're pretty good at all this."

"I wouldn't say good, but I have enough boring practical skills to survive a zombie apocalypse." She reached into the toolbox and looked through the screws until she found one the right size and handed it back to him.

"I want to see you do it. It's a bit sexy."

"Leon!" she hissed. "We're at a preschool."

"I'm not propositioning you. I like girls who have practical skills."

"That sounds incredibly dirty, and rather inappropriate," she said, but she took the screwdriver and affixed the door. She swung it back and forth. "Done."

"I'll say."

Their eyes met and she leaned closer, an overwhelming urge took over to give into those delicious cornflour blue eyes of his and kiss him. She glanced around, no-one was watching and they were shielded by the cubby house.

She put her hands on his collar and pulled him towards her, but as their lips were about to meet, she heard Leon's name being called.

"Fish and chips for dinner tonight?" His mother's round face appeared at the window of the cubby house.

Michelle pulled back and inspected a hammer. That could have been embarrassing. She shuddered. Being caught making out in a preschool playground by her boyfriend's mother? Not a good idea.

"Michelle?" Leon asked. "Dinner?"

She looked at Leon. "If you're up for it."

The thing was that fish and chips with all the family

turned out to be very much like fish and chips with her family.

The Marek's kitchen was much like her parents' kitchen —warm, comfortable and welcoming, and the noise levels were comparable as various siblings wandered in and out, talking and laughing.

The management of the fish and chips even followed the same process.

Firstly, there was the unenviable task of trying to get the order straight. Fried or grilled fish? How many potato cakes? Would anyone eat the scallops because, last time, no one did and they were thrown out? Would the shop give them lemons or did they only do that at the shop they used to go to?

When Bruno arrived with a series of paper trays wrapped in butcher's paper, Leon's nieces and nephews squawked like hungry seagulls at the beach, bringing back memories of her own father on a Friday night with the monster Fitzgerald order.

"You should get the chips first," she whispered to Leon as they held their plates and assessed the mountain of fried food.

"Huh?" Leon picked up a pair of tongs and started placing food on her plate, then his.

"Everyone gets a bit of fish and a potato cake, but the chips are communal, right?"

He frowned. "I guess."

She nodded, purposefully. Being the youngest of five hungry siblings meant she'd had to become crafty to ensure she didn't starve. "So, you take your chips first so you have optimum helping sizes."

He looked at her in amazement and watched everyone help themselves to their fish and potato cakes first. "How come I never figured that out?"

"I'm the smallest in my house. I had to fight dirty, or go hungry."

She bit into a crispy piece of fried flake. It was crunchy and oily and delicious. Hundreds of family take away nights flooded back to her.

"You can hold your own," he said, pointing to her cleaned plate a few moments later.

She wiped her hands on a paper napkin. "I'm a Fitzgerald. A stack of potato cakes doesn't last long around our table."

"Sounds familiar." He waved a hand around the bustling room.

After the dishes were stacked, Leon grabbed her hand and they snuck out to the backyard. They sat on the old swing set, behind an apple tree, looking up at the stars.

"I'm glad you came with me today."

"Me too."

"I like you in that shirt," he said, running a finger down the buttons. He put his hand on her collar and pulled her slowly to him. "You look sexy."

"I thought that was just when I was doing carpentry work."

"Don't get me started on that," he said and kissed her.

Closing her eyes, she allowed herself to fall into him, wrapped in his shirt and in his arms, a strange feeling of the past and future merging together in a moment that felt as charged and emotional as a first, stolen kiss.

CHAPTER 22

*B*ebe and Harry walked through the city and approached an alleyway covered in graffiti and paved with large, uneven cobblestones. Several neon lights indicated restaurants and bars.

"This is it," he said with a grin, gesturing towards a narrow, metal staircase.

"Are you sure?" She scanned her surroundings. "Or are you leading me somewhere dodgy?"

"It's dodgy, all right. It can't be good if they let my band play here. We're pretty bad."

She laughed at his self-deprecating humour, scaled the staircase, and lined up behind a group at the door. His lack of ego and arrogance was refreshing. Bebe found that men 'talked themselves up' to impress her, but it usually left her cold. She liked to figure out people for herself, and Harry was certainly proving intriguing.

They made their way into the bar. The venue was small and dimly lit, but elegant in an eclectic manner. A small stage was situated at the back, where a woman was sitting at a piano, playing and singing a ballad with a devilishly throaty, sexy voice. The song set the entire tone for the club—it was pure noir.

A bartender in a white shirt, sleeves rolled to expose his forearms, and with a black bow tie nestled at the base of his neck embraced Harry and they spoke for a few moments, though Bebe was too focused on the singer to pay much attention.

"I'm going to get a few things ready as our set is nearly up. Can I get you a drink?"

She shook her head. "You get sorted. I'll make myself comfortable."

He grinned and disappeared towards a stage where he chatted with a couple of guys.

Bebe perched herself on a barstool and signalled to the bartender then waited for him to make her a gin and tonic. The singer was crooning a familiar song, and Bebe tapped her foot in time to the rhythm.

The dim lighting was soothing and the warmth and sexiness of the music already relaxed her. She took the gin and tonic, sipped it, and rolled her shoulders, some tension releasing with the motion.

She cheered as the singer finished her set then waited for Harry and his band to play.

A small round of applause and a couple of whistles greeted Harry and two other guys, around the same age, as they took to the stage. One had a saxophone; the other sat at the piano. Harry sat behind at the drum kit.

He twirled the drumsticks in his hand like an expert, and Bebe put her fingers in her mouth and whistled loudly in appreciation.

She wasn't sure if he knew it was her, but he appeared to hear it as he gave a chuckle and ran a hand through his hair in a way that was sort of cool but also a tad uncertain and awkward. *Adorkable* was the word that sprung to mind as she watched him briefly confer with the pianist before counting the band in with several taps of his drumsticks.

Within a few bars of the first song, she was hooked. She sat mesmerised as the music filled the bar. She wasn't much of an expert on what was good or bad jazz, but she knew what she liked, and this she liked. The pianist had a great voice, and the saxophonist had an incredibly handsome face, yet she found herself unable to take her eyes off Harry.

He expertly tapped at the drums, his head nodding along, sometimes even closing his eyes as if being carried along by the rhythm of the music.

She tilted her head. It was always such a pleasure to watch people who were doing something they truly loved. Like the way she'd watched her mother smile in absolute peace at art that hung on a gallery wall, or designers she worked with who had been totally absorbed in their creations. Hours could pass, the seasons could change, the world could end, yet when people were immersed, it didn't matter. They were in their own bubble of joy.

Chewing on her straw, she became lost in the music, but as good as it was, she wanted Harry to herself.

Those arms beating the drums, she wanted around her, pulling her into him. Her stomach flipped at the thought of kissing him again.

She glanced around the room. There were several women in the audience, and clearly, the overall attractiveness of the trio hadn't been lost on any of them. Many were leaning forward and whispering to each other.

She looked back to Harry and found his eyes on hers as he played. He struck a grin and winked, and it was like a lightning bolt went through her. She'd thought he was cute and a nice guy, but now? He was causing butterflies to hurtle around her stomach at such speed in a way that she'd not felt for a very long time.

After the set and thunderous applause, Harry approached her and held out his drumsticks.

"For you," he said.

She took them from him. "Do you always do this? There's no shortage of attractive groupies here, it seems."

"No. First time I've handed these out."

There were so many guys she'd met whom she wouldn't have believed this from for a minute, but with Harry? No. From the way his eyes lingered like she was the only person in the room, he was being honest.

She twirled one around her fingers, mimicking what he'd done before the set. "Thank you. I love them."

"Can I get you another drink?"

She nodded, and as he ordered she ran her finger along the smooth drumsticks and placed them in her handbag. Like her mother, she wasn't always the most sentimental of people when it came to possessions, but something told her this thoughtful gift was one she'd treasure.

As they clinked glasses, Harry leaned against the bar next to her, his legs touching her knees. Like the handholding at the cinema on their previous date, the movement was small and minor but incredibly intimate.

"How long have you played for?" She stirred her straw around the drink, watching ice cubes and mint twirl.

"Since I was a kid, and with these guys for a few years."

She leaned forward. "Which one is the corporate sell out again?"

He grinned. "The saxophonist. Financial planner by day."

"That's a shame. You're good."

Harry pushed his glasses up the bridge of his nose. "It's fun."

"You were in another zone up there."

He tilted his head. "What do you mean?"

She leaned into him. "I saw it. It's like disappearing into

another world, isn't it? When you're doing something you love. I see it in my mother with art. It's like nothing else matters but that pure experience for the moment."

"That's kind of like what it is. When it all comes together like that—the music, the lights, the atmosphere—it's magic."

"It is," she whispered.

"Like when you design?"

She nodded. "Exactly."

He leaned in closer. "Aren't we lucky to have that sort of magic on earth?"

"We are."

Their eyes locked, and she fought an overwhelming urge to kiss him. She was about to suggest they leave when he took her hand and said, "Let's get out of here."

They left the club, and as they walked back up the alley, they grasped hands tightly. He gently tugged her along to the sounds of their shoes against the concrete.

Harry stopped, and she paused, their hands still connected. He gave her wrist a little pull so they were closer to the wall of a building. She leaned back against the brickwork as he stepped in closer to her, their bodies touching.

The streetlights were dim but reflected off the damp paving stones, giving the alleyway a magical feel. Was she in an old movie? It certainly felt that way—she could even hear the strains of jazz music from the club.

He ran a hand along her jawline. Her stomach cartwheeled in sheer anticipation for what might come next.

Enveloped in the darkness, the brick wall was cool against her back and the warmth from Harry's body was against hers as he leaned into her, his lips touching hers, gently at first but with increasing strength. The kiss was slow, intimate, and sexy. It was far more charged than she had ever thought possible when she had first agreed to go out with him. It was intoxicating.

He wrapped his arms around her, pulling her into him and enveloping her just as she'd fantasised about when she'd watched him play. She draped her arms around his shoulders. Her mouth explored his, tasting the whiskey he'd been drinking after his set and smelling a peppery aftershave. It was a heady mix.

She didn't want the kissing to end and pulled him closer.

What on earth was happening here? She'd chalked him up as a nice guy only a few days ago. Since when did nice guys kiss like *this*? In a knee-weakening, resolve-melting sort of way? Up-against-a-brick-wall type of passionate kissing?

She wanted him. She usually liked to really get to know people before she jumped into bed with them, but she had to admit that if that was where tonight was heading, she may break her own rules for him.

Finally, Harry moved his head back and smiled. Their eyes locked on each other, the flickers of the neon light of the bar creating a glow around him. "Come on, let's get you home." His voice was low and almost as delicious as the kiss they'd just shared.

Regaining her breath, and her composure, she grasped his hand as they walked towards the main street, and they waited at the tram platform.

Their eyes met, and lingered on each other, before she looked away at the passing traffic. When she glanced back, his eyes were still on her.

He cleared his throat, as if to say something, but didn't. He glanced at her, a smile on his lips.

The next tram was four minutes away. Something needed to be said while they waited or she risked leaning over and kissing him again. Not that it wouldn't have been nice, but she wasn't sure if she'd be able to stop kissing him this time.

And they were much more illuminated here thanks to the fluorescent lights of the tram stop. She didn't want to risk being arrested for some sort of indecent behaviour. "It's a beautiful night." The weather? Oh, Bebe.

"I like Melbourne in autumn," Harry said, running a hand through his hair. "The night has that slight chill; you know?"

She didn't. Her body was on fire. "The trees are nice colours—the oranges and browns." She fanned her flushed cheeks. Were they really here, talking about seasons when a few moments ago they'd indulged in that knee-weakening, passionate kiss?

He smiled. "Yeah." He fidgeted with a button on his shirt. "The trees are great."

"It reminds me of Boston."

"I've heard that. Did you like Boston?" He tilted his head. "It's another place on my bucket list."

"This sounds silly, but I sort of like everywhere I've been. It all has something to offer and something to like."

"You like seeing the best in things."

Did she always see the best in things? Or in people? Was she seeing the best in her mother at the moment in thinking that she'd had some sort of affair with Greg Fitzgerald and lied about who her father was? Perhaps not.

Harry was too generous in his assessment.

A tram slowly pulled to a stop in front of them, and they climbed on. It wasn't crowded, yet they stood rather than taking an empty seat. Her arm was outstretched to a bar above them and his hand grasped right alongside hers. A shiver of anticipation ran down her spine. She wasn't sure how it was possible that such minor instances of intimacy could generate such incredible jolts of electricity through her body.

As they reached her stop, they both disembarked and Harry walked her to the door.

"I had a great time tonight," he said. "Can I call you tomorrow?"

She nodded. "Are you working tomorrow? Maybe I'll come in and work for a bit. I really need to get some designs ready for Tessa."

"You can be our designer in residence," he said.

"What do I get for that?"

He moved his head from one side to the other. "Great coffee and good-looking staff. Maybe a muffin."

"Well, that is very enticing." She slipped her arms around his neck and their lips met in a tender and slow kiss, causing her knees to feel weak as she melted into his body.

"I'll see you tomorrow," he said to her, sweeping a strand of her hair behind her ear.

"Don't forget to save me a muffin."

He nodded and smiled. "Night, Bebe." He walked down the steps and onto the street, and she sighed.

She brought a finger to her lips, mentally trying to preserve the taste of his mouth on hers.

Floating upstairs, she climbed into bed and allowed herself to settle against her soft pillow. She yawned as her eyes grew heavy and fell into a dreamlike state between being awake and asleep, filled with a haunting undercurrent of the pianist's voice, and the sexy kiss with Harry against the cool brick wall brought her inspiration of flapper dresses, jazz clubs, long beads and bow ties in one sultry, neon-hazed 1920s flashback.

Fingers crossed she'd remember it tomorrow. She may have just mentally designed the perfect engagement party dress for Tessa De Luca.

CHAPTER 23

Michelle grabbed her phone as it buzzed against her nightstand, sounding her alarm. She blinked rapidly, groggy and disorientated. Had she been asleep for ten minutes or six hours?

It wasn't Monday morning already. It couldn't be.

Ugh. She inspected the time. Turned out it was and it was time to get up. She dimmed the light on her screen and allowed herself a few minutes to wake up and scroll her phone.

Stifling a yawn, she opened her Messenger app.

She could see a little green light next to Ashton's name. Of course, he was awake. It was early evening there.

As she willed herself to put the phone down and start getting ready for the day, a short, sharp beep sounded and a message appeared on the screen.

Hey. Saw you were on-line. How are you, babe?

Ashton! She gasped and pushed the phone to her chest. Why was he messaging her? She glanced at it again. Had he been looking at his phone, waiting for her to come online?

How odd. How strange. How coincidental.

Her finger hovered over the message, tempted to answer, but she paused.

Don't message him. Don't message him. Don't message him. She repeated this mantra again and again in her head and stuffed the phone under her pillow.

Throwing back her covers, she slipped into the bathroom and turned on the shower. She whispered "Don't message him. Don't message him. Don't message him," to the rhythm of the hot water splashing against the tiles.

It was hard to be strong. And it had taken her time to build up her resistance to break off all communications with him a few months earlier.

The day that he'd sent that final text message to her, telling her he was sorry but it was over, she'd sent him back a barrage of unanswered responses. It had been desperate. It had been undignified. It had been embarrassing.

She'd gone cold turkey a week after he'd ended things, perhaps faced with more challenging issues like flunking out of her final exams and running out of money, meaning she had been on the phone, in tears, begging her father to send her money to get home.

Since she'd been home, she'd managed to hold off sending Ashton anything—even when she had exciting news or a date with the gorgeous Leon—and now shouldn't be any different.

It was simply a matter of self-control and of being the better person. Dressed and ready to go, she retrieved her phone from her pillow and scooped it into her bag.

She didn't check to see if there were any other messages, though she was almost beside herself at the thought of whether he'd sent a follow-up. Was he waiting for her to respond? Was he disappointed she hadn't? Maybe she should…

No. Stay strong.

She placed her handbag over her shoulder and crept down the dark, still hallway to the kitchen.

The flicker of green light from the clock on the microwave bathed the room in an eerie glow, just enough to make out the fruit bowl on the bench.

Selecting an apple, she misjudged the way they'd been piled and several came tumbling out over the kitchen tiles. They rolled into a pair of fluffy bedroom slippers shaped like bunny rabbits with floppy ears and lifeless glass eyes reflecting against the dim light of microwave clock.

Michelle gasped as the kitchen light was switched on. "You scared me." She blinked as her eyes adjusted to the downlights.

"I scared you?" Mum brought her hand to her heart over her grey bathrobe covered in rabbits, matching her footwear. "What are you doing up at this hour? I thought it was a burglar. I was about to grab the toaster and hit you over the head with it."

"Thank goodness you didn't, because I'd rather not spend the morning in the emergency room. Is that how you treat any member of the family who happens to be up early? Clocking them over the head with household appliances?" She replaced the apples in the bowl, aside from one, which she washed and bit into.

"It's four in the morning. When have you ever gotten up at this hour?" Her mother scratched her head.

It was a reasonable question. Michelle was only ever up at this hour to catch a flight, or stumble home from a night club.

"Today, I have."

"Why?"

"For work."

"Now? What time does your café open?" Her mother sounded astonished and squinted at the time on the oven, which was probably wrong. Her father was an engineer yet couldn't figure out how to change it between daylight saving and standard time.

"Not until later, but I'm helping to do some preparation." And before she had to answer the 'why' that was no doubt coming, Michelle said her goodbyes and left.

The drive to work was short, and she slipped in the back door, a gust of wind slamming it behind her.

The lights were on in the kitchen, and she could hear the faint sound of a radio playing some peppy Latin American-style music.

"Good morning." Gabriel took a sip from an espresso cup and smiled at her. "I was thinking you might have slept in."

"Nope. I'm determined." She put aside her bag and coat before slipping into the kitchen and washing her hands. *Determined* didn't begin to cover it. She was even more adamant that she needed to win the trophy. And not just to annoy Pete. It was a matter of pride. Her pride.

"Okay." Gabriel poured flour into a large metal bowl. "I thought I'd make some éclairs today. We haven't done those for a while and they're always popular. You could see if they were something you could replicate at home."

Éclairs sounded rather fancy, and Michelle had memories of eating a beautiful, delicate buttery éclair drizzled in rich, dark chocolate in a bakery in Quebec with Ashton.

She went to reach for her phone to see if he'd messaged her again, but paused. *Stop thinking about him!* There were far more important things to worry about.

She refocused on Gabriel. Éclairs sounded like a competition-standard dish, but she had to be able to make them herself. It wasn't like she could smuggle a chef into her parents' kitchen to help her. Clare had once handed Pete a spoon during the competition and Steve had called for him to be disqualified.

The 'incident' had inspired her father to write a complex rule book, so large it had an index and appendices outlining the governance of the competition.

"Aren't éclairs hard?" She wrung her hands.

"They can be difficult, but if you get the pastry right, the whole thing falls into place. Make these and you'll win that trophy."

"Brilliant. Where do we start?" She beamed at him.

Gabriel was a little like his daughter. They shared the same dark hair and good looks. He had a little bit of a temper at times, but overall, he was high energy and had a dedication to perfection, like Tessa possessed.

His kitchen was impeccable. The stainless-steel bench gleamed, every utensil, pot and pan had a home, and spices and herbs were neatly labelled in containers and jars. They were even in alphabetical order like at the supermarket.

Food was a very serious endeavour with the De Luca Family. It was in their blood: generations of restaurateurs, butchers, chefs, orchardists, fishermen, and wine importers.

It was certainly a big part of life with the Fitzgeralds, but it seemed more based on the fact that they needed to somehow satisfy enormous appetites than any great genetic affinity for the preparation of food.

She watched Gabriel like a hawk, trying to take in the techniques, measurements and timings. It was like spinning plates. He had saucepans boiling, cakes in the oven, and mixers whizzing with ingredients, yet the whole kitchen was smooth and organised.

"That was fun." Michelle wiped her hands on a tea towel, amazed that more than two hours had zoomed by.

"You did well," Gabriel encouraged. "You're very focused."

That was perhaps the first time anyone had ever said that to her, but it was amazing how she'd been able to block out the world and solely concentrate on the work.

Maybe it was a good omen. She was going to be focused, on her job, on Leon, and on her future. Not on Ashton and her broken heart. Not on his callous dismissal of her. Not on her many, many failures.

"I really appreciate this. Thanks, Gabriel."

He grinned. "It's a pleasure. I'm happy for you to come in anytime if you want to try the recipe again."

She looked around the kitchen. Maybe she would take Gabriel up on the offer. It wouldn't hurt to keep on refining her skills ahead of the competition and as a way to stay busy.

Slipping her phone from her pocket, she looked at the message again and was even prouder of herself for not having responded. Take that, Ashton!

Maybe, just maybe, she was curing her addiction to him and rebuilding her life.

CHAPTER 24

Harry placed a large chocolate and cherry muffin next to Bebe's sketchbook.

She blushed, and smiled at him. "Thank you." She picked up the plate and took in the smell of vanilla and cherry. It was intoxicating.

"The least we can do for our designer in residence." He winked and walked back to the counter to serve a customer.

A little jolt of lust hurtled through her.

The muffin wasn't the only thing that was intoxicating around here.

She broke the muffin into quarters and popped a piece into her mouth and drew some embellishments on the dress she had thought about for Tessa.

Since her dreamy half awake, half asleep state after her date with Harry to the club, her mind had gone into overdrive for Tessa and she had refined the design to the point it was almost ready to be made.

Reaching out to pick up another piece of the muffin, she gasped as her eyes locked on a man who had walked into the café. It was Greg Fitzgerald. She ducked her head. What he if recognised her? She hadn't thought he'd seen her that day at the office, but what if she'd been mistaken and he had noticed her peering around from around the pole.

Surely he'd be suspicious of running into her twice.

He sat at a table and opened a newspaper, flicking through the pages.

Shoving another piece of muffin in her mouth and draining the last of her coffee, she slipped her phone into her handbag and stood, turning towards the back of the café, where she knew there was a back exit near the kitchen.

Raising a hand to wave good-bye to Harry, she took a footstep before she heard a male voice call out, "Excuse me?"

Was it Greg, talking to her? She gulped and took another step towards the back of the café.

"Excuse me, miss?"

She paused and turned slowly, clutching her handbag, meeting Greg eye-to-eye. "Yes?" she croaked.

He pointed to the table she'd vacated. "Did you leave your book?"

She picked up the sketchbook, stuffing it into her bag. "Thank you," she mumbled and turned, rushing towards the hallway, and her escape.

She glanced around the hall until she found the fire escape door. She pushed it open and slipped through, letting it slam behind her with a metallic clunk.

That was close. Far too close. If she was going to play this game, she'd need to do it carefully or the whole thing could blow up in her face.

Bebe walked arm-in-arm with Harry as they left a rooftop cinema he'd taken her to that night for their date.

"You left the café quickly today."

"Oh, yes. I needed to get back to work. I'm sorry, did I owe you money for the coffee, or the muffin?"

He shook his head. "You paid for the coffee and the muffin was on the house as always. Are you okay?"

Not really. "I'm fine. And thanks for the movie, that was a lot of fun." She'd enjoyed sitting on deck chairs on the fake grass on the top of a building with fairy lights strung above them and an old movie showing. They'd bought hot, salty souvlakis from a pop-up stand for dinner, and washed them down with glasses of rosé.

"I'm glad."

"You know all the good places here." His creativity in their dates was impressive. Jazz clubs and rooftop cinemas were much more than your standard dinner or drinks.

"I grew up around here. So, your mother lived here when you were born?"

"Yes." She nodded.

"And your father?" Harry asked. "Is he from here too?"

"He was." She exhaled. "He died."

Harry flinched. "I'm so sorry."

She looked straight ahead. "It happened before I was born. I don't really know that much about him."

He didn't say anything, but took her hand and gave it a comforting squeeze. "You don't?"

"Not really. My mother doesn't really talk much about him. I sometimes ask questions, but I don't get much response."

"Maybe it's painful for her."

"I understand that, but I wish I knew more."

"Is there anyone else you can ask?"

"No." She shook her head. "There's no-one else to talk to. He didn't have any family in Australia. He migrated here from Sweden when he was a kid with his parents, but they're both deceased now."

"That must be hard, but it sounds like you're close with your mother." He squeezed her hand again.

"We are." That wasn't the issue. "I'm grateful. I've had a lot of opportunities thanks to her hard work."

"You've been to more places than I've had hot dinners."

Bebe looked down at the pavement. Crisp brown leaves were strewn in front of them. A gust of wind picked them up and they danced down the street. Sometimes she felt like that. Like she was a leaf pushed along the path by the sheer force of her mother's ambition and career. There was no base to return to. The tree couldn't take back a fallen leaf. And like the leaf, she'd go where the wind took her.

Or at least, that's what she always thought, but she didn't need to live like that, did she? Could there a base for her here? Was that why the winds of change had brought her back to her hometown?

"Bebe?"

She glanced at Harry. "Sorry. I was miles away. I always have a lot of thoughts, and get a bit lost in them."

"It seems like a nice place to be."

"Sometimes it is," she said. "Sometimes, it's just confusing."

He frowned. "Confusing?"

"I move so much. It's hard to feel at home. I find things to make me comfortable, but it can be hard to be grounded."

"I understand."

"You do, don't you?" She paused. She wasn't sure why exactly but his thoughts and hers did seem similar at times. Maybe it was a past life connection, or maybe a similar energy, but there was something about him that she felt like she could tell him the darkest fears that lurked within her, the greatest uncertainties and regrets.

He stopped, and pulled her into him. He wrapped his arms around her waist and their noses touched. His felt cold as it rubbed against hers. She closed her eyes, the sound of the street fading into nothing as she became lost in him and their lips met.

His hands stroked her hair and she grasped at the back of his jacket, pulling him further into her body.

She wasn't sure how long they were like this, but when a noisy gaggle of teenagers passed and giggled, she cleared her throat. What was it about him that made her unable to control herself when it came to public displays of affection?

He grinned and took her hand. They continued to walk. "Do you want to take the tram home, or get an Uber?"

She paused and bit her lip. It was too early for her to end this evening with just a kiss. She wanted more. She wanted him. "Could we go back to your place?"

He smiled. "I'd like that."

They held hands as they took the tram, exchanging small glances at each other and smiles that made her heart flutter with anticipation.

His apartment was furnished with a dark brown leather couch, a 1960s style, oval coffee table, a tall lamp and a rug with a geometric brown and aqua pattern on it. The whole effect was cool, effortlessly cool, actually.

He brought over two small, white espresso cups on saucers and sat next to her, and the closeness of his body next to hers made her feel charged up.

He cupped her chin, and their lips met in a slow and tender kiss. It was like they had all the time in the world compared to the fast and frenzied kiss that had shaken her entire world outside that jazz club.

His hand skimmed across her thigh, and he pushed at the fabric of her dress up, only a few centimetres. She moved his hand further along her thigh.

She wanted his hands on her body and to feel as close to him as she could. The undeniable mental, or perhaps spiritual connection needed an earthly element to feel even more real.

Tugging at his shirt buttons, she moved her hand up against the warm, smooth skin of his torso and let out an involuntarily moan as his mouth moved across her face, kissing her jawline and neck. She grasped at his back, digging her nails in, urging their bodies closer together.

She felt for the zip on the side of her dress, when Harry's hand met hers. He raised his eyebrows, as if seeking approval. She nodded, and pushed his hand so the zip parted.

He stood up, and paused. "You are so beautiful." He held out his hand.

She took it and he pulled her to her feet. As they made their way to the bedroom, she felt the pure chemical reaction take over, leaving her feeling light-headed and a little love-drunk as he slipped her dress over her head and lay her down on the bed.

As his lips moved down along her bra, down her stomach, she allowed herself to close her eyes, and for the first time since she landed in Melbourne, her mind fell silent.

CHAPTER 25

"This is awesome." Leon ate the rest of the pasta Michelle made him as they sat on the sofa in his living room.

"I'm learning a lot from Gabriel." She placed her bowl down on the coffee table. She'd gone in early four times over the past few weeks and each time had learned a lot, and enjoyed herself.

"But you still made that by yourself. You must be a fast learner." He took a sip of his wine and removed his phone from his pocket. He pulled her into him and snapped a selfie of them together.

"Are you putting that on Instagram?" she asked as he flipped back to the shot and showed her.

"Nah. Just for me to remind me what a beautiful girlfriend I have. Or do you want me to post it?"

"Goodness no! Look at me!" She pointed to her hair, scooped up in a messy bun, and wiped flour dust off her top.

"You look cute," he insisted. "I like it."

"Are you on Instagram?" She'd searched for him a couple

of times, but had been unable to find him, or more specifically, any evidence of any former girlfriends.

"Yeah, but I use a handle and don't have a profile picture. I should look you up though."

He hadn't looked her up on socials? Really? "Here I am." She pushed her phone towards him.

"How do you have that many followers?" His mouth was open. "Are you a celebrity in Japan?"

She giggled.

"Oh, there's my noodles from the other day!" He squinted. "You know moving that chilli really did make it look better. Who's that guy?" He held up her phone to her, revealing a photo of her and Ashton.

"Oh." She ducked her head. Was Leon the jealous type? "An ex of mine. Sorry."

He tilted his head. "Don't be sorry. We all have exes. What was his deal?"

"I went out with him in Canada. It didn't end well. I should delete it."

"Nah. Exes are part of our history."

She held out her hand. "Okay. Your turn. Hand it over."

He tapped on his phone and handed it to her. "I have thirty followers and I've probably posted one picture in my life so there's not much to see on my account."

Thirty? He was right. And he most certainly didn't post anything. There was one photo of a beach somewhere and one taken at the football. "Why even bother to have an account?"

"I like to keep in touch with people. Sometimes if mates go overseas, it's handy for touching base. But that's about it. I guess I don't really want people to know my every move."

"Are you on the run from the law?" she teased.

"No."

"Why don't you post anything?"

"I don't know. I forget to take photographs, and some I like just to be my memories, you know."

She glanced at him. "You're not into posting pictures of the girls you date."

He cleared his throat. "Is that a sneaky way of asking me to open the ex-files?"

Yes. "Only if you want to."

He rubbed his neck. "Not much to tell. Pip was my longest relationship. We broke up last year. Nice girl, but it was like being with a friend."

"Is that a bad thing? Friendship is a good basis of long-lasting relationships." That's what her parents always said. They'd been married for well over thirty years and they still snuggled together on the sofa while watching television and gave each other mushy cards for Valentine's Day.

"I don't disagree, but you need that spark there. That little buzz that's more than just hanging with a mate." He held her phone out to her. "Why do you post so many photos?"

She took back her phone and scrolled through her feed. "I like to show people what I've been up to. I want people to know I've been doing exciting things."

"Why? Why do you care what they think?"

She put down the phone. Why did she care so much? "I don't know. There's something satisfying about people liking my photos."

He frowned. "Why?"

"It makes me feel good. When I see that little icon lit up with comments and likes, it makes me feel special."

"You shouldn't need likes or comments to feel like that. You are special." He leaned forward and dusted some flour off her nose. "Your photos look great. But I really like the real you, not a virtual version."

She crawled onto his lap and ran her fingertip along his

jawline. "I guess a virtual person can't do this." She leaned forward and kissed him, allowing her body to melt into his.

"No, they can't," he agreed.

"And they definitely can't do this," she whispered, with a flick of her hair and puffing out her lips in a way that she hoped looked pouty and seductive.

At that point, Leon shifted and she lost her balance. She shrieked as she crashed to the floor and her shoulder slammed into Leon's polished floorboards. "Ouch," she whimpered.

"Michelle!" He leaned forward and helped her up to a sitting position. "Are you okay? Anything broken?"

"No, I don't think so." She sighed. "I was trying to be sexy."

"You are sexy." He sat next to her on the floor and massaged her shoulder.

She raised an eyebrow. "Really? Even when I fall over?"

"All the time."

She hesitated. "What about spark?"

He scoffed. "Are you kidding me? You're a firework."

She blushed as he leaned into her and their lips met and he brought his arms around her.

Her feelings for Ashton had been like an out of control bushfire, Leon had felt more like a friend in many ways so far, but as they kissed, his tongue exploring hers and his hand skimming along the curve of her waist, she wondered if maybe friendship, plus spark, was the secret to a successful relationship.

CHAPTER 26

What time was it? The hours had blurred together before Bebe had fallen asleep, lying in the crook of Harry's arm.

She grimaced. Her head was throbbing. She felt along the floor for something to put on and when she hit buttons, she picked up a garment. It was Harry's shirt. She pulled it on and crept into the living room. She brought her arms around her as the coolness of the apartment left goosebumps on her skin. It had been cosy in that bed with Harry, and she was loathed to leave, but she'd never fall back to sleep with her head aching.

Switching on his kitchen light, she removed a glass from the cupboard, filled it with water and fumbled around in her handbag for some aspirin, and returned to the bedroom with the tablets.

A lamp by the side of his bed illuminated the room. Harry sat up. "Headache?"

She nodded, took the aspirin and a big gulp of water, and climbed back into bed with him, bringing his arm around her.

"Are you okay?" He stroked her hair back as she snuggled into him.

She felt tears well in her eyes. It was so warm and comforting and happy here with Harry, and despite the thumping in her head, things felt calmer when she was next to him.

"Yeah. I don't know. I've been getting a lot of headaches. I thought it was jetlag or tiredness or not enough water, but I wonder now if it's stress. I've been going through some stuff since I got here."

"Work?"

She shook her head. "It's about my father." She'd never told this to anyone. It was one of the things about moving so much. She'd had friends, and boyfriends, but there was always a distance. An emotional barrier of sorts. She smoothed out the bedsheet. "I've been undertaking some research into his past. I want to know more about him."

"What sort of research? Can I help?"

She shook her head. "That's so nice of you, but not really. I went to the State Library to see if I could find a newspaper article about when he died." There was no way known she could take Harry on such trips, despite his generous offer to help. What if he noticed a link with Greg Fitzgerald?

"And did you find out anything?"

"Not much. It was what my mother had said, that he was killed in a motorbike accident."

Harry stroked her arm. "I'm so sorry. What are you hoping to find out about him?"

"I need to know….err…well," She sat up. "This is where it gets a bit complicated."

He frowned. "Complicated?"

"When I was a child, I overheard my mother talking to a friend. We were still in London, but we moved to Paris shortly after. It's all just bits and pieces, some of which I barely remember." She closed her eyes, recalling the conversation she'd heard through the kitchen door of their London apartment. "They were talking about a man. A man who couldn't be a father to me as he wouldn't leave his family."

Harry narrowed his eyes. "Okay. That must have been hard for a little kid to hear."

"I think I blocked some of it out, or didn't sort of realise what it meant at the time, but over the years, along with some information, I've begun to wonder who that man was and whether he was actually my real father."

"This man who wouldn't leave his family?" Harry rubbed his chin. "You think your mother lied to you about the identity of your father?"

"I wonder."

He paused. "That's a big deal. Why would she have done that?"

"If he couldn't leave his family, maybe they had an affair and she wanted to protect me from that. Maybe it was easier for me to think my father had died rather than a man who didn't want anything to do with me." Her voice wobbled on the final words.

"How old were you when you heard this?"

"I was small. Maybe five. I wondered if perhaps she'd been in touch with him and tried to make it work, but he wouldn't leave his wife."

"Perhaps. Did you ask her?"

"I was five. It didn't mean much to me. As I got older, I remembered it and started asking questions about Arne, and she'd always get cagey and so adamant that it would always just be the two of us. You and me. Me and You. That was our mantra." She snuggled into Harry.

"That's a good mantra."

She nodded. "I know, and I'm grateful for everything my

mother has done for us. I've lived an incredible life and I know that, but sometimes you can't help but wonder…"

"About whether this other man is your father?"

"And what life could have been like. Could I have had that suburban, family life if they could have been together? But what could that have done? Could that have deprived another family of their father?" She swallowed. She wanted to tell Harry her fears about Greg Fitzgerald, and how if he left his family, he would have left Michelle.

But it was too crazy. She trusted Harry, but he was also friends with Michelle.

She wasn't sure what any of this meant, and it could have far-reaching consequences if something ever came out about it. It could tear a family apart.

"Maybe you should ask your mum a few more questions. You could be worrying yourself over nothing. Maybe there's a simple explanation for what you heard."

Bebe shook her head. "Every time I even mention anything about my father, she shuts down. She doesn't want to talk about it. I think she's hiding something. Something big."

"Or maybe it's just painful for her, but I'm sure she wouldn't like you getting stressed about it."

"I also don't want her to think I'm ungrateful. She has given up so much for me and shown me the world. I studied at amazing schools and universities. I've ridden camels in Egypt, I've been to palaces and galleries. I've met artists and actors and been to glamourous parties, but at the same time…"

"You never felt home?"

She blinked back tears and shook her head.

He drew her in close to him and kissed the crown of her head, leaving her in no doubt that at that moment, there was nowhere else in the world she'd rather be.

CHAPTER 27

When the alarm went off a little after four-thirty, it hadn't bothered Michelle as it had the first time she'd worked in the kitchen with Gabriel. Was she turning into an early riser?

It certainly helped when Leon brought her a cup of coffee to help her wake up, rather than her mother mistaking her for an intruder and threatening to hit her over the head with a kitchen appliance.

"I could get used to this," she said as she sipped the coffee, snuggling up to him in bed.

"It's not as good as you make."

She smiled. "Not just the coffee, but being here with you. It's nice."

"It is."

"Meet you back here later?"

He grinned. "Sounds good. What's for dinner?"

"Let's see what Gabriel teaches me today." She flung back the quilt cover and handed him the coffee cup.

"Tell him that I really like lamb," he mused, kissing the top of her forehead.

They both got ready, and he dropped her off at Espresso Walk.

"Thanks for the lift." She leaned over the gear stick and kissed him.

"My pleasure. I'm going to go to a couple of jobs but I'll come back for coffee at lunchtime."

"I'd like that." She gave him another kiss and climbed out, closing the door as he gave her a wave and whistled a cheery tune.

There was something delightfully domestic about their situation in the morning—something she always thought she wanted to run from, but could it be just wanted she needed?

"You're good at this," Gabriel said later that morning as Michelle pulled a chocolate orange cake from the oven. He had his arms folded and was watching her carefully. "You've made great progress over the past few weeks."

"Really?" Michelle had never considered herself a cook, let alone a good one. She'd learned a few basics, but she'd always thought that Pete was the chef of the family. She took in the smell of the cake and her stomach rumbled.

"You are. Have you practised the éclairs at home? Remember the oven will vary. These are commercial ovens here; they will heat differently to your one at home"

She nodded. She'd carefully made notes about the steps in the process and had thought about the difference in temperatures of the ovens. "Yes. I need to find a time when no-one will be home so they don't get suspicious."

He quirked an eyebrow. "It sounds very competitive."

"Everything in my family is."

"If you want to come in early on Thursday, I'm happy to run through them again here."

She paused. "Thanks, Gabriel. That's so nice."

He smiled. "I have an ulterior motive. Last time we made éclairs they sold out by nine-thirty."

"You're a good teacher."

"You're a good student," he said.

"I don't think anyone has ever said that about me."

"I think you're going to prove yourself to your family in this competition." He grinned. "Sometimes the black sheep comes through, yeah?"

She laughed. "Sometimes they do, don't they?"

CHAPTER 28

It wasn't going to be easy to get a sample of Michelle's hair.

And it wasn't simply the logistics involved, it was the uneasy feeling whenever Bebe thought about it. Breaking Michelle's trust and being sneaky—it didn't sit well with her. In an ideal world, she'd just ask, but how could she suggest to Michelle that maybe her father cheated on his wife? And how would she feel about taking a quick DNA test to prove this?

Bebe placed her head in her hands. This was ridiculous, but perhaps it was the best way. Michelle need not know anything about it, and if it turned out as a no-match, she'd be none the wiser. It was far better than raising it with Michelle and causing hurt and confusion if there need not be any.

She slipped a clean comb into a tissue and placed it into an empty pocket in her handbag. She also placed a fresh, clear, Ziploc bag alongside it. She wasn't sure what she'd be able to get, but given they were going to spend the day together, she wanted to be prepared to either offer her a comb or be able to grab something of Michelle's, like a takeaway coffee cup that could be tested.

Her phone rang. Michelle.

"Hey. I know we were going to go shopping, but would you mind coming over to my house?

Bebe tensed. Go to the Fitzgerald family home? She swallowed. What if Greg were there? What if he recognised her from the day outside his workplace or the café?

A cold hand gripped her heart. What if he recognised her and drew the connection? She didn't look that much like her mother, but surely he could have an inkling, right?

She chewed her nail. Or maybe he was blissfully unaware of who she was, the fact he'd run into her and her connection with Petra. He'd not seemed to make any connection to her that day at Espresso Walk. "To your house?" she clarified.

"Yeah. I need to test making these éclairs for my family cooking competition and you can be my guinea pig."

"Éclairs?" she asked, as a way to stall while she considered the upside to the situation—it would be much easier to get a sample of Michelle's DNA from her home. And that would once and for all prove things, one way or another.

"Yes. Gabriel has shown me how to make a dish and I want to test it out."

"Err. Okay."

"Excellent. I'll text you the address."

She hung up the phone, uncertain as to whether she'd made the right decision. Her debate of the pros and cons continued until she arrived at Michelle's house.

It was just as she had expected—the suburban dream. Solid house. Nice block. Calm street. A house full of kids. And nothing like she'd ever experienced.

She held her breath as she rang the doorbell. Would Greg open it?

The door opened, and it was Michelle with a tea towel over her shoulder and flour on her nose.

"Thanks for coming over," she said, gesturing for Bebe to come in. "Everyone is out so I knew this was the only time I could make this recipe in this kitchen. I need to make sure I have the settings right on the oven. If they know what I'm doing, they'll try to sabotage me."

They walked through to the kitchen.

"Who lives here?" Bebe looked around the room, taking in the faint smell of pumpkin soup and the sun filtering through a window, giving it a cosy glow. It wasn't an expensive-looking kitchen with flashy European appliances, but it had been built to last with wooden cupboards and a generous bench.

She pulled up one of the stools at the counter. She could imagine kids sitting up here, eating bowls full of cereal or doing their homework.

"Mum, Dad, and me, the loser of the family, right? Still with my parents."

Bebe shrugged. "I live with my mother." It was hard to imagine not living with her. It had always been just them and would be at least for the next six months while they were both in New York.

"That's a bit different. You've lived all over the world. This is my childhood home, and all these years later"—she waved a wooden spoon around the kitchen and leaned forward against the bench—"I'm still here."

Bebe smiled. "It's nice."

"I'd love to get my own place, but I'm so broke after Canada. I'm trying to save a little bit now." She gestured towards a block of chocolate. "Here, can you break this up for me?"

"Of course." Bebe stood and washed her hands in the sink. "I'm sorry about Canada."

"Don't be. I got distracted and didn't study well. My grades were terrible, and when I returned, I couldn't get my head into classes here and I got so many fails that they asked me to leave."

"Why were you distracted?" Bebe picked up the block of dark cooking chocolate and broke it into small pieces.

"His name was Ashton." She frowned and paused, her spoon hovering over ingredients in a large ceramic bowl. "*Is* Ashton, I guess. Strange how I just put him in the past tense."

Bebe smiled. "Perhaps that's a good thing that you're putting him behind you."

"It wasn't long ago that I never thought I'd be able to do that."

"Break-ups are hard."

"This one in particular. I thought I'd found the one, that he could give me everything. His family are rich, *really* rich. And powerful and they're a bit famous. I thought my life would be nothing but parties and private planes, but it was as if, at the stroke of midnight, everything turned into a pumpkin."

Bebe was silent. She'd seen their relationship play out on social media, but it was weird to admit she'd been cyber-stalking Michelle and her Canadian quasi-royalty boyfriend. And her family here. Come to think of it, she knew nearly everything there was to know about Michelle, but she couldn't admit that. It was vital to play it cool.

Michelle levelled off a cup of sugar and poured it into the bowl. "He kept on delaying me meeting his family. I didn't think too much of it at the time as I was busy between university and skiing and working and partying, and then finally, I overheard him on speakerphone with his mother, who told him that she had no interest in meeting some ski bunny from Australia and that he needed to think of the family image."

Bebe's mouth fell open. "The family image?" she repeated, slowly.

"Yep. I guess I wasn't … I don't know … rich enough? Connected enough? Cultured enough?" She continued to mix the ingredients with a wooden spoon. "Anyway, after that, he went cold on me and ended things with a text message. He's now dating a stick-insect called Gretchen whose parents I think own half of Canada and a couple of Islands too."

"You're better off without him." What a bunch of stuck-up snobs.

"I guess. But it still hurts. I shouldn't say that when I'm seeing someone else, and I really like Leon, but it does still hurt. Is that wrong?" She tilted her head to the side.

"If it still hurts, it still hurts. You can't deny that. Maybe Leon will be a way that you can move on from that and realise you deserve better than how Ashton treated you."

Michelle flashed her a beautiful smile, but it quickly faded. "I don't want Leon just to be a rebound thing."

Bebe shook her head. "I didn't say he was, but it could be nice to see where it goes."

"We're taking it pretty slowly." She tipped the contents of the mixing bowl out and rolled the pastry. "Dating Ashton was a bit of a blur, to be honest. We were always out and doing things. When I think about it now, we didn't actually talk much." She held the rolling pin up and tilted her head to the side as if trying to recall.

"I understand that."

"How are things going with Harry? He's nice to talk to."

"He is." It was one of the things she liked most about him.

"He's mad about you." Michelle flashed her a smile. "He always looks so pleased when you stop by Espresso Walk."

"I like him." Bebe frowned as these words came out of her mouth. She'd not really articulated it like that to herself, or anyone, but there it was. She did like Harry. A lot.

She cleared her throat. She had to stop daydreaming about Harry and focus on why she was there. "May I use your bathroom, please?"

"Of course. Go down that hallway and it's second on the left."

Bebe slipped past a wall of family photos. School photos. Wedding pictures. Family holiday snaps. It seemed overwhelming as she stared and tried to imagine herself in them, lined up in a school dress or around the Christmas table. Everyone looked so happy, and her heart ached.

The bathroom counter had bottles of perfumes, hair products and make-up, and it smelled of Michelle's perfume. She carefully opened a cupboard next to the vanity, and saw a hairbrush sitting on a shelf.

She inched her hand forward to pick it up before she snapped her hand back.

What was she thinking? She pinched the bridge of her nose. She couldn't do this.

She glanced at her reflection in the mirror. She was going to see the best in this situation, just like Harry told her she did.

She'd had a great, interesting and exciting life, and Michelle was a good person who clearly needed the support of her family unit. She didn't deserve to have her life blown apart, even if it were true. Why should she pay for the sins of her father?

Bebe should be grateful she'd been able to meet Michelle and become friends with her. For someone who had always lived out of a suitcase, connections like Harry and Michelle had been hard to come by.

Was it worth not knowing some things in order to have so much more?

CHAPTER 29

Michelle drizzled chocolate over the éclairs and stood back as Gabriel leaned over to inspect them.

"I tried so hard. I did them at home the other day too. I think I got the oven right. Ours isn't a commercial one like here, but I did your calculations…" She was rambling.

A smile curled over Gabriel's lips. "Not bad." He glanced back at her. "Not bad at all. The colour of the pastry looks good, the chocolate looks glossy and the cream doesn't appear to be runny.

"Are you going to try one?" She wrung her hands on a tea towel. Bebe had raved about them at her house, which was lovely but Gabriel was the expert.

He nodded and picked up a pastry. He inspected it and bit. Chewing slowly, he continued to nod. "Perfect."

She gasped. "Perfect?"

He gave a thumbs up. "Don't tell Tessa but I think these are better than hers."

"Yay!" She flung her arms around Gabriel's neck. She pulled back. "I'm sorry, that wasn't very professional."

"It's okay." He leaned a hand on the bench. "I think you're a certainty for your family cooking competition."

She probably was, thanks to him, but more than that, perfecting the recipe over time and thinking about all the elements had been far more interesting than she'd expected.

It was quite amazing to make something out of nothing. It must be how Bebe felt when she designed and sewed a gown from nothing more than basic fabric.

"Thank you for helping me, Gabriel. I really appreciate it."

"It's been a pleasure. As I said, you're a natural."

She hesitated. "I'd love to keep learning from you, but I don't want to get in your way."

"You're not in my way." He flipped a tea towel over his shoulder. "I can always use some help. Why don't I talk to Tessa and we can see if we can come up with some sort of arrangement?"

She smiled. "That would be great, but if it's okay, I'd like to ask Tessa myself."

Later that morning, Tessa walked through the café. Michelle paused, took a deep breath, straightened her apron and approached her boss.

"Tessa?"

"Hmm?" Tessa looked up from an iPad. "Sorry, I'm dealing with a real estate agent who is trying to gouge me on this new place. Seriously. I wish my cousin Lottie had something on her books."

Lottie was a real estate agent. Harry had pointed her out in the café and she regularly stopped by with clients for coffee.

She spoke rapidly like Tessa did and had the same intimidating, feisty personality. The De Luca family seemed as high-energy, large and noisy as the Fitzgeralds, and there always seemed to be uncles, aunts, and cousins coming and going.

"I don't want to interrupt, but I'm wondering if it is okay to help Gabriel in the kitchen sometimes?" she asked.

Tessa frowned. "I thought he had enough staff?"

"No. It's just I want to learn more about food and cooking. I won't get in his way, and I'm happy to come in on my day off. The more I know, the more useful I can be to customers when they have questions about the food."

Tessa tilted her head. "Come in on your day off? That's keen."

"I'm interested in cooking, pastry in particular."

"How interested?"

She wasn't sure what this meant. "Very?" she asked, hesitantly.

Tessa chuckled. "You've been a great employee, Michelle. You work really well with Harry and the crew, and it's wonderful to see you taking an interest in what we cook here. I've been impressed, and I always believe in using people's talents." She brought a finger to her red lips and narrowed her eyes. "I'm more than happy for you to help in the kitchen, and we can move some of your shifts around to do that, but I'd like you to try it and in a few weeks' time, let's check in on how you are going. If this new place gets off the ground, I'm going to need more chefs."

Michelle's heart sped up. "Chefs?"

"If it was something you were interested in learning, I'd be happy to look at a career pathway for you. My father has worked with apprentices for years."

An apprenticeship? She thought back to the conversation at the family dinner table when she was first kicked out of uni. The idea hadn't been that appealing then, but that was a plumbing apprenticeship. Cooking was far more interesting.

And learning more from Gabriel? That was certainly a wonderful opportunity.

"I'm not sure if I'm ready for that." Was she good enough to make this a career? Or commit to studying again?

"Consider it an option. In the meantime, that's fine for you to work with my father." Tessa walked to the kitchen.

It was certainly nice to have options. Michelle straightened her shoulders and walked to the counter. Those had felt few and far between in recent times.

The café door opened, and Bebe gave her a wave as she entered.

"Hey. Nice to see you. You know it's Harry's day off," Michelle said, pouring her a glass of water and setting it down in front of her at Bebe's favourite table—the one near the window with the cushions and where the light filtered in no matter what time of day.

Bebe smiled and slipped into her seat. "I know. I like it here."

Michelle looked around. She did too. "Harry said that I need to give you a muffin when you come in? Do you want one?"

"Did he?" Bebe blushed. "Not today, but thank you. Just a latte, please."

"No worries. How's work going?"

"Not bad." Bebe held up her notebook, revealing a delicate sketch of a woman with a lace skirt, each fold of fabric so beautifully shaded that even in pencil, the design leapt off the page.

"Fashion block has clearly gone." Michelle whistled.

"Pretty much." Bebe gave herself a contented smile, and pulled a pencil from a small case in front of her.

"That's great. You know, I was wondering if you wanted to go with me to …" She paused as she saw *Ashton*.

She blinked. It couldn't be. She'd thought she'd seen him

everywhere after they had broken up. At the airport, at the supermarket, filling a car with petrol, or catching a bus. Could this be the real version, or just her imagination?

He smiled through the glass window. That smile was far too real to be an illusion.

Michelle pulled open the door. A cool breeze hit her face. If she had been dreaming, that would have woken her up.

But it wasn't an illusion. It was real. He was here.

"Hey, Michelle," he said softly

Hearing his voice again was surreal. "What are you doing here?" she asked, staring at him.

Leaning into her, he kissed her cheek. "I'm here to see you."

"But what about Gretchen?"

"Gretchen? What about her?"

"I thought you were dating her?" All those photos on Instagram? What had those been?

"She's just a friend. I told you that from the start."

She folded her arms. "It didn't seem like that."

"I'm sorry if it did, but that's all she was. Besides, these past few months, I haven't been able to get you out of my mind."

Their eyes met and familiar feelings washed over her as when they'd first met.

But this was different. The pain he'd caused hurtled through her. "You hurt me."

"I know." His face softened. "I'm sorry. If I could go back and change things, I would, but I can't so that's why I'm here now. I'm trying to make amends so we can start again." He took her hands and gave them a squeeze.

She looked down at his hands over hers. "I don't know."

"Michelle, I love you. Please tell me you still feel the same way."

Her mouth fell open. He loved her? He'd never said that when they were together.

But why now? After all this time? She rubbed her temple. Her brain hurt. Her heart hurt. She looked around the street. It wasn't the time or place to have this conversation.

"What do you say?" he asked, hopefully.

"I'm at work. This isn't the time to talk about it."

"I understand. I've caught you off guard. What time do you finish? Maybe we can get a drink and talk properly."

She was going straight to Clare and Pete's house after work to babysit Timothy. "I'm busy tonight."

"Tomorrow?"

"That sounds …" she began before she remembered the family Master Chef Trophy. She couldn't back out of that, and especially not as she'd asked Leon to come over for it. Oh goodness. Leon. Her shoulders slumped.

"Busy? Wow. I knew you would have moved on." He frowned. "Maybe this was a mistake." His shoulders fell and he looked somewhat lost. He'd come all this way for her. She could at least hear what he had to say.

"What about tomorrow night?" she offered. "We can have a drink."

"That would be great." He leaned in and kissed her cheek, sending a shiver down her spine as she took in the smell of the woody aftershave he always used. "It's so good to see you. You look so cute in this." He flicked the edge of her apron.

She swallowed and murmured something about him looking good too. There was always something about his compliments that made him very hard to resist. The cheekiness of his voice coming from his soft kissable lips combined to make any sweet little words just seem even more glorious.

She had to be careful. "I'll see you tomorrow night. I'll message you with some details."

"I can't wait." He flashed her another smile, which was as expensive as the watch on his wrist, and walked away.

She wrapped her arms around her waist as her teeth chattered. Was she cold or just in shock? It had been like seeing the ghost of relationship past come back and disturb her at work. But was he really in the past, or could he be part of her future again?

"What about Leon?" a little voice in her head reminded her, persistently. She paused at the door. Ashton disappeared into the distance.

She walked back inside the café, her head overrun with thoughts.

"Was that Ashton?" Bebe asked, appearing at the door. Her violet-painted mouth formed an 'o' shape.

"How did you know that?"

Her friend blushed. "You seemed surprised, I guess. What's he doing here?"

"He says he wants to see me. He wants me back. He told me he loves me."

Bebe's eyes widened. "What are you going to do?"

"I said I would talk to him tomorrow night, but…" She brought her hands to her hips and tried to take a deep breath. "I don't know what to do."

"He treated you badly."

"I know, but … as soon as I saw him, the feelings came rushing back at me. That's stupid, isn't it?"

"But," Bebe paused. "What about Leon?"

Michelle hesitated. "I don't know," she whispered. It had all seemed so straightforward with Leon and everything she was working towards, but Ashton's appearance brought back a hint of exhilaration that was both painful and breathtaking, unpicking months and months of hard work to rebuild her life in only a few minutes.

CHAPTER 30

Bebe closed the door behind her at the apartment and picked up an envelope addressed to her from the hall table. It was large and official-looking with United States postage stamps covering the top corner.

She tore it open to reveal a glossy folder with the L'Or Master Class emblem printed on top. Flipping it open revealed a stack of paperwork inside.

The words swirled in front of her as she thumbed through the pages, yet she was able to make out that it was the receipt of her payment for tuition and paperwork to complete for her student pass and class timetable.

The start date was printed in big, bold letters across the top. Three weeks from today. It had come up much more quickly than she had anticipated.

She flicked through the pages before shoving it all into her handbag. Her visa had arrived, but she was yet to book her flight. Removing her phone from her bag, she typed in a flight booking website she used, but instantly pushed her phone back in her bag. She'd do it later.

She pinched the bridge of her nose. Tea. She needed a hot

cup of tea with lots of lemon stirred into it. Sometimes citrus helped clear her aching head.

With the kettle boiling, she opened the cupboards and inspected the contents. There was coffee, but no tea.

Where was Cole when she needed him?

She tilted her head from side to side. She barely had the energy to make a cup of tea let alone go to the store.

She'd go without. She shed her shoes, jacket and bag.

Her head throbbed and red light flickered in the corners of her eyes. She needed to take something else for the pain.

Her jacket and bag dropped to the floor, and she kicked off her shoes as she walked to the bathroom. Fumbling through the cupboard in her en-suite, she found a packet of aspirin and swallowed a couple.

She flopped on to her bed and drifted off, caught between awake and asleep. It was a place where inspiration often struck, but there was no such inspiration now. The pain in her head was uncomfortable, and coloured flecks lit up like fireworks behind her closed eyelids. She scrunched them tight to block out the colour and light, but it made it worse.

Her phone beeped. She reached over and picked it up. The brightness of the screen further aggravated her head and appeared blurry in the darkness. Despite this, she could see it was Harry.

"Hey." She stretched out her arms.

"Want to go out? Can I take you to a movie, or maybe we could see if there—"

"Oh. I'm sorry. That sounds nice, but I have a headache. I'm lying on my bed. I don't think I'll be awake much longer, even though I could kill for a cup of tea with lemon."

"Does that make your head feel better?"

"It usually helps, but I'm out of tea and we don't have any lemons."

"Can your mum get it?"

"She's out, but it's fine. I've taken some aspirin and I'm going to rest up."

"That sounds like a good option. I'll speak to you tomorrow."

After she said goodbye, she held her phone to her chest and thought about Harry. She wished she felt up to going out with him. Maybe to a movie at that old-fashioned cinema, or perhaps the jazz club.

Three weeks left with Harry. That was it. After that, she'd be in New York, and he'd be here.

Sadness settled over her. They hadn't really spoken much about it, but it would be hard to say goodbye to him. Especially after everything they'd shared.

Her daydreams of sexy kisses and soulful crooning caused her to drift back into the space between awake and asleep. This time it was a beautiful dream-like world where her head didn't seem to ache, and her whole body felt lighter.

The buzzer at the door sounded, waking her from her blissful safe place. She groaned. Who was it?

The bell sounded again and she sat up. Her head was so heavy she felt off-balance as if she would topple over like a doll she'd try to have stand by itself when she was a kid putting on make believe fashion parades.

Reaching the hallway, she pressed the intercom and smiled when she saw Harry's face appear on the screen. Her heart leapt. Had he been thinking of her as she had him since they'd said goodbye?

She opened the door and waited for the elevator doors to spring open. When they did, he stepped out and held out his hands to her. "I brought you this." He handed her a box of English breakfast tea and two lemons, bright yellow and bursting with a fresh, citrus scent.

She looked down at the gift, and between the aching of

her head and the kindness he was showing her, she wanted to cry.

"Stay with me." She grabbed his hand and pulled him towards her. "Please?"

He rested a hand against the side of her face and stroked her cheekbone. "You should rest."

"Please."

He hesitated. "Okay. I'll make you the tea at least."

Inside, she lay down on her bed while Harry moved around the kitchen. The sound of the kettle boiling was so comforting, and even just having him there was reassuring. It wasn't charged and sexy like the last few times they'd been out, but it was cosy and romantic in a sweet sort of way.

He appeared at the door of her bedroom and she moved to the side of the bed. He handed her a mug and propped himself next to her.

She sipped the tea and allowed the hot liquid to warm her throat and her body. "Thank you." She sighed. "This is so good."

"Feeling a bit better?"

"A little."

"Have you always had a lot of headaches?" he asked.

"Lately I have. I mustn't be drinking enough water or getting enough sleep." She snuggled into him.

"That's no good. Maybe you should see a doctor. I can check if my GP can see you?"

"That would be nice. That's the thing about moving around, I don't really have *my* doctors or dentists or anything like that. It's always someone new to explain everything about myself to."

"How do you feel about moving around so much? I like travel, but I also like having a base."

She took another sip of the tea. It was the perfect balance

of sourness and zest. "It's never bothered me that much. I don't know any different."

"I suppose not." He stroked her hair back behind her ear. "You are the ultimate citizen of the world."

"Yes. My passport is Australian, yet it doesn't really feel like I belong here."

This was it. This was a good moment to help manage expectations and lay down exactly what was happening between them.

After all, she was a citizen of the world, and she trotted around the globe like a leaf blowing in the wind.

It was the absolute ideal time to remind him she was off to New York in a few weeks, yet even though she opened her mouth, she couldn't form the words. Maybe her head hurt too much for those sorts of conversations, or maybe she was worried that he would leave.

"How's the tea?" he asked.

And like that, the moment was gone. She'd missed her chance, but relief swept over her. She wasn't ready to have that conversation.

Were things as clear-cut with Harry as she'd once thought?

She handed him her cup and snuggled into the crook of his arm. She wasn't sure if she was ready to leave just yet, or give him up. His body was warm against hers, and safe. And in a cocoon of blankets, the sound of rain falling, and the smell of lemon tea lingering, she slipped off to sleep with Harry stroking her hair.

CHAPTER 31

Michelle's phone performed a merry jig across her bedside table, waking her up. She picked it up and squinted. It was a text message from Pete. Actually, more like a dozen text messages, accompanied by photographs of Timothy wearing a baby chef's hat and a T-shirt that said 'My Dad is the Best Chef'.

Very cute, if not mildly aggravating, given she was hoping for a lie-in. Especially as she'd not gotten much sleep the night before.

She texted a short response, rolled back, and looked at the ceiling. She'd been awake long into the night thinking over and over about the Ashton-related events of the day before.

She flung back the covers and went into the bathroom. It was time to get ready for the day, and the competition. Nerves pooled in her stomach but she took a deep breath. And not just about the competition. There was also Ashton to deal with.

While she had been in the shower, the circus had arrived. Laughter and loud voices burst from the kitchen, a hive of activity as she walked into the room.

She reached into the bottom drawer near the dishwasher. It was a drawer that, over the years, had become a resting place for any item that someone didn't want to throw out but which had no other clear use or home. Remote controls to VCRs long gone, phone chargers to models that no longer existed, CDs with no covers and keys to goodness knew what.

"What are you doing?" Pete walked into the kitchen with a box, which landed with a thud on the bench.

"My secret ingredients." She removed the brown paper bag she'd carefully hidden there the night before. She'd ran through exactly what she'd need with Gabriel and stashed all the dry ingredients, like the fine dark chocolate imported from Switzerland, in the drawer to avoid any suspicion. The eggs and butter were in the fridge and, thankfully, they were common items. No one would raise any eyebrows at a few dairy products, but the expensive vanilla pods and tools Gabriel had loaned her would raise much conjecture, gossip, and carry-on amongst her fellow competitors.

Shock and awe was her game here.

They were expecting little from her. She'd never delivered before, but today she had a sense of steely determination. And mad skills thanks to Gabriel's tuition.

"Secret ingredients? What are you making?" Mum asked, setting lemons out in a neat row. Ah, she was making lemon slice—Dad's favourite. She was trying to win him over with tried and true old school classic recipes.

Michelle organised her butter, flour, and sugar into little bowls on the kitchen table. "Éclairs."

"No!" Pete looked up from the kitchen bench where he was removing a pasta-making machine from the box. "Last time you competed you made instant noodles with frozen peas and soy sauce."

"And they were delicious," Michelle insisted, as she

sprinkled flour on her chopping board with a flourish that she hoped looked impressive to her siblings. "But this year, I thought I'd take it up a notch."

"Choux pastry?" Pete let out a low whistle. "That is taking it up a notch. That's tricky stuff to get right."

"Step aside, sister." Lauren appeared with her arms laden with groceries. She dumped them on the table and pushed Michelle's flour out of the way. "The dessert queen is here."

"Queen of burnt chocolate tarts more like," Luke said, walking behind them, a pair of BBQ tongs in one hand and a bag of vegetables in another.

He snapped the tongs together in a quick, short, sharp motion like the claws on a crab. "I don't know why you lot bother. We all know the path to success is simple: charcoal, heat and meat."

"Not everyone likes your caveman food," Lauren huffed. She was clearly still sensitive about last year's oven heating issues.

"Caveman?" Luke's mouth fell open. "This is prime Wagyu steak. This is real food, not that fluffy nonsense." He snapped the tongs again at the array of flour and sugar on the kitchen table. "That's just air and dust."

"I was thinking that was a fairly accurate description of you," Michelle said.

"Oh, trash talk. Bring it on." He puffed up his chest. "We all know the judge likes meat."

"He can't have parsley, you idiot." Lauren pointed at the bag of vegetables. "He'll come out in a rash."

"Thanks for reminding me," he said. "If I don't win, I hope you do, Loz," he added in a way that didn't sound particularly sincere given how much Lauren had just saved his dish.

The doorbell sounded and everyone looked at each other.

"That'll be Leon," Michelle said.

Lauren waved a wooden spoon at her. "That's cheating."

"He's not cooking. Just hanging out. Like Clare is."

"I'm not getting involved," Clare said, walking past with Timothy at her hip, who was still wearing his 'My Dad is the Best Chef' outfit. "I'll be in the living room reading a book."

"What's the book? Better not be a cookery book and you're sneaking Pete measurements and things." Luke gave a warning snap of the tongs.

Clare shook her head and kept on walking. Even Timothy seemed indignant of the accusations and turned his head away from his uncle.

Michelle wiped her hands on a tea towel and answered the door.

"Hey, Leon."

He smiled and her stomach did a pleasant, happy cartwheel. Who was she kidding? Ashton's return may have thrown her, but Leon was the one she wanted.

Friendship plus spark. That was the key. He was right.

She threw her arms around him and kissed him. "Thanks for coming to cheer me on."

"Thanks for inviting me." He held up a brown paper shopping bag. "I brought you something."

"You did?" She took it from his outstretched hand, peeped inside, and let out a laugh as she removed a crisp, white chef's hat. "For me?"

"For you." He took it from her and placed it on her head. "Looks good, I reckon."

"Leon Marek!" Mum appeared at the hallway, wiping her hands on a tea towel. She brought him into an embrace. "How is your mother? And your sister?"

Lauren stood next to Michelle and gave her a poke in the ribs. "That's Leon? When did he become Alexander Skarsgård's body double?"

Michelle blushed, and snuck a look back at Leon. He really was very attractive, and it felt nice to have earned the admiration of her family that day—in attempting to cook a complex dish and bringing home a hot dish.

Dad appeared with a stopwatch and waved it in the air. "Preparation time is nearly done."

She grabbed Leon's hand and scurried back to her position at the table where she assessed everything she needed to do and made a mental note of the time.

"Good luck," he whispered to her.

"Thanks."

The rolling pin fell off the edge, Leon caught it. He handed it back to her.

"He's not allowed to help!" Lauren hissed.

"Clare helps Pete!"

"I'm not getting involved!" Clare's voice rang through from the living room. "I'm in here with Timothy."

"I might go in there too," Leon said. "I don't want you suspended from the competition," he added with a whisper. He ran his hand against her lower back, which was perfectly innocent enough for her family's kitchen, yet sent a delicious, lustful chill down her spine.

The bell rang, and in a flash, the family kitchen and meals area converted into a frenzied movement of Fitzgeralds clamouring about and bickering over space, utensils and oven temperatures.

Despite the chaos around her, she ticked off every step, remembering temperatures, techniques and timings, having committed Gabriel's instructions to memory.

As she removed the pastries from the oven (which she'd watched the temperature of like a hawk, even shooing away Mum when she saw her hovering), she returned to the table to allow them to cool, before she could fill them with cream and ice them with chocolate.

Sneaking a glance in the living room, Leon was sitting on the floor waving a rattle in front of Timothy as he chatted with Clare.

She'd nail this competition, deal with Ashton tonight and then it was all going to be roses from there.

Her life would be back on track thanks to her newfound cooking skills and a gorgeous man by her side.

After all these years of losing, she was finally winning.

CHAPTER 32

*B*ebe awoke to daylight streaming through the curtains, and Harry, lying next to her, fully-clothed and asleep, his arm around her. He'd stayed all night to care for her.

Gazing at him for a moment, she briefly wondered what it would be like to settle in with him and make a home. Would it be nice to stop for a while? For the world to stop spinning?

His eyes fluttered open.

"Sleepyhead," she said, giving him a poke.

"What's the time?" he asked, groggily, stretching his arms above his head.

Glancing at her clock, she told him the time.

"Hey, thanks for taking care of me," she said.

"It's no problem," he said, giving her a kiss on the cheek. "Can I see you after work?"

She nodded. "That would be nice. I'll buy you dinner to say thank you."

He hesitated. "Bebe?"

"Yes."

He rubbed her shoulder. "If you ever want to talk more about your father and that situation, or if I can help, let me know. I worry these headaches may be stress-related if you are carrying that around."

She nodded. But it wasn't just that. How on earth could she walk away from him in a few weeks' time? "Maybe you're right."

He kissed her cheek as they stood in the doorway, prior to him leaving. "Have a good day and I'll speak to you later, okay?"

She rubbed her temples. Time for a shower and a strong coffee to tackle the day at work, yet for some reason, that felt like the least of her problems.

"Are you okay?" Cole narrowed his eyes as she walked into the studio later that morning. "You look pale."

Still? She'd bronzed and contoured and rouged. And she still looked pale?

"Nice to see you too."

"You know what I mean. Now you're here, can we please go over the designs for Andrea? I'm not sure if I have the fabric right and we need—"

"Do you think they would extend my contract here?" she interrupted.

He scoffed. "In a heartbeat. You're brilliant." He frowned. "What happened? Did your visa fall through?"

"No. It's …" She looked down. "I wonder if maybe I should stay in town for a bit longer."

Cole folded his arms. "Stay? I would love for you to stay, but you have been given an opportunity of a lifetime in New York. It's near impossible to get into L'Or."

True. It had taken several attempts, despite an excellent

portfolio and impeccable references, yet, was her enthusiasm waning? "I know, but …"

"But what?" Cole's eyes widened. "Is it hipster boy?"

"Hipster boy?"

"You know, barista boy? Henry?"

"Harry," she corrected him. "You know his name."

Cole smirked. "Okay. I'm teasing. Yes, Handsome Harry. Is he the reason you are re-thinking your destiny?"

"I'm not re-thinking it, but maybe I wouldn't mind seeing where things go with him."

Cole heaved a sigh and crossed his arms. "Cute baristas grow on trees. Master classes like this don't. Is it really worth giving up your dream for him?"

"I like him." The first time they'd shared a bed, it had been pure lust. But last night? That had been something else. Tender, caring and loving.

Surely that was the foundation of something real and long-lasting? "We have chemistry."

Cole held up his hands defensively. "I'm not saying you don't, but go and do your thing. If he loves you, he'll follow. Or he'll be here afterwards. You have been given a gift from the universe to create art."

"I can do that here."

He shrugged. "You could, sure. But you could be huge. Go to New York. Chase your dreams. Send him a first-class ticket to meet you in Europe when you're designing for Prada. You need to do this."

"But…" She wanted to be with him now. "Long distance is difficult."

"Let him tag along if he likes you as much in return. He can pour coffee for the Manhattanites. It's hardly an insurmountable problem."

She inspected her nails. There was a chip in her violet nail varnish. She should slip down to the salon at lunchtime, but the exercise seemed exhausting, as did so many things right now. Being wrapped up in the linen sheets of her bed with Harry stroking her hair was the only place she wanted to be, or had the energy to be.

What did that mean? Was it simply that she was feeling tired and unwell and she wanted to retreat into a nice world of swirling sheets, old movies, honey and lemon drinks, jazz music, and Harry? She rubbed her temple, trying to break up the discomfort. Should she go home and go back to bed? Maybe she could see if Harry would come over too.

Or was it more than that? Did she need a break? To land somewhere for a bit after an endless life on the road. As fascinating and interesting as her life had been, was her body aching for some routine and familiarity?

"Oh, I saw this in the newspaper while I was waiting for coffee." Cole tossed her a copy of *The Age*. "The arts section."

She picked it up and flicked through the pages. There was a lengthy feature article about Petra Baranov, her career and her latest exhibit. It was accompanied by a large photo of her mother, looking blow-waved and impeccable in a crisp white shirt and Ferrari-red lipstick.

"You got a mention."

"*Petra lives with daughter, Bebe, a fashion designer.*" She paused. "Wow. One for the scrapbook." She tossed the newspaper aside.

"What is going on with you this morning? You're all over the place!" Cole paused and tilted his head. "Do you have another headache?"

"Yes." She winced. Despite Harry's tender, loving care the night before and a dose of aspirin gulped down with her double espresso, a painfully familiar ache spread over her temples.

"Oh, Bebe. Not again. I'm worried about you. Have you seen a doctor about this?"

"It's not just the headache, it's this!" She pointed at the newspaper, the photo of her mother staring at her. "I always feel like I can never live up to my mother's name. I have been given everything and every chance to succeed—the best universities, the most amazing experiences, internships—and I'm still a mere passing mention in the amazing life of Petra Baranov."

"I doubt your mother would see you as a footnote."

Bebe scoffed. "She doesn't notice anything I do. Maybe I should just give up and stay here."

"Oh." Cole pursed his lips. "That's what all this is about, is it? You're going to stay here because you think you can't live up to her? How can you achieve greatness when you won't even try?"

"I wouldn't be giving up. But maybe it would be nice to be in one place. I've never known that sort of life, and maybe it's not bad."

"Of course, it's not bad, but you're selling yourself short if you think it's your only option. If you want to stay with hipster boy and work here and buy a house in the suburbs, good for you, but I don't think you do."

Her mother certainly hadn't wanted that. And look at all she had achieved. The sheer enormity of it weighed on Bebe's shoulders. "I don't know."

"Well, think about it, but quickly. This is a big opportunity. I'm going to make you a special tea concoction for your head and I'm going to make an appointment for you to see a doctor." He walked into the kitchen, murmuring something about chamomile and jasmine and antioxidants.

She took a deep breath and opened up an app on her phone, searching for flights to New York. Cole was right. This was an opportunity of a lifetime, and how could she throw it away for a guy she'd only known for a few weeks.

Her finger hovered over a link that said *purchase tickets*. It wasn't time to get cold feet now. She pushed her finger against the screen.

This was her moment. She'd be more than one of the accessories in her mother's closet—the perfect Chanel brooch or the neat silk scarf. She'd carve out her own name. She was Bebe Baranov, and she wasn't just going to live up to her mother's reputation—she was going to exceed it.

CHAPTER 33

The Fitzgerald house was never as quiet as it was when Dad tested each dish in the competition. He awarded marks for presentation, taste, technique and a raft of other categories that made scoring complex and time-consuming.

"Okay. I'll tally the scores." Pete smirked when each dish had been tasted.

Mum was right. His face *was* smug.

"Hurry up then," Dad said.

Pete produced a calculator from his back pocket.

"Is that your old scientific calculator from year-twelve math class?" Steve asked.

"Yep. Still works."

Steve scoffed. "All that university and you can't add up a few single-digit scores?"

Pete input the numbers. "There are those weird half points."

"They're constitutional," Dad reminded him. "We added those in two years ago."

"All right. No-one is disputing that, get on with it, Pete." Steve held up his hands in surrender.

Pete tapped away at the calculator. Silence fell upon the room as everyone drew a collective breath.

"Yes! We won!" Pete jumped up and down. "By one point! I told you! That spanner crab ravioli never fails!"

"One point? Come on, let me see that!" Michelle took it from him. She'd really hoped she'd done enough to win.

She ran her eye down the score sheet. "That doesn't add up!"

"What?" Pete had his arms around Clare, but looked up when Michelle waved the paper at him.

"Pete! Add it again. It doesn't look right."

His eyes skimmed the page and his face fell. "Oh. I didn't add that up correctly."

Groans and a chorus of jeers followed.

"Oh, good work, *Professor*," Steve said. "You're clearly not a doctor of mathematics, though I'm now absolutely terrified about taking any drugs that come out of that pharmaceutical company of yours if you can't add up five scores."

"The half points are confusing." Pete scratched his head.

"Never mind that, who won?" Lauren asked. "I have to get to work. I'm on night shift."

Pete ran his finger down the page and looked up while everyone watched him with bated breath.

"Need a calculator, PhD?" Luke teased.

"No." Pete gave a huff, and shoved the paper towards Michelle. "You won."

"I did?" She added up the score in her head. She didn't want to make an idiot of herself the way her brother just had and jump the gun on her celebrations. She hugged Leon. "We won!"

"*You* won. I don't think I was much help." He planted a kiss on her cheek.

"He shouldn't have been any help." Her sister folded her arms. "That's cheating."

"Congratulations!" Dad pressed the trophy into her hands, which was one of Mum's wooden spoons—spray-painted gold—and mounted on a piece of chipboard.

She held it up and beamed at her siblings, who by now looked either grumpy, tired, or simply over it. But she didn't care. It may have just been a homemade trophy, but it meant the world.

"Should we go out and celebrate?" Leon asked. "My shout."

"Oh. Thanks, but I'm meeting a friend tonight." Her voice wobbled on the word 'friend'.

She looked down at the trophy. Should she tell him about Ashton? He'd been open about his relationship with Pip, but then again, that was just them talking. It wasn't like he was catching up with her for a drink.

Best to say nothing. Deal with it and move on. What he didn't know, couldn't hurt him.

She sat at a table at the restaurant she'd told Ashton to meet her at. She checked her make-up in her compact. Was she too dressed up, or not dressed up enough? She'd wanted to go for worldly and sophisticated but in a casual, 'I always look this way, and oh, boy, am I over you, Ashton James!'.

She'd taken a sip of water but nearly choked on it as she realised Ashton was there.

He'd shown up. It would have been easier if his inner-flake had taken him off to a nightclub, but clearly not. He must really want to talk to her.

They exchanged a kiss on the cheek and some mundane chatter as they ordered a glass of wine.

"You look so good," he said.

So did he, but her inner voice tried to push that thought away, "I should let you know, I'm seeing someone else," she said.

He tilted his head. "Really? And here I was thinking you were pining over me? Well, I guess it's my own fault for letting you go. Who is he?"

"He's a guy I went to school with."

"Childhood sweetheart. How cute." His tone was dripping in sarcasm, which startled her for a moment.

She'd never, ever seen him jealous before. After all, there was little for Ashton to be envious about between his looks, money, and power.

She tilted her head. Was he really that hurt she was seeing someone else?

"Is it serious?" he asked.

She considered Leon her boyfriend. They hadn't had serious discussions about their future, but it felt like it was heading that way given how much time they spent together. "I care about him."

"Guess that's my own fault, right?" Ashton ran a hand through his hair, and looked down. "I never meant to hurt you. There was just so much pressure from my family to step up."

"And get rid of me."

He exhaled. "It wasn't like that."

She leaned back. "Oh, so that's why you broke up with me."

"I needed some space."

"Space to be with Gretchen?"

"She doesn't mean anything to me."

"Your family love her."

He rolled his eyes. "You know what my family are like."

She raised an eyebrow. "Not really. The only time I ever

met them was a rushed introduction on a ski slope." The pain of that afternoon came crashing back when she'd finally thought he'd introduce her to his wealthy and powerful family, yet instead, he'd hurriedly explained that she was 'someone he'd met here.'

It was true, they had met there originally, but he'd said nothing about how they'd been dating, or spending time together or how they'd been falling in love.

"What do you mean?" he asked, seemingly confused.

"They looked blank when you introduced me. They had no idea who I was or what I allegedly meant to you. It was clear that you'd never mentioned me to them at all, and apparently, as soon as you did, it was over." A bitterness rose in her throat as she remembered his mother's humiliating words about her.

How different it had been with Leon's family? To be included and hugged and invited to dinner?

It was how her family treated her sibling's partners. Her parents would never treat someone the way the James's had treated her.

Taking her hand in his, he ran his thumb over hers. "I'm sorry. It wasn't like that. Come back with me. It'll be a fresh start, just you and me. I miss you."

Her mouth fell open. "Go back with you to Canada?"

"Yes. The truth was," he said, a sheepish look on his face, "I was confused. I felt so much for you, but I convinced myself that I didn't. I shouldn't have sent you that text message."

The message that had sent her life crashing down around her? "The text you dumped me with?"

He winced. "That was so wrong of me. I wasn't thinking straight. I was confused. I was overwhelmed with how I felt about you and so very wrong to let you go."

She looked at him. He wasn't one to admit his failings so

she knew that eating the humblest of humble pies wasn't something he had ever really had to do.

Whatever Ashton James had wanted, he had. Money, looks, opportunity…his parents had served up everything to him on a silver platter.

"But what will change with your parents? They hate me."

"They don't hate you. They don't know you. They have survived this long in the public eye because everything we do is calculated and perfect. You just threw them."

"Because I'm not calculated and perfect. Because I get lost and fall off boats."

"Because you're different and free-spirited. And I miss that."

She rolled her eyes. "And the falling off boats?"

He chuckled. "I even miss that as I wouldn't get the chance to rescue you if you're here and I'm back home." He grasped her hand more tightly. "I mean it, come back with me. We'll start again. Look, don't say anything now, okay? Take some time and think it over."

Pull away. Pull AWAY! She screamed at herself yet it was as if her hand was stuck in place. Leon! Think of Leon. But as she tried to focus, Ashton leaned in and gave her a kiss.

A sweet kiss that brought back so many memories. Familiar feelings washed over her taking her back to the ski slopes, the fluffy beds of eye-waveringly expensive hotels, the taste of liquor from expensive cocktails at exclusive parties…She pulled back.

"Think about what we could have together. How much fun we could get up to. It'll be just like old times, but better, I promise," he said.

What was he handing her here? It was like the keys to the universe, yet it left her cold.

She took a deep breath. She no longer wanted the universe. She wanted her job at Espresso Walk, Saturday afternoons at the football with Leon and that dinky, spray-painted trophy now sitting on her bedside table.

"Ashton, I'm sorry that you've come all this way if you were under the impression that I wanted to try again, but I'm seeing someone else. I really don't feel the same way about you anymore."

She removed a ten-dollar note from her purse and slid it onto the table.

"Good luck, Ashton." She stood. "Safe travels home."

A light-headed dizziness set over her as she walked away.

She didn't look back despite him begging her to return. She didn't need to look back. She didn't want to listen to his pleas.

Ashton James no longer meant anything to her.

CHAPTER 34

Bebe carefully applied her winged eyeliner while watching herself in the large gilded mirror in the living room. She took a deep breath. While there was little doubt she was looking forward to the engagement party, part of her wished she could lie on Harry's couch and watch an old movie with him. Her stomach churned. Perhaps she hadn't eaten enough throughout the day. Surely Tessa, being the foodie she was, would have some lovely food at the party. She'd make sure she had something to eat before she had anything to drink.

"Where are you going tonight?" Her mother was working from a small, sleek laptop at a desk on the other side of the room. She was bathed in the light of a desk lamp that was giving the room a golden hue.

"Tessa and Matthew's engagement party."

Her mother took a sip from a glass of champagne and looked thoughtfully at her. "Tessa?"

"I designed her that red dress I showed you, and she invited me to the party." Bebe examined her mother in the reflection of the mirror, waiting for a moment of recognition, but when there wasn't one, she refocused on her eye make-up.

"Lovely." Her mother turned back to her computer and continued to type.

"The dress, or the invitation?"

"Both."

Bebe placed her eyeliner back in her make-up bag. There was no point in pressing. Her mother never noticed her work, or remembered it. She smoothed over her own dress she'd made, a baby-doll style with a high lace collar and a swinging chiffon bodice. She'd piled her hair high on her head and swinging earrings to give it a 1960s mod look. Harry always had a vaguely mod look to him with his dark-framed glasses and a penchant for those skinny ties he wore when they went out.

They'd look cute together. They always did.

Thoughts of her conversation with Cole from the day before flooded back to her. As cute as Harry was, she had to take advantage of this opportunity. Maybe if she did make it to the upper echelons of the fashion industry, finally she'd be more than a postscript in her mother's life.

She removed some aspirin from her make-up bag.

"Headache?"

"I'm not feeling that great, to be honest." Bebe swallowed the tablets. "I've been having a few headaches since we arrived, and today, I feel a bit off."

"Flu?"

She felt her temple. She didn't have a temperature. "I don't think so."

"Have you seen a doctor?"

"No, but I will though."

The buzzer to the door sounded.

Her mother continued to type. "Are you expecting someone?"

"Harry is picking me up."

"The boy from the café?"

That made him sound like he was a kid with a paper route compared to an adult with a job, a life, and hobbies. But there was no point in starting an argument. Bebe mumbled, "yes" and moved to the front door, where she pressed the button that would allow Harry to enter the building and their floor.

She waited at the door, looking forward to seeing him. As the elevator sprung open, her heart leapt and they locked eyes.

He walked towards her and kissed her tenderly on the lips. "You look beautiful."

"You look pretty sharp yourself." She eyed his suit, grabbed his hand, and lowered her voice. This was not ideal given the uncertainty between them, but she also didn't want to be rude and bundle him out of the building like he was a secret. "I didn't know this when we made plans, but my mother is inside."

"The apartment or jail?"

She smiled. He had a way of diffusing any tension with his humour. "Inside. If you'd like to meet her, you'd be welcome, but if not, that's fine too."

"I'd love to meet her."

She nodded and they walked back into the apartment. "Mum?"

Her mother looked up and removed her glasses when she saw Harry. She never liked attractive men to see her wearing her spectacles.

"Oh, good evening," she said, smoothly, as if she had been expecting him all along. She sailed across the room, a kimono-type blouse swooshing behind her. She held out her hand and they chatted, before Bebe reminded Harry they had to leave.

Her mother stood in the doorway as Harry went ahead of them to push the elevator button.

"I like him," she whispered to Bebe.

Bebe tilted her head. "You do?" she whispered back.

Her mother raised an eyebrow. "You're surprised?"

"I don't know; I guess …"

"That I want you to be alone like I've chosen to be?"

She stared at her mother. "I don't think that at all."

"Good. Have a nice night." Her mother kissed her on the cheek and quietly closed the door behind her as Bebe walked to the elevator, Harry holding it open for her.

"Everything okay?" he asked.

"Yes." She slipped her arm through his.

Arriving at the party, Bebe spotted Michelle and Leon, and immediately Michelle had gathered them round for a selfie.

"Look how cute we are?" Michelle turned the phone around for them to see the photo. "Such squad goals!"

Harry glanced at Bebe. "We're her squad?"

"How did the cooking competition go?" Bebe asked.

"I won!" Michelle beamed.

Harry gave her a high five. "Nice work. I hear the Fitzgeralds can get pretty competitive."

"Horribly. It really brings out the worst in our family."

"I wouldn't have believed it if I hadn't seen it for myself. They seem like such nice people." Leon rubbed his neck.

"That's what we'd have you believe."

"Can I get anyone a drink?" Leon asked them.

Bebe put a hand to her stomach. The nauseated feeling from earlier that day had not abated. It was as if she'd been on a boat for a few hours. "I might have something to eat first."

"There's a cheese tower." Michelle's eyes were wide; childlike and delighted. "It's like a cake." She paused. "But made entirely of cheese! You have to see it."

As they admired the cheese tower, Bebe watched Tessa and Matthew as they spoke to their guests and exchanged loved-up glances with each other. Matthew leaned over and whispered something in Tessa's ear. She gave him a feisty smile, then whispered back before catching Bebe's eye and waving. Tessa grabbed Matthew's hand and approached them.

"Bebe, thank you so much. The dress is just perfect." She ran her hand along the folds of fabric. The gown had come together perfectly. It was highly structured with a pull-in waist and the deepest scarlet colour that popped against Tessa's olive skin and dark waves of hair, which were cascading over her bare shoulders.

"You look stunning," Bebe said.

"She does." Matthew looked at his bride-to-be admiringly.

Tessa smiled. "If I get this many compliments, I might need you to design me a wedding dress too."

"Are you still thinking next year for the wedding?" Harry put his arm around Bebe.

"Next year," Matthew said, firmly.

"Late next year," Tessa corrected him. "I have another place to open before we get to the wedding."

Matthew rolled his eyes. "My fiancée, the workaholic."

"You can talk," she poked his shoulder, affectionately.

Bebe knew this game was totally in jest by the way their eyes lingered on each other. She cuddled into Harry, thinking about Cole's words. She liked Harry very much, but enough to throw everything away for?

"Thanks again for the dress, Bebe," Tessa said. "I'll be in touch about the wedding gown."

"Of course." She was about to say that she wouldn't be in Melbourne by then, but she hesitated. There was no reason she couldn't help with the project, even if she was overseas.

As Tessa and Matthew moved on to greet more friends, Harry suggested they dance together. He held out his hand and she took it. They moved onto the dance floor.

"I never thought I'd be at Tessa's engagement party," Harry said, placing one hand on her waist and holding her other hand as they began to dance to the pleasant ballad being crooned by the band.

"No?"

"I have never met a bigger commitment-phobe in my life. She was out of control, dating guys who were just not good for her. I don't think she wanted to see that there were nice guys, but then she met Matthew and things changed."

"You adore her," Bebe said.

"Of course. She's the best boss. She's like family, in a way."

Bebe rested her head on his chest. "Family is important," she murmured.

You and me. Me and you. That was the only family she had, and given she was giving up her search for the truth about Greg, it was all she may ever have.

Harry had his life here: a job he loved, a hobby he loved, and workmates who were like family. She couldn't just 'send' for him the way Cole had suggested.

She breathed him in, looking forward to curling up with him later back at his place. She would enjoy every moment they had before she got on that plane.

CHAPTER 35

"I don't always drink the alcohol," Clare's words were starting to run together. She leaned forward and in a conspiratorial whisper added, "but when I do, it's delicious."

Michelle hadn't seen her sister-in-law this tipsy, but found it somewhat endearing to see the straight-laced, mouse-like Clare swaying from side to side in a blue prom-style dress and silver heels.

Pete walked up to them and handed his wife a gin and tonic, who took it and immediately gulped a mouthful.

"How much has she had?" Michelle whispered to her brother.

He shrugged. "Enough for the moment. Hence the water."

"I thought it was a gin."

"This one tastes different. It must be the mint." Clare hung her arms around Pete's neck. "And you, Mr Fitzgerald, when you drink the alcohol, you dance so good."

She sounded like a drunk meme.

"You don't need to ask me twice." Pete took the glass from his wife, who hissed 'boo' at him.

Clare looked at her brother dreamily, and then turned to Michelle. "Your brother is soooo sexy. When I first met him…"

Michelle didn't need, or want to know where that sentence was going, but thankfully Pete had escaped with her to the dance floor.

Leon returned from the bar with two glasses of wine, and handed her one. "Clare and Pete are great."

"They're a bit tipsy. I guess that's what a night away from the baby does." She looked down at her phone and held it up. "Look how many likes our selfie got already."

Leon took a sip from his glass. "Probably more than I have followers."

"Correct." She stared at the photo. They looked adorable together. She glanced up at the real thing and a sense of relief swept over her. What if Ashton being back had caused her to end things with Leon? She shuddered. It wasn't worth thinking about. She put her phone away.

"I'm going to go to the bathroom, but when I get back, what about a spin on the dance floor?"

He grinned. "Can't wait."

She walked through to a corridor that led to the bathrooms when she heard someone call her name.

Ashton?

She turned to find him leaning on a staircase railing. "Hey, babe."

Her mouth fell open. "What are you doing here?"

He held up his phone and shook it. "Saw this on your Instagram. It looked a bit boring so I thought I'd spice things up. You are so easy to stalk!"

She closed her eyes. Why had she posted that photo? She opened them again and Ashton walked over to her. He placed his hand on her waist. "Nice dress. Have I seen this before?"

She pulled his hand off her. "Ashton. I mean what I said

last night, I'm seeing someone else, and this is a private party, you'd better leave."

A thunderous look crossed his face. "A private party?" He scoffed. "Come on, don't be stupid."

He'd probably never been refused entry to anything in his life.

She crossed her arms. "Please, go. I thought I made myself clear last night."

He stepped forward, and lowered his tone. "I flew a lot of hours to be here and you—"

"Michelle?"

She looked up as Leon walked towards her.

"Are you okay?" he asked.

Her heart raced and her mouth went dry. She mumbled a 'yes'.

"Ah-ha!" Ashton pointed at Leon. "Childhood sweetheart dude?"

Michelle brought her hand to her forehead. She needed to diffuse this situation quickly.

"Canadian dude?" Leon narrowed his eyes.

Ashton smirked. "Yes. Michelle told me all about you and her last night."

Leon looked at Michelle and raised an eyebrow.

"When I told you that I didn't want to see you," she hissed at Ashton. "Please, leave." She glanced back at Leon, an ill feeling settling in her stomach. "I'm sorry, I'll explain everything in a moment."

Ashton looked between them and his mouth fell open. "Oh, so you didn't know that Michelle and I caught up last night?"

"This is your friend." Leon's tone was so neutral that Michelle felt her blood run cold. She would have preferred him to be angry or upset, but this coolness was terrifying.

"And she was very friendly last night." Ashton raised an eyebrow.

Leon took a step towards Ashton. "Look mate, Michelle asked you to leave. This is a private party."

Ashton moved forward, puffing out his chest. "I don't need to listen to you."

"You do. She doesn't want you here. You're trespassing. Get out." He grabbed Ashton by the collar.

"Leon!" Michelle gasped. She didn't want this to descend into chaos. "No!"

"Get your hands off me!" Ashton protested as Leon pushed him against the railing.

"Leave then. Nobody wants you here." Leon let go and took Michelle's hand, and led her back into the party.

They paused back inside the room. "I'm so sorry about that. He tracked me down on Instagram and I told him to leave…"

Leon turned to her. "He was the friend you were catching up with last night."

"I didn't want to hurt you." She should have told him Ashton was back in town and that she'd agreed to have a drink with him, or better yet, she should have told him to leave her alone when he tracked her down at Espresso Walk.

"And what did he mean by 'friendly'?" Leon crossed his arms.

Michelle exhaled. "He kissed me, but that was it. I ended it with him."

Leon took a step back. "Why didn't you tell me this happened?"

"It meant nothing. I told him I wanted you."

"It doesn't mean nothing." He looked at her. "Thank Matthew and Tessa for having me, but I need to get out of here."

"No, please, Leon, stay." She grabbed his hand. "Please, let's talk about this."

He pulled his hand back. "No." He walked away.

"Leon!" she called, but he kept walking. She followed him out. "Please!"

He turned to face her. "No, Michelle. I want to be alone."

Tears stung at the back of her eyes as he disappeared down the stairwell. What had she done? She took a deep breath as she felt the arms of Bebe around her, telling her everything was going to be okay.

CHAPTER 36

"He'll be fine." Bebe squeezed Michelle's hand as Pete hailed a taxi. She'd been able to discretely find a place for Michelle to tell her what had happened while Harry found Clare and Pete to help comfort her after they saw Leon storm out.

"Leon hates me." Michelle's eye-makeup was smudged. Tears further dissolved what was left of her mascara.

"No. He's just upset. Give him some time to cool down." Harry's voice was calming and reassuring. "Call him tomorrow and be honest about what happened. He adores you too much to let this get in the way."

Bebe glanced up at him, her heart filling with warmth at his kindness.

"Come on, let's get you home," Pete said as he held the door open of a car that had pulled up, and helped Michelle into the back as Clare got in the other side. She reached out and gave Michelle a hug.

Bebe waved and blew Michelle a kiss as the car drove away.

"Poor Michelle, I'm sure they'll work through it." Harry took Bebe's hand.

"I agree. Ashton coming back threw her a little, but she really cares about Leon."

"I'm glad Pete and Clare were here for her." Bebe was pleased Michelle didn't have to leave on her own.

"And you. You really helped comfort her. You're a good friend to her."

They were silent for a moment.

She breathed in the night air. Was she a good friend to Michelle? She didn't feel like it with the sneaking around and cyberstalking.

Harry put his arm around her. "Aside from that, did you have a good night?"

"Wonderful." Bebe wound her arm around his waist.

He pulled her towards him and gently flicked at one of her earrings. "You look incredible. The number of eyes on you tonight rivaled Tessa. I don't think you are meant to upstage the bride-to-be."

"Hardly. But what choice did I have? I had to keep up with you." She ran her hand over his lapel. He looked good, as he always did.

As they walked towards Parliament Station, the streets were busy. There were people leaving restaurants, sitting out on rooftop bars, and scores of people in footy scarves and jumpers were out in a beer garden.

"Do you want me to take you home?" he asked.

"Can we go back to your apartment?" she nestled into his arm.

"If you can put up with my snoring."

She laughed. "More like if you can put up with mine."

"Of course, I can. I love you."

She froze. He loved her? She swallowed. The sound of blood pumping rapidly through her eardrums overtook the noise of the streets. Love? No. Surely he didn't just say that. She'd misheard him.

But he did say it. She knew that was what he said. She glanced at him, and he looked down at the pavement as they continued to walk. His hand was tense and rigid in hers.

Taking a deep breath, she tried to steady herself. Should she say something, pretend that she hadn't heard it? Or address it? *Love?* No. She liked him. She thought he was cute and funny and fun to be around. But love? No. That was something completely different.

They walked half a block in a strange silence before he stopped and turned to her. He pulled her into him.

She played with the button on his jacket.

"Bebe, look at me."

She glanced up. Their eyes met.

"I have to be honest with you. I didn't mean to say that to you now."

Relief swept over her. "I thought it was a bit soon. I love hanging out with you, but love? No, this is just fun, isn't it? I'm going to New York soon, and it's not like this was going to last forever." She gave him a bright smile. There was no reason for things to be awkward. Sometimes things slipped out accidentally, or the wrong thing was said. It wasn't a problem. It wasn't the end of the world. Maybe they could even have a bit of a laugh about it.

But Harry wasn't laughing. His face had fallen and even in the streetlight, he looked pale. He removed his glasses and rubbed the bridge of his nose before replacing them.

"Harry? Please say something," she pleaded. There was a way out of this. It could be 'unsaid'. It wasn't too late.

He blinked a couple of times. "I didn't mean to tell you that now, as in today, but one day …"

It was like being hit in the stomach by a baseball bat. Swift and brisk, but the pain rippled, causing little waves of nausea. She'd frozen when he'd said it, and then after he'd raised it again, she'd laughed it off. If there were a way to hurt the man any further, she didn't know it.

He walked to a bench that was near a taxi rank and slumped down. "I never thought of you as just a bit of fun," he said, quietly.

She took a deep breath as she sat next to him. "I didn't mean it like that, but I don't want to hurt you or lead you on."

"I take it back then," he said. "Just pretend I never said it. Pretend I said that I loved your earrings or your dress."

"You did say it," she said. "And I'm not sure if we can ever have that. I am leading you on."

"I'm not imagining what we have though?"

No. He wasn't imagining it. There was an undeniable spark, but what good was that? Or what was to say it would last? Perhaps it would come and go as quickly as things had escalated between them. "No, you're not. But we always knew this wouldn't be forever. I'm going to New York soon."

Harry took off his glasses again and rubbed his eyes before replacing them. "I knew that, but I thought that maybe …"

"What? I'd stay here and give up everything?"

"No." He said this slowly and carefully. "I didn't think about the logistics."

"I've lived my entire life on the move. I don't know, settling down just seems like something that may not ever happen for me."

"Settling down? I never asked you to 'settle down'. I'm not asking you to give anything up, but I thought you wanted to see where this went and then figure things out, not mark it up as a fling and forget about it."

"I never said it was a fling," she protested.

"That's what you meant."

Had she? Perhaps she had, but when it was said with such

a bitter tone in mid-argument, it sounded far different from what she'd ever intended.

Harry removed his mobile phone from his pocket. "I'll call you a taxi."

"I thought you were going to come back with me on the train."

"That's not a good idea." His voice was flat. His usual energy had evaporated. "I don't want to confuse things further, and if that's how things are between us, I think it's best to walk away now."

"Oh." She swallowed. She didn't want to walk away, but she couldn't give him what he wanted. "Of course. I'm sorry."

"Me too."

He gestured to a taxi that pulled up to the curb.

"I'm so sorry, Harry. All the time we've spent together means so much to me." She leaned in to kiss him but he didn't move. She planted a kiss on his cheek and got into the cab.

Harry leaned through the front window and gave the driver the address. He looked in the cabin towards her, and gave her a solemn nod before stepping back to the sidewalk.

The driver pushed the indicator down and pulled the car into the next lane.

Bebe looked back, watching as Harry went farther and farther away, her heart and head trying to catch up with what had just happened.

It was over. She had wanted that, hadn't she? She'd known it couldn't go on, but why did it feel so painful?

CHAPTER 37

Michelle looked at her reflection in the mirror and shuddered. Her eyes were dark and puffy. She looked like a panda thanks to the eyeliner and mascara smudged across her face.

She heard the doorbell ring, followed by a knock on her bedroom door.

"It's Alfred for you," her father said when she opened it.

"Who's Alfred?"

"Tall guy." He gestured to his own height. "He was here the other day." He frowned, as if now uncertain.

Her heart leapt. "Leon?"

"That's the chap. He's in the living room." He rubbed his chin. "I'm not sure why I thought his name was Alfred."

Michelle looked down at her pyjamas and brought her hands to her black-streaked eyes. "Now?"

"Now."

"I look terrible," she hissed, throwing a dressing gown around herself. She plucked a tissue from the box on her dresser and rubbed at her eyes.

Her father shifted his weight. "Should I send him away?"

"No!" She had to speak to him and as much as she wanted to make herself presentable, she couldn't risk him leaving before she'd apologised. "I'm coming."

She walked out to the living room, where Leon was talking with her mother about someone called 'Bob.'

"I'm not sure if he still lives here, but I can ask Mum," he was telling her.

"Leon?" Michelle asked, pushing her hands into the pockets of her gown.

Here he was looking hot in jeans and a polo shirt, and she looked hungover with last night's make-up smeared over her face. She hadn't even brushed her teeth that morning, or her hair.

"Can we talk?"

She nodded, relieved he was here. This was a good sign that he'd calmed down. Maybe they could apologise and start again, and take away this heavy feeling that sat in her stomach.

Her parents were still standing in the living room and she gestured at her father, who nodded back.

"Ah, Jennifer. I need you to help me with something in the garage." He put his arm around her mother's waist and led her out of the room.

"What do you need my help with?" her mother asked loudly.

"I'll explain out there."

"Sorry," she said, focusing on Leon. "I wasn't expecting you, but I'm glad you're here. I'm so sorry about last night."

He ran a hand through his hair. "I don't play games. I knew you had exes. I wish you had told me you were seeing him."

"I didn't want to upset you."

"He kissed you?"

She swallowed, and nodded. "It didn't mean anything."

"I still wish you'd told me. I stood there like an idiot while he bragged about it."

Michelle's heart ached at Leon's hurt and at Ashton's cruelty. "I'm so sorry."

"If you told him it was over; why did he show up last night? Did he think that he had a chance?"

"I don't know. He'd come all this way and I rejected him. He's a brat. He's used to getting whatever he wants."

Leon exhaled. "Look, Michelle. I care about you, but I need to be able to trust you, and after last night, I don't think I can."

Her heart froze, and when it started beating again, it was so loud it was all she could hear. "You don't trust me?"

"I'm sorry," he mumbled, and walked towards the door. He paused, and looked back. "I really wanted this to work."

"Leon, please!" Michelle heard herself plead as the door slammed.

She brought a hand to her mouth and ran back to her room, where she fell onto her bed, and cried as she cursed Ashton for not only hurting her, but causing her relationship with Leon to destruct.

But as she rolled onto her back, she chastised herself. Ashton wasn't to blame. She'd hurt Leon by hiding the truth from him and broken his trust in her.

And for that, like failing her courses, getting thrown out of her degree and finding herself broke back on her parents' doorstep, she had to take responsibility.

After she'd cried so much that she gave herself a headache, she heard voices in the living room and walked down the hallway to find Mum, Dad, Pete and Clare were sitting on the couch, looking over at the entrance to the 'good' room.

It was formal dining room —they only ate in there at Christmas. The rest of the year they ate at the kitchen table.

"What's going on?" she asked.

"Look!" Pete stabbed a finger towards the 'good' room where Timothy was crawling around the table, cooing in amazement as if extraordinarily impressed by his own feats. He paused and looked back towards his adoring audience and gave them a gummy, dribbly smile, as if perfectly cued for the camera before continuing on, making surprised-sounding gurgling noises.

"He's crawling." Tears stung at the back of Michelle's eyes. "That's amazing."

"He's so clever," Mum beamed. "I told you he was. Just like you were, Pete."

"Were? I'm not clever now?" Pete asked.

"Oh, you know what I mean."

Michelle watched as Timothy explored the floor of the 'good' room, and the legs of the chairs. He seemed so impressed with himself, and overawed by the dining table as he strained his little neck up to examine it, a somewhat confused look on his face.

He turned and crawled back, eventually falling into Clare's waiting arms, and was welcomed back by his parents with warm praises and kisses over his chubby cheeks.

Michelle let out a sob, and everyone looked up at her.

"Are you okay, honey?" Dad asked.

She used her index finger to wipe away a tear. "That's so amazing he went off exploring the world and then wanted to go home where it was safe and his parents were." She struggled over the last word as she hiccupped.

"Michelle, are you okay?" her brother asked, almost hesitantly.

"Things are over with Leon." She let out a sniff as the

tears clogged her eyes and caused a lump to form in her throat. How were there still tears left to cry?

"Oh, no! What happened?" Mum asked. "He's such a nice boy."

"Too nice for me."

Clare raised an eyebrow and looked sideways at Pete. Mum stood and pulled her into a hug. "Sit down and tell us what happened."

"Maybe we should go," Clare offered.

Michelle shook her head. "It's fine. I was stupid. Leon is a nice boy and I broke his heart, and mine." More tears filled her eyes, and she wiped them away with her sleeve.

"So, I take it that he didn't calm down after last night?" Pete asked as Clare fumbled around in a giant baby bag, produced a small packet of tissues and handed them to her.

Michelle stared at them absently. Her sister-in-law was always so prepared with things like that. It was probably why she had a degree, a solid career, a husband, a baby, and a lovely house. All those things required a certain level of practical wisdom that seemed to elude Michelle. She wasn't even sure where one would purchase such neat little packets of tissues. The supermarket? A pharmacy?

"What happened?" Mum looked around the room. She narrowed her eyes. "Did something happen last night at the party?"

Michelle sniffed.

"Honey?"

She looked up from the tissues to her father and shrugged. "Ashton arrived from Canada asking to get back together the other day. I met him for a drink after the cooking competition and he said he wanted to try again and he kissed me." She blushed at having to say this to her family. "I told him no and it was over, but last night he showed up at the engagement party, and Leon was hurt that I didn't tell him any of this."

"How did Ashton find you at the engagement party?" Dad asked.

"He tracked me down after I posted some photos online."

"That's what happens when you put every moment of your life on the internet." Pete shook his head.

Clare put her hand on her husband's arm. "It wasn't her fault. Ashton shouldn't have crashed a private party."

"I don't care about Ashton. It's Leon I hurt." Michelle knotted the tissue into a ball. "He won't forgive me."

"Did you tell him the whole story?" Mum asked. "He seems like an understanding—"

"I did. He said he couldn't trust me if I keep things from him. I thought I was protecting him, but clearly not."

"Maybe I could talk to his mother."

Everyone looked at Mum. Pete's mouth fell open. Even baby Timothy let out a harsh squeal as if to chastise his grandmother for such a hare-brained suggestion.

"Mum! He's not a kid in the playground who you can march up to and demand to be my friend," Michelle hissed.

"Well," Mum scoffed and clasped her hands together. "It worked when that Alice was being a little madam to Pete here. I made that princess apologise for throwing apples at him."

Michelle had forgotten about that. Yes, her mother had form on this.

Pete groaned. "Mum!"

"Or was it oranges? I can't remember." Mum looked to Dad for guidance.

"I think it was apples." Dad patted Mum's leg. "Was it the whole apple, or just the core?"

"Does it matter?" Pete muttered.

"How are you feeling?" Clare asked.

Pete rubbed his neck. "I'm fine now, I mean, it hurt when I was hit on the head with them, but it was so embarrassing when Mum told her off at pick-up time."

Clare gave him a reassuring pat on the shoulder. "Okay. I meant, Michelle. How are *you* feeling about this?"

The sound of her name seemed to refocus the attention on Michelle away from Pete's school day woes.

"Like I've destroyed yet another thing in my life. Michelle Fitzgerald: the screw up of the family." She shrugged. "It's time I take responsibility for all the terrible choices I make."

"Don't say that," Pete said. "You've had a bad run of luck, that's all."

"Losing my phone or breaking a heel—that's bad luck. This is just hurting people and wasting everyone's time and money. No wonder no-one believes in me."

She stood and retreated into the kitchen where she could try to find a snack and prepare to eat away her feelings. How much cheese could she manage to eat in one sitting, and more importantly, would it make her feel better?

She heard footsteps behind her and knew it was her dad. Would he finally tell her he was disappointed in how everything had been for so many years? All the failures and wasting of family money spent on her in Canada and university fees, and for what? Or about hurting such a decent man like Leon.

"I believe in you, honey."

She turned to him and hugged him as further tears fell.

When all the pieces of her life fell shattered, she could always rely on her family.

CHAPTER 38

Bebe swallowed two smooth, white tablets with her coffee. Aspirin was next to useless these days with her headaches, yet the act of taking it made her feel she was at least doing something to fight the pain.

Aside from her headache, she knew the pills wouldn't take away the heavy feeling at the pit of her stomach, which had been firmly in place since she'd ended things with Harry. There was no tablet to ease the uncertainty and emptiness.

She ran a hand through the dresses in her wardrobe and finally settled on one she'd made a few months earlier. It was pink and covered in sequins. And despite working in a highly creative industry, it was still a bit much for work. But today, she needed sequins. She needed something to set her spirits soaring in such a miserable time, and if a beautiful dress couldn't help, she was well and truly in trouble.

After accessorising it with a bright pink cardigan and white boots, she walked towards the tram stop, trying to breathe in the cool morning air to ground herself and connect with the earth and its cycles.

"Good morning." Cole looked at the dress as she walked into the studio. "Did you just put that on or have you come straight from a club?"

"I put it on today." She looked down. "I ended things with Harry on the weekend, and I needed a bright look that didn't make me feel terrible."

Cole's mouth fell open, but he promptly shut it again and gave her a concerned look. "I'm sorry to hear that. Are you okay?"

She placed her bag down at her desk and ran her hands through her hair. "I'm fine. It was the right decision."

"Let me make you a tea, and we'll talk."

She didn't want tea. Hot drinks reminded her too much of Harry, but Cole was already boiling the kettle and selecting mugs.

"What happened?" Cole placed a cup in front of her.

"I realised you were right. I can't let anything get in my way." She breathed in the scent of peppermint and jasmine. She wasn't sure what concoction this was, but it seemed fresh and vibrant and leapt out of the cup at her. As much as she had resisted the idea, it did seem to be calming her.

"What are you talking about?"

Bebe took a deep breath. "The other day, you said that I couldn't let anything stand in my way, that I needed to go to New York. You said that boys like him were everywhere."

"I didn't mean if you really liked him!" Cole leaned forward. "Do you really like him?"

"I did, but he told me he loved me. He said he wanted to take it back."

Cole made a face. "You can't take that back. Once that genie is out of the bottle, it's out."

"Exactly!"

"Well, better now than down the line, and while I'll be

very sad to see you go, along with all the fashionistas of Melbourne, you deserve to fly."

Bebe sipped her tea. Cole was right. Of course, he was right. She couldn't let these sorts of things stop her from accomplishing her dream. "I'd better get back to work." Broken hearts or not, she had things to do.

As she sketched and planned, she allowed herself to get lost in her work.

"A visitor for you." Cole's voice startled her.

"For me?"

"For you." Cole waved towards the front of the studio. "You're the only one here!"

Bebe looked up to find Michelle standing in the small lounge area they used for consultations. She looked a little pale but put on a smile.

"Hello. What are you doing here?" Bebe walked over to her.

"I spoke to Harry."

"Oh." Harry and Michelle got on well. It hadn't occurred to her that the break-up might hurt her friendship with Michelle.

"I'm sorry to hear about what happened and I wanted to check you were okay."

"I'm okay. How are you? What happened with Leon?"

Michelle shook her head. "It was a disaster. He dumped me."

"I'm sorry."

"What a pair we are!" Michelle sighed. "I think we're cut from the same cloth!"

Bebe froze. What did she mean by that? "I'm sorry?"

"You know, both of us dating nice guys, too scared to commit. Or something. I don't know, maybe I'm just stupid."

"You're not stupid," Bebe soothed.

"I have a university transcript and a dating record that would suggest otherwise. I seem to muck up everything I touch." She inspected her nails before turning back to Bebe. "At least you had a reason to end things."

Bebe wasn't sure what Harry had told her. "Well, yes, New York."

"Long-distance would have been hard and you're leaving, in what?"

"Two weeks."

"Exactly. Harry's really sad, but I guess there's a reason it wouldn't have worked out."

That was what she'd told herself time and time again. Still, why did doing the right thing feel so miserable?

They needed something to take their minds off the omnishambles that was their love lives, and she knew exactly what that was. It was the physical embodiment of sequins. "We're going out. This weekend!"

Michelle scrunched up her face. "I don't feel like it. Unless it's somewhere we can go and eat chocolate."

"I'm sure there's a cocktail with chocolate in it somewhere in this town."

"But I can't wear pyjamas. Believe me, getting dressed for work is a hassle right now."

"Come on!" Bebe cajoled. A night of dancing and drinks with a friend was exactly what she needed. That usually sorted out a broken heart nicely. "We both deserve a little fun."

Michelle groaned. "I think too much fun is usually what gets me into trouble."

"Come on. We should treat ourselves."

Michelle puffed out her cheeks and exhaled. "Okay."

"And Michelle? I want your measurements."

"My measurements?" Michelle brought her hand to her chest. "What for?"

"I want to make you a dress."

"You're going to make me a dress?"

"A dress. Come on, step over here, Cinderella. We're going to a ball this weekend. And I guarantee you, at midnight, this won't turn into a pumpkin!"

CHAPTER 39

"It's not him," Harry said as Michelle's head turned to the door of Espresso Walk as it opened.

Her shoulders dropped. All week she'd hoped that Leon might come in, silver travelling coffee mug in hand, whistling a tune and ready to forgive her, and try again.

But no.

She glanced sideways at Harry. She'd seen him look at the door too, little doubt longing for his designer in residence to make a stylish appearance. But Bebe hadn't been in. The chance of a reconciliation between them over a chocolate and cherry muffin was appearing as remote as her eating fish and chips around the Marek's wooden kitchen table again.

"How are you?" she asked Harry.

He stacked a pile of coffee cups and rested his hands on the bench.

"I've been better. I guess trying to make things work between here and New York would have been impossible."

He'd said that several times this week. A coping mechanism perhaps?

"That doesn't make it less difficult," she said.

He shrugged and flicked a couple of leavers on the coffee machine. "Yeah," he muttered.

"You should tell her that you could go with her. I'm sure Tessa would give you a leave of absence."

He raised an eyebrow. "Well, thanks for your input, but I don't think I'll be taking your relationship advice anytime soon." He walked towards the kitchen. "Not that I'm sure it's not well-meaning," he added in a tone that Michelle wasn't sure was sincere or sarcastic.

Harry was right—whether he was being ironic or not. She was hardly in a position to be dishing out advice.

She glanced at the clock. She was meant to meet Bebe in a few hours. And despite her friend's enthusiasm earlier that week, Michelle still didn't really feel like getting glammed up tonight, but she'd been so adamant at the time, and had since shown her photos and sketches of the dress she was making, that Michelle had to go out. She couldn't let Bebe's generous offer and lauded tailoring skills go to waste.

And with the clock ticking on when Bebe would return to New York, it might be one of the last chances they had to go out together.

She sighed. Bebe and Leon hadn't been in her life very long, but she'd come to adore both of them.

And like that, both were being taken away from her. At least maybe one day she could visit Bebe in some exotic location for a catch-up, unlike Leon who wouldn't even come back to Espresso Walk in order to avoid her.

That night, Michelle straightened her hair and applied her make-up, pulling her robe and slippers on as she waited for Bebe and her dress to arrive.

There was a high level of activity from outside the

bathroom door. The dull roar sounded like the entire family was there.

She walked into the hall, stepping back to avoid getting bowled over by a nephew, which one she couldn't see as he raced off. "Careful!" she shouted after him.

"Those kids nearly took me out," she told Steve when she walked into the kitchen.

"Kids. Calm down," Heather said half-heartedly to no child in particular, between sips of a glass of champagne. She didn't seem too fussed about their behaviour, however, as she hadn't moved from her spot at the bench.

"Sure you don't want to come with us?" Mum pushed a large container filled to the brim with some sort of chocolate slice into the basket she was packing with snacks and thermoses.

"It'll be fun." Clare jiggled Timothy in her arms. He bobbed his head as if in agreement with his mum. "Though I'm not sure how long this little guy will last at a night match. He'll probably be asleep by quarter-time." She looked doubtfully at Pete.

Michelle smiled at the sight of Timothy in his little Kangaroos jumper and a tiny beanie that fit snuggly against his head. "I would come, but I'm going out with a friend."

"In that?" Dad asked, pointing towards her robe before continuing to tune a small radio he took to the football with him so he could listen to the commentary during the game. "Are dressing gowns the new fashion?"

"No, but I'll tell you what is." She paused for effect. "Bebe is bringing me a dress. She's the most talented fashion designer, and I'm sure whatever she makes me will be cutting edge. It will be amazing."

"Like couture?" Heather's eyes widened.

"What's couture?" Steve asked his wife.

"Like tailored, just for her by a designer." Envy dripped from Heather's words.

"Sounds expensive." Steve's voice was flat. He was probably dreading that couture gowns were going to be another thing added to his wife's 'wish list' after the new car, private school fees and the trip to Fiji his wife had mentioned. Several times.

Michelle turned the tap on for a glass of water, enjoying the reaction. "Yep. A design just for me." She couldn't wait to see what the outfit would be, but given how amazing Bebe always looked, and not to mention the stunning dress she'd designed for Tessa, her expectations were running high.

"Bebe? That's an interesting name," Mum said, thoughtfully. "Is it her real name, or a nickname?"

"No, her real name. Her surname is Baranov. Bebe Baranov. Doesn't she sound like a designer? I can so see her name in *Vogue* magazine one day."

"Baranov?" Dad interrupted, looking up from the radio.

"Yes, that's right." Michelle took a sip of water.

He frowned. "Her mother isn't Petra Baranov, by any chance?"

Michelle nodded. "Yes, she's an art curator. She's in Melbourne for the latest exhibition at the National Gallery, but she's curated exhibits all over the world."

"Well." He grinned a sentimental smile. "That's amazing. She did it, did she?"

"Who is Petra Baranov? And what did she do?" Mum asked.

"How do you know Petra?" Dad usually knew blokes from the footy club with names like Phil and Wayne who were tradesmen or who owned hardware shops. How did he know about glamorous, world-renowned Russian art curators?

"Petra used to work in the office. I don't know, twenty-five, maybe thirty years ago." He rubbed his chin. "A long while back anyway."

"In your office?" Michelle scrunched her face. The office in question was a suburban engineering firm that looked like a 1970s classroom and smelled of old carpet and instant coffee. It was situated out the back of an industrial estate surrounded by warehouses that imported machinery parts and tyre repair shops. It didn't seem a place that someone like Petra Baranov would voluntarily be spending her time.

"Yep. She was at university, but did some filing for us on Fridays. Her parents knew the boss's wife …"

"Oh, Sandra?" Mum interrupted.

"Nah, boss before that. What was his wife's name?" He paused.

Michelle didn't want to get side-tracked into a conversation about the wives of Dad's former employers. "You knew Petra?"

"Wendy!" He snapped his fingers. "That was it. She was married to Craig and they had that place up at Bonnie Doon."

"Oh, yes." Mum nodded. "She was lovely. She'd always send over hand-me-downs for you kids. And some of it was pricey, you know."

This was spiralling out of control. Michelle raised her hand. "Hang on. Can we get back to Petra? Are you sure it's the same person?"

Her Dad made a face. "I don't really know any other Petra Baranovs who were studying art."

Fair call. Michelle blinked. Bebe's mother—a highly sought-after art curator who travelled the world—had once done a bit of admin work at her father's engineering firm.

She had a new wave of admiration for Petra. Perhaps it wasn't impossible to completely reinvent your life.

"Bebe is her daughter?" Dad asked, as if suddenly

remembering the start of the conversation. "Is she an only child?"

What a strange question. "Yes."

Her father frowned. "How old is she?"

"Twenty-six."

"Unreal." He let out a whistle. "Small world. It's hard to believe that baby is all grown up."

"What are you talking about?" Mum demanded, likely verbalising the thoughts of everyone in the room. "What baby?"

"Don't you remember what happened?" He shot her mother an inquisitive look.

"Remember what?"

"Petra had a baby." He said this slowly and carefully.

"I don't even remember the woman, let alone her baby!" Exasperation rose in her mother's voice.

"Arne!"

Mum's mouth fell open. "Oh, my goodness. Arne!" She brought her hand to her heart. "Poor, poor Arne."

"I have no idea what is going on," Pete said, looking between his parents. "Who are you talking about?"

"Arne." Her mother sighed. "He was a lovely man. He used to work with your father and he died in a motorcycle accident. I was so heavily pregnant with Lauren and my hormones were going crazy, so I remember being in floods of tears even though I'd met him a couple of times."

"He was a good bloke," Dad agreed.

"What does he have to do with Petra?" Michelle asked.

"He was dating Petra and he was riding his motorcycle to work one day and he was in an accident. He passed away at the scene."

Mum shook her head. "It was on the news and everything. Awful, awful."

"Petra had to identify his body," Dad explained. "I offered

to do it, but she was adamant she wanted to go. She was a tough cookie, but I didn't realise how much. She later told me she was pregnant, and she and Arne had been planning to marry and move overseas so she could pursue a job at a gallery in London."

Michelle brought her hand to her mouth. How incredibly sad for someone to lose their partner before their child was born. Bebe hadn't mentioned her father, and Michelle hadn't pried, assuming perhaps her parents had been separated or divorced. She'd never considered anything like this.

"How awful." Clare looked on the verge of tears. "Poor Petra. Poor Arne."

Michelle shot her a comforting look. Clare had her own complicated family history with her mother passing away at a young age, and understandably, these sorts of stories seemed to affect her at times. "What happened to Petra?"

Dad rubbed his neck as he appeared to think. "She finished her degree and left the job. She wanted to go overseas afterwards to work. I thought it was a pretty brave thing to contemplate with a little baby."

"What about her parents?" Mum asked. "Did they go with her?"

He shrugged. "No idea. I never saw her after that."

"What a small world that you're now friends with Bebe," Clare said. "That's rather amazing, isn't it?"

Michelle nodded. It was a coincidence. She felt uncomfortable, like she had discovered some secret about Bebe's family. "It is."

"I wonder how long she's in town for. Maybe we could have them over for dinner?" Mum said.

"Why not?" Dad asked. "It would be nice to catch up. I'd wondered how she got on."

Pete looked up at the clock. "Right, we'd better go or we'll miss the opening bounce."

"Go?" Mum's voice rose. "Now?"

"Now, come on!" Pete said, gesturing towards the door, which then set off a few moments of pure pandemonium as people ran through the house looking for scarves and bags, and Mum nearly did her back in lifting the giant basket of food they were taking with them that would probably not only feed the Fitzgerald family, but the team, the coaching staff, and the cheer squad.

"Have fun!" Michelle called, closing the door behind them and taking in the glorious silence of inside the house while hearing Steve and Heather bicker about something outside and Pete trying to figure out who was going in which car.

She did love them, but they were so noisy. It certainly wouldn't have been like anything Bebe would have grown up with.

Michelle turned the television on while she painted her toenails. Bebe had certainly had a hard time never knowing her father, and how challenging it must have been for her mother.

Inspecting her nails, she wished she was getting dressed up for Leon—not that she thought Leon would have paid much attention to the colour of her nails. She should have made more effort with him and she should have blocked Ashton out of her life when he came crawling back.

As familiar feelings of sadness crept over her, she stood and raided the bar in their rumpus room.

It had been the centrepiece of many boisterous Fitzgerald family gatherings, and the source of a couple of alcohol-induced injuries like when Pete copped a piñata stick to the jaw, or Steve attempted to flip a rum bottle like Tom Cruise in *Cocktail* to impress some girlfriend of the time and chipped a tooth as it landed on him.

She helped herself to a vodka from the top shelf and sipped slowly, trying to push all thoughts of Leon out of her mind. She was going out. Getting a fancy new dress. And maybe she'd meet some hot guys tonight.

But none of it brought the same feelings of joy she'd experienced when relaxing with Leon. Part of her wished she were making the most of a quiet, empty house with a bottle of wine and a movie, and snuggling on the sofa with Leon.

There was little point in thinking about that though. It was too depressing.

She looked around the empty room. For so much of her life, she'd been desperate for everyone to be out so she could enjoy the silence, but she wasn't really enjoying it that much tonight.

It was a good thing to go out and Bebe needed to get a bad break-up out of her system too, though she wasn't sure how bad it had been for Bebe. It had been hard for Harry, little doubt. He'd seemed so hurt. He had a sensitive streak beneath his cheery countenance, and Michelle had felt heartbroken as he absently swept the floor that afternoon at work, seemingly a million miles away.

Either way, Bebe and Michelle were both post-break-up, and they could comfort each other and revel in this weird, shared connection they had via their parents. It was almost cosmic that they'd become friends.

Rallied, she settled in front of the television, flicking the channels while she waited for Bebe, satisfied that a night out was the best course of action.

Her phone beeped. *Bebe wants you to follow her trip!* It was a message from Uber. Michelle examined the map. It wasn't too far. She wouldn't be far off. Switching off the television, she placed her empty vodka glass in the dishwasher.

The sound of a car pulling up and with a message arriving on her phone that Bebe had arrived, Michelle opened the door.

Bebe emerged from the car with a garment bag, and once

again, Michelle's expectations grew as she saw the violet-coloured dress her friend was wearing. It was short, showing off Bebe's long legs, and had a fringe, giving it a flapper-style. It was matched with a little black jacket and purple Doc Martens. She looked like a roaring twenties biker chick.

Bebe gave a wide smile and shook the garment bag as Michelle opened the door for her. "I don't want to sound arrogant, but, hey, I don't care because this is perfect for you."

"Really?"

Inside the living room, Bebe ran the zip down the bag, and with an excited flourish removed a black dress. It was 1950s style with a pull-in waist, and a sweetheart neckline. It was dusted with little sequins and beads and finished off with tulle skirting. It was pretty and romantic, and utterly divine.

Michelle ran a hand over the fabric, taking in the little bumps of sequins and beads scattered throughout. It must have taken hours upon hours to make. "It's beautiful." She looked at her friend, tears in her eyes. "It's … it's …" She couldn't even find a word to articulate how amazingly generous this handmade gift was.

"It'll look awesome," Bebe said. "Come on, go and try it on."

Michelle took the dress and walked to her bedroom. After fishing out a pair of red peep-toe shoes and slipping it over her head, she inspected herself in the mirror. Had she ever looked more glamorous? She picked up her phone to take a selfie when she glanced over at the teddy bear she'd won in the arcade game with Leon on their first date.

She put away her phone in her clutch bag. The selfie wasn't for her. It was to present an image to the world about how amazing she looked, which was true, but the truth was, despite the dress, the shoes, and the make-up, she felt empty on the inside.

Bebe applauded when Michelle walked into the room. "You look stunning."

"Thanks to you!" She ran her hand over the dress. "It's so beautiful."

"You deserve it. Oh!" Bebe looked at her phone, then at Michelle. "That's the car."

"Fantastic." Michelle switched off the lights and locked up as they left. Sliding into the car, the conversation of earlier came back to her. "Guess what? I was so distracted by the dress that I totally forgot. You'll never believe this! My dad used to work with your mum!"

She looked at Bebe, expecting a puzzled look or one of surprise, yet her face appeared to be frozen in fear.

CHAPTER 40

A cold hand of fear crept around Bebe's heart and grasped it. This was it. There was no hiding from it now.

"Oh," she murmured and looked out the window at the other cars on the road as they zoomed towards the city.

"Isn't that amazing? What a small world!" Michelle seemed so pleased with her discovery.

It was as if Bebe's head was suddenly empty; she couldn't think of anything to say.

"Bebe?" Michelle questioned. "Isn't it an amazing coincidence? And to think we've become friends and we didn't even know."

She couldn't do it. She couldn't pretend anymore. Michelle was so close to learning the truth, and as much as Bebe tried to deny it, there was no turning back now.

"I knew about it." She swallowed.

The driver glanced at her in his rear-view mirror.

"You knew?" Michelle's voice rose. "Why didn't you say anything?"

Bebe turned to face her friend and examined her perplexed face.

"Why didn't you tell me?" Michelle repeated. "Bebe? What's going on? You look pale."

"I've known for some time. I found a card from your father to my mother, many years ago."

"What card? Like a birthday card?"

"Not quite. It was strange."

"Strange?" Michelle echoed. "I'm not sure what you mean. How was it strange? They worked together; it sounds like they were friends."

Bebe's heart lurched. Was all this insane? What she was about to tell Michelle was based on little more than the fact her mother had always been so vague, and so unsentimental that a card felt like a big deal, but it was just a card.

She closed her eyes. This was madness. It *was* just a card. And the photo? Lots of people put their arms around a friend for a photo. And the blood type? It was rare but it wasn't like only the Fitzgeralds had that blood type …

But what if it wasn't? What if none of it was a coincidence or didn't mean anything? What if a common allergy to parsley meant something? Something important had led her here, at this time, to find the answers to the questions that had haunted her for years.

She opened her eyes and looked at Michelle. "My mother told me that my father was a man called Arne."

"I'm so sorry," Michelle said, putting her hand on Bebe's. "Dad told me he passed away before you were born. That must have been so hard."

Bebe cleared her throat. "That's what Mum told me. But there's this card."

"The card from my dad?" Michelle prompted. "I'm still confused. What did the card say?"

"It made me wonder if maybe …"

"Maybe what?"

"If she was telling me the truth." Bebe looked at her friend. "I would ask her about my dad, and she'd never say anything or was so vague. And she has so little that was his—like two photographs. I began to wonder if he really was my father."

Michelle rubbed the bridge of her nose. "I don't understand. Why would she lie about that? That's a pretty big thing to do to you."

Did she have to tell her friend her thoughts exactly? Michelle seemed so perplexed that she feared she'd have to spell it out.

"I thought maybe she was protecting someone else, someone who was married. I once heard her talk about a man—one who was married and had a family, who hadn't left his wife, so …"

"Bebe! Dad is the most committed family man, father and husband you could find. There is no way he had an affair with your mother. He wouldn't do anything like that."

"People do strange things. Maybe it was just something that happened one time," Bebe protested.

"Don't say that. There is no way he would do anything like that." A tear ran down her face. "He loves my mum, and all us kids. He wouldn't jeopardise that for anyone."

Bebe nodded. "I know, but doesn't it seem odd?"

Michelle crossed her arms. "You have a card, and what … some conversation you overheard when your mother talked about some former lover? Did she mention my father's name?"

"No."

Michelle scoffed. "I don't understand why you would jump to these conclusions with so little information. Is there anything else you have?"

"There's a photo of my mother and your father."

"Doing what?"

"They're at work, and he has his arm around her."

Michelle rolled her eyes. "I've put my arm around workmates for a photo. So what?"

Bebe exhaled. She wasn't getting anywhere with the photograph. "We're…we're the same blood type."

"What?" Michelle's mouth fell open. "How do you know that?"

"You put it on social media when you fell off the boat in Montreal, and I saw a message from your sister and I figured out we have the same blood type. And we're both left-handed, like your father, and you're allergic to parsley like I am."

"But lots of people can have the same blood type and are left-handed or have food that doesn't agree with them. It means nothing! Okay, what else do you have? Do you have anything else? Anything concrete like a birth certificate or a DNA test?"

"No." That was all she had—that and a hunch. Nothing more. She'd chickened out of the DNA test. "I considered a DNA test."

Michelle's eyes widened. "What does that mean? Were you going to sneak a strand of my hair or something?"

"I thought about it," Bebe admitted. "But I couldn't go through with it."

"This is unbelievable." Michelle raised her hands to her temples. "It's a card! I have cards from all sorts of people, it doesn't mean I had love affairs with them."

"You don't understand." This was so hard to explain. "My mother keeps nothing. She is so unsentimental. Why would she keep this card?"

"Did you ask her?"

"She doesn't know I know about it."

"I can't believe this." Michelle's mouth was set in a hard line. "That is so ridiculous."

"But it's not only that. I don't look anything like him, or my mother."

"So? Lots of people don't look like their parents. It doesn't mean anything. Besides, you don't look like anyone in my family."

This wasn't going well. Now that it was all being said out loud, it did sound ridiculous. "I'm sorry. I've clearly jumped to conclusions."

Michelle pinched the bridge of her nose. "I'm confused." She looked up at her. "I don't understand. You knew all this and then realised who I was after we met?"

"Not quite."

"What does that mean?"

"I looked up your dad, and I found you on social media."

Michelle brought a hand to her mouth. "Oh, my goodness. So this is why we're friends? You were stalking me?"

"I wasn't stalking you."

"You didn't come into the café by accident, did you? You knew I worked there, and ..." She shook her head. "I don't believe this. I thought you were my friend." She gave Bebe a desperate look.

"I am your friend. Your friendship has meant so much to me. I didn't want to break your trust."

"You've done that already. Sneaking around, looking us up and intruding in my family's life. Making up these outrageous lies about my father." She leaned forward and tapped the Uber driver on the shoulder. "Can you please pull over here?"

"Here?" The driver looked around at their surroundings. "It's dark. I don't think it's safe to leave you here."

"It's fine." Michelle pulled her phone out of her bag.

Bebe looked around. She agreed with the driver. They were on a busy road, but there weren't many pedestrians around and the street lamps looked dim. "What about we turn around at least and go back to your house and talk?"

"There's nothing to talk about. Please, stop the car." Michelle leaned forward to the driver again.

"But?"

"Please, don't worry about me. I'll get another car." She tapped away at her phone.

"Wait, Michelle. Please!" Bebe's head was hurting, as was her heart. In a few days, she'd managed to hurt and isolate two of the people who meant the most to her since she'd arrived in Melbourne.

The car pulled to a stop and Michelle got out and slammed the door behind her.

"Can we please wait until the car picks her up?" Bebe asked.

The driver shrugged. "That's okay, but where to after that?"

Bebe rubbed her temple. Her head was getting worse. She blinked back tears, partly due to the pain, and partly as she glanced up at her friend, waiting outside for another car.

It had been so hard to make friends when she'd always been on the move, yet Michelle had become a friend. And in one fell swoop, she'd made a terrible accusation that had hurt her friend.

She put a hand up to the cool glass of the window, longing to run to her friend and apologise for everything, but as she saw Michelle's cold eyes, she brought her hand back to her lap.

She'd turned a crazy hunch into an all-consuming obsession that had caused her to alienate a friend. She put her head in her hands and let out a sob for everything she'd lost in a few short weeks.

CHAPTER 41

Michelle could see Bebe and the Uber driver watching her. She tried to ignore them and refreshed her app, hoping her newly-ordered Uber would arrive shortly and whisk her away from the most ridiculous, ludicrous idea she'd ever heard in her entire life.

Oh no. Her heart skipped a beat as she looked at the app. The order hadn't gone through as her credit card had maxed out. She opened up her banking app but her accounts were empty.

There wasn't a train station nearby. Was there a bus stop? She brought her arms around herself. Perhaps she could get a cab to the train station. That could work. She'd removed cash from her account that afternoon to pay for the night out and pay Lauren back for some money she'd loaned her. She'd just have to use that and ring for a taxi. The driver would take cash.

Opening her bag, the blood drained from her face when she realised that her wallet wasn't inside. With the excitement of the new dress, she'd thrown her phone and keys in, but that was all.

She was stranded. With no cash, no credit cards and no money in her account there was no way of getting a taxi or train or anything.

Bebe was still looking at her. She turned her head. *Quick*. She needed a plan to escape.

All her family were at the football game, and Leon? She couldn't see him dropping everything to come and collect her after how she'd treated him.

She tried Harry, but he didn't pick up. Was he still a bit cool with her after her 'advice' of earlier? She wasn't sure so she tried a friend from school, but it went to voice mail.

Her social media accounts boasted thousands of followers, yet right now, she didn't have a friend—a real friend—she could count on.

Finally, with no other choice, she called her father. The football crowd buzzed in the background when he answered. She explained briefly she'd been stranded with no cash, no credit and no way of getting home.

It was a really sad thing to admit to her father, and to herself. She wasn't an adult, she was a wayward teenager.

"Where are you?" he asked over the sound of the siren.

She explained her location. "I can wait until the end of the game."

"No, I'm on my way. Pete and Clare can drop your mother home." She could hear Pete yelling about a free kick in the background.

"I'm sorry."

"If you need me, I'm there." His voice was firm, but comforting and she struggled back a tear as they said 'goodbye'. She could always rely on her father. He was dependable and caring and always there for her.

Anger bubbled up inside her as she looked back to Bebe. How dare she say those things about him? She had no idea what he was like.

With the MCG not too far away, her father's car pulled up and she gave Bebe a final glare as she climbed in.

"I'm sorry for dragging you away from the match," she told him.

He shrugged. "We were losing anyway and it's much warmer in here."

She held her hands up to the heater vent on the dashboard. "Still it's a shame to have to leave early." She knew her father liked to stay to the end win, lose or draw. "I'm sorry."

"These things happen and it's more important to me that you're safe. You know you can always call me, right?"

"I know. Thank you." She could always rely on him.

She looked out the window as they drew closer to home. Familiar streets, familiar take away food shops lit up, familiar parks. She'd been desperate to escape, looking for adventure. To live a life like Bebe, but yet what had it all brought Bebe?

Her father groaned as the other team scored another goal, and turned down the football commentary.

"As I'm not missing anything there, are you going to tell me what happened? I thought you were going out with Bebe?"

Should she dance around the truth? She looked at her father. She trusted him. She loved him. She knew he'd not done anything wrong.

"Bebe made a terrible allegation and we had a fight."

"An allegation?" He scrunched up his face. "That sounds serious."

She looked down. "It was about you."

"Me?"

Michelle let out a sigh. This was perhaps the most awkward conversation she could ever have with her parents. She didn't even want to think about them sleeping together, let alone anyone outside of their marriage. She shuddered.

"Bebe isn't convinced that Arne was her father," she said carefully.

"No?"

"She wondered if you were."

There was silence before her father let out a laugh. A full, belly laugh.

"Are you right?"

He wiped a tear from his eye. "I'm sorry. I shouldn't laugh, but no. Petra? Goodness. What a crazy notion! Why does she think that?"

"She says that you wrote her mother a card."

"Did I? When?"

She shrugged. "I don't know."

He paused and finally sighed as they pulled up at a red light. He tapped his fingers on the steering wheel as if trying to recall. "I could have," he said. "I don't know. I do remember I wanted what was best for her. I thought it was so hard with all you kids when you were little, I feared for her alone with a baby in another country. I may have written her a note when she left just to let her know that if she ever needed anything that we were here. She was a smart woman, but didn't seem to be the sort of person who accepted a lot of help—I mean, we offered to identify Arne, but she wanted to do it herself. It was admirable, but also, grief is hard to handle."

"It would have been hard."

"Very. And she proved me wrong in doing things her own way." He gave a contented smile. "Good for her."

"Why do you think she kept the note?" Michelle asked. "Why did it mean that much to her."

"I don't know. Maybe she kept it as a reminder there were people here in case she ever needed. It's tough being overseas when you're on your own." He glanced sideways at her. "I gathered you found that out in Canada."

Michelle nodded. "I screwed up big time over there."

They pulled into the driveway and her father turned off the car.

"I've made so many terrible errors of judgement," she said.

"You made some mistakes, we all do. But I love the fact you wanted to try something different."

"I spent a lot of your money. I wasted it." She laced her fingers together.

"Having five kids was never going to mean we were rich, but we have never wasted a cent on you. You're all worth it. Giving you kids a good base, a solid foundation in life was what mattered. We paid the mortgage and didn't lash out on things we didn't need."

"Is that why Mum cut all our hair?" she asked.

"Partly. And don't tell her this, but she thought she was quite good at it."

She made a face. "We looked like we were in some sort of weird cult."

"I always thought Steve looked like a convict." He smiled, but it quickly faded. "Around the time Petra lost Arne, I was worried for her. But I thought about it a lot, you know. It made me realise that I wanted to give you kids the solid foundation but as a springboard. It's solid and there, but it should enable you to fly. In whatever way you wanted. So, no, what happened in Canada or at university, it wasn't a waste. Do I wish you would have paid more attention? Yes, I do."

She grimaced.

"It was a great opportunity for you and it sounds like you attended more parties than lectures," he added.

She shifted in her seat. "I'm sorry."

"But you learned from it. Not the lessons I thought you might, but it was a life experience."

"You still believe in me."

He smiled. "Of course, I do."

"I think I want to do something different. It's early days and I'm talking to Tessa, but I think I might like to become a chef."

"Did winning the Master Chef Trophy have that much impact on you?" he asked.

She laughed. "Maybe."

"I think you'd be good at that. What's the plan?" He rested his arm on the steering wheel. It was the engineer in him—he liked a blueprint.

She took a deep breath. "I'm going to shadow Gabriel at work sometimes, go in a bit early and help with the preparation."

"Early? How early?"

She grinned. "Yeah, early. Not really me, is it? But I'm excited for it. If it goes well, Tessa said she'd be happy to look at me doing an apprenticeship."

He nodded, thoughtfully. "We may need to update the by-laws of the competition if you're a professional."

She smiled. "It would be a while until I was considered a professional, but that's the plan."

"It sounds sensible. I'm proud of you."

Michelle leaned back in her seat. She was proud of herself. "I think so." The plan seemed smart, and cautious and considered. It was the sort of plan that Leon would have agreed was sensible and solid. That was Leon, sensible and solid. She pushed him from her mind. "But what if I fail again?"

"We'll catch you."

Tears prickled at the back of her eyes.

"I know why Bebe envied what we have here. I couldn't figure it out at first when her own life seemed so amazing to have lived all around the world, but she's right. I am lucky."

Dad frowned. "Poor Bebe. I hate to think that she had this impression all this time. Arne was a good guy. He would have made a great father if he'd had the chance. It must have been upsetting for her to think her mother was hiding something."

Michelle shrugged. "Petra told her that, but she seemed to take this card as some sort of sign."

"I'm surprised she kept it." He scratched his head. "I don't even remember writing the thing. Would it help if I spoke to Bebe, or to Petra?"

"I don't know and I'm not sure I can ask." She hesitated. "Things didn't end well tonight. I stormed off on her."

He frowned. "Stormed off?"

"I was angry."

"Always a bit dramatic, Shell." His tone was warning, but not mad. "We raised you kids never to leave your mates alone."

She sighed. "I know. I'll apologise I promise. Maybe it would help if this could all be cleared up. Maybe she'd like you to tell her more about Arne."

"I'd be happy to if that would be okay with Petra. I don't want to get in between their relationship."

She nodded. "Thanks, Dad. I don't know what I'd do without you."

"You'd be fine but if you're ever not, you're here. Now, I'm going to have a beer to commiserate this terrible performance," he gestured towards the radio, where commentators were talking about another brilliant goal scored by the opposition, "before your mother gets home. Join me?"

Michelle nodded and walked slowly back into her house, pausing as she viewed the photographs on the wall of their family, of wonky haircuts, homemade birthday cakes, dance concerts and graduations.

But something she had never noticed before was that in every photo they were smiling.

For so many years, it had felt her family were a boring prison that she longed to escape from and find a more glamorous life, yet, someone as worldly and brilliant as Bebe had potentially harboured longing for what she had.

She closed her bedroom door and looked down at the dress Bebe had made her, unsure whether to be angry at Bebe, or feel sorry for her.

CHAPTER 42

Bebe stood in the doorway of Harry's apartment block. She buzzed his apartment but there was no answer.

Her head had been sore all day, but her disagreement with Michelle had left flecks of colour exploding at the sides of her eyes and a feeling that her brain was simply too large for her skull.

Something wasn't right. She'd see a doctor tomorrow but now, she needed someone. No, that wasn't true.

As she'd seen Greg Fitzgerald rescue his daughter from the street, Bebe had gasped and told the Uber driver to depart.

She'd sunk back into her seat and tears had streamed down her face. She was alone, but she didn't want to be. She needed him. Harry. *Her* Harry. Well, not her Harry anymore, but he'd been her Harry. She wanted to feel his arms around her and for him to tell her everything was going to be okay. He'd made her feel safe and secure, and that was what she needed now. She had to find him.

Why wasn't he answering his buzzer? She wiped a tear

from the corner of her eye and checked the buttons again to make sure she had the right one. She did. Was he ignoring it, or simply out?

Pulling her phone from her bag, she called his number, but it went straight to voicemail.

Creeping around the side of the building, she could see light shining through the slits of the blinds that covered his windows. He was home. Maybe he had the music up and hadn't heard the bell or his phone.

She needed to see him.

Glancing around, she located small pieces of white gravel in a nearby garden bed and threw one up so it hit the glass safety rail that edged Harry's balcony. She threw another, and another.

As she was looking for further pebbles, the light on the balcony sprung on, and a figure emerged from the doorway.

"Harry!" she called.

He leaned over the railing. "Bebe? What are you doing?"

"You didn't answer your bell. I needed to speak to you."

"I was in the shower. What are you doing here?"

How on earth could she explain it from the garden? "Can I come up?"

There was a silence.

"Please, Harry. I know I ended things and you have every right to be mad, but I need your help. Please can I come in?"

There was another moment of silence before he heaved a sigh. "Okay, of course. I'll buzz you up."

Relief swept over her, and she made her way to the door. He was letting her in, but she cautioned herself. He was a gentleman; there was no way he'd leave a woman stranded in his garden, asking for help.

Her headache was getting worse. Thoughts swam slowly around her head. She was a little unsure of where they started or where they ended. She needed to get inside to

Harry, where she could sit down. He always made her feel at ease.

A buzzing noise sounded and she opened the front door. She pushed the lift button but couldn't be bothered to wait in the brightly lit hallway, instead walking up the flight of stairs until she came to the second floor. He was at the door of his apartment, wearing a robe, and his hair was wet and slicked back.

"Sorry," she said. "I didn't mean to disturb you."

"Why are you here?"

Her shoulders slumped. He was less welcoming than she'd anticipated.

"I haven't had a good night." She wrung her hands.

"Are you okay?"

She choked back a tear. "No."

He held the door open and gestured for her to come through. "Do you want a drink?"

"May I have a cup of tea?"

"Okay. I'll put some clothes on and boil the kettle. You sit down and we'll talk."

She walked into his apartment, sat on his leather couch, and stared at the poster he had on the wall. *Vertigo*. She looked away. The circles on it were hurting her eyes and aggravating her headache.

Thankfully, he only had a lamp on, but even that seemed bright. She turned her back to it and rested her head on her arm, which she slung over the back of the couch, and listened to the whistling noise of the kettle. It was domestic and simple. The sound of home. Her eyes fluttered shut.

"Bebe?"

She opened her eyes to see Harry dressed in jeans and a long-sleeved Henley tee. With his hair slicked back and his glasses on, he looked like he usually did: sort of retro and staggeringly handsome. She wanted to dive into his arms, have him stroke her temple and assure her everything was going to be okay.

"Sorry. Just resting my eyes." She tried to sit up, but her head felt so strange. What on earth was happening to her?

Harry moved into the kitchen and made two large cups of tea, and sat next to her. He handed her one, but the cup felt heavy in her hand so she rested it against her leg.

"Are you okay?" He inspected her. "You look pale."

"I had a big fight with Michelle."

"With Michelle? What about?"

It was a long story. And there was no place to start other than at the very beginning. "Do you remember that first day I came into the café? When I raced out so quickly and you came after me with the change?"

He gave a small smile and nodded. "I don't think I'll ever forget that day."

Their eyes met and Bebe felt like crying. She'd hurt him so badly, and for what? Because he'd expressed his feelings to her? Why had she been so afraid to stay and see if she felt the same way?

"What about that day?" he asked.

"I didn't come into the café by chance." She looked down into her cup. It was perfect. Milky and hot, and she could smell the sweetness wafting up.

"Why did you come?"

She swallowed a mouthful from her cup. "I was following Michelle on social media and I saw she'd started working there. I wanted to meet her."

He rubbed his chin. "Michelle's nice and a good laugh, but I'm confused as to why you wanted to meet her after seeing her on social media."

"Her father used to know my mother, and the topic of my father has always been one that was a bit vague growing up.

Years ago, I found a note from Michelle's father, and I wondered if there was more to the story."

"More to the story?" he clarified. "What did the note say?"

"That he was there for my mother. But this is my mum; she keeps next to nothing of sentimental value. Why keep a card from an old co-worker?"

"Maybe they were friends."

"Perhaps." She said this carefully.

"Oh, and then you thought maybe this was the man who you overheard your mother talking about?"

She nodded. "I became curious. I looked him up and saw his family and started following Michelle on social media. Something clicked. We had all these things in common, like the same blood type and her family! It felt like the family I never had and I wondered …"

Harry frowned. "And you thought that he was your father? The man who your mother had spoken of?"

"I don't know." Her eyes welled with tears. "I was so confused. I became a bit obsessed with what I saw. My life has always been so busy, and it was just us. I love my mother, but it's also hard living in that shadow. I used to look at Michelle's photos on social media and imagine and wonder what it would have been like to grow up with siblings and the same school and family events."

He put a hand on her leg. "Did you ever talk to your mother about this?"

"I asked her about family and my dad, and she always shut down. Over time, I wondered if that was because there was a secret."

"You should talk to her. You've gotten yourself tied up in knots about something that might just be a note to a co-worker and a coincidence."

It all seemed so outlandish when she said it out loud, but

for years it had rattled around in her head, growing bigger and bigger until the thoughts couldn't be stopped.

"You told Michelle all this, I gather?" He sipped from his cup. "And she got mad at you for accusing her father of having an affair, and you had a fight?"

She nodded. "I didn't mean to, but her father mentioned to her how he knew my mother and it all came out."

"That would have been upsetting for her. They're a close family."

Bebe rubbed the bridge of her nose. "I never intended it to be like that. I tried to take a sample of her hair for a DNA test—"

"What?" Harry's mouth fell open.

She grimaced. "I know what you're thinking. I didn't. I couldn't bring myself to do it, and I tried to ignore it, but then it came out and she stormed off."

"I'm sorry to hear that. I know you two get along well."

"We do." Bebe sighed. She'd always moved around so much that she met a lot of people, but making friends had been hard. She glanced up at Harry. And falling in love had been difficult too. "I miss you." A tear ran down her face.

"I miss you."

She wiped her tears away with the back of her hand. "I'm sorry about the other night. I don't know why I said what I did."

He shrugged. "It's my fault. I came on too strong. It was too soon to be saying things like that. I understand that you probably thought I was rushing things." He rested his hand on hers.

"I panicked." She gripped his hand. "I was worried I was leading you on because I'm going to New York. I even thought about cancelling to spend more time with you here, but I don't want to give up my dream."

"You shouldn't have to do that. Definitely not for me."

"When you said…"

He cleared his throat. "When I told you that I loved you."

Her heart leapt at hearing the words. How she wished she could go back to that moment and react differently. "Yes."

"You panicked, and didn't want to make me believe you felt the same way. I get it."

"No." She squeezed his hand. "You don't get it as I'm falling in love with you."

"You are?" He blinked.

She nodded. "Do you still feel the same way? I know you said it accidentally, but you said that you meant it."

"I love you."

Tears prickled at her eyes. She leaned forward and wrapped her arms around him, his body warm against hers.

Home had never really been a clear concept. It had just been whistling kettles or her mother's capsule-collection wardrobe, or that little wooden box full of memories, but with Harry's arms around her and her head on his shoulder, she wasn't sure if it was home, but it certainly felt like a nice place to stop for a moment.

She closed her eyes, a wave of fatigue sweeping over her, her body slowly winding down and becoming almost numb.

Harry was saying something. It sounded nice, but she couldn't follow the exact words. She was too tired to understand. They were simply a pleasant buzzing noise in the background. It felt comforting and reassuring, just like that place she sometimes went to before she fell asleep.

This time she didn't see fashion or ideas or inspiration—a warm light that she was being carried towards.

The sound of Harry's voice became faint as the light finally went out. She slipped into that space between waking and sleeping, enveloped in a heavy darkness.

CHAPTER 43

The sound of her phone buzzing against her nightstand woke Michelle. She fumbled for it, blinking as her eyes adjusted to the screen.

It was Harry. She brought the phone to her ear. Had Espresso Walk burned down? Why else would he be calling in the middle of the night?

"Hello?" she croaked.

"Michelle. Something is wrong with Bebe; she's at the hospital."

"Hospital?" She blinked and groped for the switch, turning on her bedside lamp. "Is she okay? What happened?" She had visions of the Uber Bebe had left in being involved in an accident, or her falling over, or, heaven forbid, being attacked on her way home.

"No. She's not."

Michelle's heart lurched. "What happened?"

"She came to my place after she had a fight with you, and we were sitting on the sofa. She rested her head on my shoulder and then I thought she'd nodded off, but I realised she'd passed out, and I couldn't wake her so I called an ambulance."

"What's the matter with her?"

Harry went silent for a moment. "They think she might have bleeding on her brain."

Blood drained from her face and nausea pooled in her stomach. "A stroke?" No. It was impossible.

"Or a tumour, or a knock to the head, but they can't see anything that suggests that, and I'm not aware of her sustaining any injury. Did she say anything to you about hitting her head?"

"No." Michelle shivered. Could she have knocked her head after she had stormed off?

"She hasn't regained consciousness. They're doing tests," Harry continued.

"Which hospital? Can I come and see you?" She threw back the covers.

"It's late. I'm sorry. I shouldn't have called."

"No, you did the right thing. I want to come down. Please, tell me the details and I'll be there. Can I bring anything?"

"No." His voice wobbled. He told her the details of the hospital and she promised she was on her way. She found a pair of jeans and a T-shirt from the day before and threw on a long cardigan over the top and a pair of shoes. She didn't know if it matched, and couldn't care whether it did or not.

She glanced at the dress Bebe made her, crumpled over the back of a chair. She physically ached at their disagreement only a few hours before, and Bebe's obvious pain over not knowing her father. Michelle had been so harsh on her. It had been wrong.

She threw her clutch bag from that evening into her bigger handbag and grabbed her keys. She tiptoed through the house so as not to wake anyone else and slipped out the back door, locking it securely behind her.

The drive was mercifully quick thanks to the lack of traffic. She found a car park and made her way through the corridors to where Harry had said he was, momentarily becoming lost before spotting him, leaning against a wall.

Her heart ached. His usually friendly, smiling face was pale. Pure fear, pain, and uncertainty were written all over it.

She rushed to him, calling his name. He looked up and she flew into his arms, clinging to him tightly. His tears spilled into her hair, but she didn't care. He needed to get this out.

He'd once told her that Tessa was like family to him, and she'd thought that a little unusual for a work colleague, but right then, he felt like family to her, and his pain was hers.

"How did this happen? I don't understand. She's so young and fit."

"I don't know." He ran a hand through his wavy hair. "It's all a blur."

"Let's sit down," she said, taking him by the arm and leading him to a series of hard, plastic chairs lined up against a wall. "What happened?"

"She came over to my place, and she told me she was sorry and missed me. I was thrilled. It was like we were going to talk about getting back together." He swallowed and rubbed his forehead. "She was in my arms, and I thought she'd fallen asleep. I moved my arm to lay her down so she could rest but when I did, I realised her face had drooped. I tried to wake her, but I couldn't." He swallowed and brought his hands to his face.

Michelle exhaled. "I'm so sorry."

"I called an ambulance and we came straight here."

Michelle's entire body went numb. Had her disagreement with Bebe triggered this? She didn't know if this sort of issue could be caused by shock. Maybe she should ring Lauren and ask her. "We had a fight. Could the stress have caused this?"

Harry shook his head. "I'm no doctor, but I doubt it. She'd complained of headaches before, but she'd always chalked them up to not getting enough sleep or not drinking enough water."

She grasped Harry's hand and gave it a squeeze. "I'm so sorry. I know that you care about her."

"She's the one. I know I came on too strong and she panicked. I don't blame her. It was too soon. I should have waited and let things happen more slowly, but when you know, you know."

Michelle wasn't sure if she did know. She had convinced herself Ashton was the one, but he most certainly wasn't. And Leon? She couldn't stop thinking about him, but she didn't think he considered her the 'the one'. If he did, he would have given her a second chance.

She took Harry's hand and squeezed it. "She'll be fine. It's destiny, you know. The world can't be deprived of her yet."

"It can't. I don't know what I'll do."

"Can I help? Is there anything I can do?"

He shook his head then paused. "Actually, I need to reach her mother. I have Bebe's phone but it's locked and I can't get into it. I don't have her home number. Should I go over there?"

"How about I go?" Michelle didn't want to leave him by himself, but she also didn't want him on the roads in his current state. She could get to Bebe's apartment quickly at this time of night, and then bring Petra back with her. It would be the simplest solution. "It's not far. I'll take my car and be back before you know it. I think it's a good idea if you stay here." She squeezed Harry's hand and gave him what she hoped was a reassuring smile.

"Thanks," Harry said, his shoulders dropping. "You're a good friend to her, Michelle."

"Not as much as I should have been," she said. The guilt made her feel physically ill.

"I know about her confusion over her father. She told me everything." He hesitated. "I think she was looking for something she never had. You're lucky, Michelle, you know, and I can't blame Bebe for maybe thinking your family would be something nice to be involved in. She wouldn't have meant any harm."

Michelle was lucky to have her family. "I'm sure she didn't mean any harm." She swung her handbag over her shoulder. "Let me collect Petra. She needs to know."

"Thanks, Michelle."

She gave Harry another hug, and walked back to her car. "I'll be back before you know it."

"I'll text you the address." His hand shook as he keyed in the numbers.

After retrieving her car from the car park, she drove towards the address Harry had texted her. There was no traffic on the roads and she arrived at the apartment complex quickly. She buzzed the apartment, but there was no answer. She buzzed again, and finally, a cranky voice answered, "yes?"

"Petra? It's Michelle. I'm a friend of Bebe's. Something has happened. She's in the hospital."

"What?" Petra's voice crackled and gasped. "Come up."

The door opened and Michelle entered, pushing the lift button and cursing how long it was taking. She emerged from the lift and saw Petra in a robe, white-faced at the doorway. "Bebe? Where is she?" she whispered.

Michelle's heart broke, not only for Bebe and Harry but also for Petra. For so many years, her large family had been a hindrance and she'd longed for peace, but she'd always had lots of people around her to love her and care for her.

Looking at Petra's scared and uncertain face, Michelle realised she only had Bebe in this world, and there was a risk she could lose her forever.

CHAPTER 44

In a world between being awake and asleep the mind played funny tricks on one's thoughts. Bebe could hear people talking, sirens and feel her body being moved.

Conversations, words and sounds buzzed around her, little making sense.

She'd slip in and out, but finally, she awoke in a bright room. She gasped for breath.

Looking around, she still wasn't sure what world she was in—the real world or a strange mismatch of being half awake and half asleep. She was in a hospital, lying on a bed and hooked up to a machine. She tried to swallow, but her mouth was dry.

"Hello?" she croaked, and within moments, the room was bustling with doctors and nurses. It was a blur of activity.

"What happened to me?"

A doctor appeared and pulled up a chair next to the bed. The words mushed together. A tumour, but they had undertaken a CT scan, where it appeared to be small and contained, which was a positive sign. They were going to perform surgery as soon as they could.

She felt tears rolling down her cheeks. "I want my mother."

The doctor nodded, and within moments, her mother was there.

"Oh, darling. I should have taken you the doctor myself, I was so worried about these headaches, but you'll be fine, I know it."

Bebe looked down. "I don't know."

"It's not your time."

More tears splashed down her cheeks. "There's something I need to know."

"What?" Her mother grasped her hand tightly.

"Who is my father?"

Her mother stiffened. "What do you mean?"

"Please, you have to tell me the truth. Is Arne my father?"

"Of course. What is all this about? Why would you think that he wasn't?"

"You never talk about him."

Her mother sighed, and sat down, her shoulders more rounded than usual, making her look less like the fierce, and elegant art curator Bebe had lived her life with. "I find it hard to talk about him. I loved him. I still love him." She swallowed. "I never felt that I could move on, and certainly have never met anyone who measured up to him."

Bebe felt tears prickle in the corner of her eyes. She'd never had any idea her mother had felt that strongly about him. "Why didn't you tell me that?" she whispered.

"I only ever sought to protect you from the feelings of loss that I had over him. I felt that if I always went on about him that you would feel so terribly sad, but I didn't realise that you were so curious."

"I asked and you shut me down. You always changed the

subject. I thought you were hiding things, and when I heard what you said once about…" She paused. "What about Greg Fitzgerald?"

"Greg Fitzgerald?" Her mother sounded bewildered. "Oh, I used to work with him."

"I found that card in your things, and I thought…"

Her mother gave an explosive snort. "Oh goodness, no. A nice man and he was very caring, but no."

"Why did you keep the card from him? I mean, you keep nothing. There're so few photos of my father. There's two and Greg is in one of them."

"That's all I had. I wish I had more, but we didn't take many." Tears appeared in the corner of her eyes.

"But the card?" Bebe whispered.

"I kept that card as I needed to remind myself of what I left behind. I kept that as inspiration when I had moments wondering if I was doing the right thing dragging you around the globe. I wanted to give us the world. But now I fear you are disappointed." She frowned. "No white picket fence?"

"I'm not disappointed. I just wondered what it would be like."

She swallowed. She had to ask. "So, the man who wouldn't leave his family? That wasn't Greg."

"What?" Petra's tone was sharp.

"I heard you talking with a friend, years ago when we lived in London. You were in tears and said that this man couldn't be a father to me as he wouldn't leave his family."

Her mother's eyes became watery and she brought a hand to her mouth. "Oh, my darling. I'm so sorry you jumped to conclusions."

"I wondered."

Petra looked down and gave a regretful sigh. "It wasn't one of my finest hours. When you were small, I had a relationship with a director of the gallery I worked at in London. He said he'd leave his wife, and move to Paris with us and we'd be a family together. I had hoped that he would be like a father to you in a way. Of course," she gave a nonchalant wave, "he didn't, so we went without him."

"You and me. Me and you."

Her mother smiled. "Exactly. I knew at that moment that it was only us and it always would be."

"And I've loved it. You've given me an amazing life. It's hard to keep up with you."

"I wanted to inspire you and give you the world."

"You did." Bebe gave a sob.

"But I never meant to rob you completely of your father and I'm so sorry if you felt I did." She stroked some strands of Bebe's hair back. "You remind me so much of him. He would have been so proud of you."

"What was he like? I'm sorry if it hurts but I want to know."

Her mother smiled. "He was a good artist. He could draw well."

He did? "What did he draw?"

"Just sketches, really. Faces. Your drawings remind me of his."

"What else?" She had to know everything. All the things she'd never known about her father, were now hers to find out.

"It was his idea to call you Bebe. It means baby in French and Spanish."

"I know." The name had been a little tedious when she'd lived in France.

Her mother smiled. "But it also means 'traveller' in Latin."

She didn't know that. "That's sort of appropriate."

"It was the most perfect suggestion he could have made." Her mother took her hand and squeezed it. "He'd been so excited that we would all explore the world together. I wanted to keep that dream alive, but I should have kept the memory of him alive by telling you about him. He was a wonderful man, Bebe. I'm so sorry you never had the chance to meet him."

"I'm so scared," she whispered. Would she live? She still had so much she wanted to achieve. And Harry? She'd only just got him back, she wanted a chance with him.

"Don't be," Petra soothed. "I won't let anything happen to you. I promise you that."

They grasped hands and Bebe knew that if any of this was in her mother's power, she knew that she wouldn't let her down.

CHAPTER 45

The words hit Michelle like a truck. A brain tumour? She exhaled as Petra told her. "I'm so sorry. Is she going to be okay?"

"The doctors are confident that we have good treatment options. She's strong and otherwise healthy. She's well-placed to take the surgery and follow up treatment well."

"She is."

Petra frowned. "You're Michelle *Fitzgerald*. I didn't realise when you appeared at my door." Her tone was curious, but her expression emotionless. She was an interesting woman. Tall and thin with a narrow face, even with no make-up in the early hours of the morning there was still a certain gravitas to her. She gave Michelle a once over and raised an eyebrow. "You have your father's nose."

Michelle brought her hand to her nose, uncertain as to whether this was a compliment. Did she want her father's nose? She wasn't sure there was anything wrong with it for a man, but for her? "Err. Thanks?"

"Bebe told me what happened." Petra's voice was smooth.

"We've had a talk, but I'm sorry if she caused you, or your family, any stress in this idea she had about your father."

"It's fine." The disagreement with Bebe felt like a lifetime ago now. And with what Michelle knew now about Bebe's health, it simply didn't matter.

"Greg was a nice man."

"He is."

"He was very kind to me when Arne died." Petra frowned. "What is he doing now?"

"The same. Same job. Same house."

Petra gave a considered nod. "Hmmm. A man of routine. He used to eat the same sandwich every day at lunchtime."

"He probably still does."

Harry came from the room, and while he still looked pale, he was smiling.

"How is she?" Michelle asked.

"She's okay. I'm just glad she's awake."

"Can I see her?" She looked at Petra, then Harry.

"For a few minutes," Petra said. "She's tired and they said she might have some memory loss, but she's not showing any so far. They are going to prep her for surgery soon."

Michelle crept through the corridors until she found Bebe's room and saw Bebe lying on a bed, her eyes closed, but as they fluttered open, Michelle raced to the edge of the bed. "I'm so sorry, Bebe. I know you'll be fine."

Bebe nodded. "I hope so. They think it is contained and hopefully benign. They will operate though and I'm so scared."

"We're all here for you." Michelle grasped her hand. "I promise you. Is there anything we can do?"

"Will you forgive me?" Bebe asked.

"No. I should be asking forgiveness for storming off on you like that."

"What I said about your father was out of line."

"It doesn't matter," Michelle soothed. She didn't want Bebe upset at a time like this.

"The truth was I was envious of what you had. I'd see your family and life on social media and think, maybe that's what my life would have been like."

"But you had so much more." Michelle was astounded. Bebe had the most amazing life. "You've lived a million times the life I have."

"It doesn't mean the grass is always greener. Or maybe it was, I don't know, but I wanted to know what that path may have looked like. I guess I was never convinced of anything, though I did wonder."

A nurse bustled in and told Michelle that Bebe needed some rest.

"I'll visit you soon," Michelle promised. She walked from the room, and finding the first chair, collapsed into it and into tears.

That card her father couldn't even remember writing so many years ago had all been for a reason—so she could find a friend like Bebe, and the thought of anything happening to her was as painful as losing a real sister.

After splashing some cold water in the bathroom over her eyes, Michelle returned to where Petra and Harry were waiting. A doctor had spoken to Petra, and the surgery would be taking place soon.

"You should go home and get some rest," Harry said.

"How long until we know more?"

"We will call you as soon as we know anything," he promised her.

Michelle nodded and walked slowly back to her car, wishing she could call Leon to talk to him and to help her feel better, but she couldn't. Not after what she'd done to him.

Arriving home, it felt like she'd been gone for days, and it felt like weeks since her ill-fated night out with Bebe. She let herself in the side door and walked through the kitchen.

"Hi, honey"

She started. "Dad! I didn't see you!"

He was at the kitchen table with a large mug of tea and a copy of the newspaper folded over. "Sorry. I didn't mean to scare you," he said. "You've had a big day. You were gone long before your mother and I were up. Working early again?"

She sat down next to him. "No. I got a call at two in the morning. Bebe collapsed. She has a brain tumour."

"That's terrible. Is she going to be okay?" He frowned.

"They are going to operate. Apparently, it's small and they are hopeful it is benign. I really hope she will be all right."

"Poor girl. Are you okay?"

Michelle nodded. "I think so. I felt terrible after the way I'd left things with her, but thankfully I was able to see her and apologise."

"I'm glad you got to do that. Is there anything we can do?" he asked.

She shook her head. "I'm going to try to get some rest. Maybe I can go back and see her later."

Wandering back to her bedroom, she sat on her bed. It was unmade from where she'd leapt up the night before, and cold. Very cold.

Thankfully she wasn't due in for work, and with nowhere else to be, it was time to rest and sleep. She pulled off her clothes and pulled on the shirt she had borrowed from Leon when they had attended the working bee at the preschool.

She'd washed it, and folded it, intending to give it back to him, but when things ended so dramatically, she'd taken to sleeping in it.

Slipping it over her head, she sat down on her bed and picked up the teddy bear from the arcade, and hugged it to her. It was soft and felt comforting and homely. After a moment, she picked her phone up, and looked at her social media accounts and one-by-one, she removed the apps from her phone.

She wouldn't go as far as deleting her accounts, but perhaps it would be nice to live her life as it was meant to be seen, not through a lens, filtered beyond all recognition. Life was so precious, why try to alter the reality of what was a really beautiful thing on its own?

CHAPTER 46

Bebe sunk back into the hard hospital bed, her body aching. The treatment following the surgery was going well, yet she still felt tired and weak from the drugs.

"You're doing well," her doctor said, ticking off something on a notepad.

Harry knocked on the open door, holding a bunch of purple tulips wrapped in brown paper.

Despite her frustrations over her how tired she felt after the surgery and the ongoing treatment, she couldn't help but feel a lift in her spirits as she saw Harry's smile. He was there for her. No matter what. Many would run after recent events, but he was still there. With flowers. And a smile.

And sometimes a chocolate cherry muffin from the café.

"L'Or will be starting soon." She looked up at him. "I have my visa and everything is ready for me."

He squeezed her hand. "I know."

The tumour had been benign and had been removed with great success, but there was still a lot of recovery and follow up treatment.

Risks also meant that flying was off the table for her potentially for six months.

She stared at his hand in hers. What if the doctors hadn't been able to save her? What if the tumour hadn't been benign? She'd never have felt Harry's hand on hers, or seen these beautiful flowers, or smelled the freshly-roasted coffee he sometimes brought her, or her mother's perfume.

"But I'm alive, I should be grateful," she said. She was grateful, yet, still. It was hard to say goodbye to a dream.

"It's okay to be sad at what you're missing. But they did say you could go into next year's intake."

"I know," she said, and rested her hand on his. She wouldn't be able to travel for many months so she couldn't even imagine next year, but for the moment, none of that mattered.

She squeezed it. "I sketched again today."

"Don't overdo it," he warned. "It's not a race."

She smiled at his concern. "I'm fine."

"Cole messaged me. He's going to visit tomorrow, if that's okay? Michelle said she'd come in today after work, and she'll bring some muffins with her," he said.

"Yay! The hospital hasn't been as interested in giving muffins to a designer in residence as Espresso Walk was."

"Well, thank goodness we offer a delivery service for our favourite customers." He smiled. "I helped your Mum move those boxes today."

"Thank you."

"She's kind of a taskmaster. I've never worked so hard in my life."

"I know." They had taken a longer lease on an apartment near the water. Her mother had also had a discussion with a local university and a gallery about some work while she was here, but it would be part-time. They were going to have a break while Bebe undertook treatment, and spend some time together, perhaps go down the Great Ocean Road where her father's ashes had been scattered. "Is the apartment nice?"

He nodded. "It's a great place. You'll see it for yourself in a few days."

"They're really pleased with how everything is going."

"You seem so much better." He cupped her chin. "I'm so proud of you."

"I know it's a way off." She hesitated. "When I go back to New York, I want you to come with me, if you'd like."

He smiled. "Are you sure?"

She nodded. "My mother lost my father, and then I nearly lost myself. I want you in my life, but I also don't want to give up my dreams."

"Then don't."

"But what about your job? And your band?"

He grinned. "I'm sure there's a jazz bar in New York and a coffee shop with my name on it."

Their eyes met and they shared a kiss. She wasn't going to go on her next chapter in life without Harry.

"Knock, knock!" Michelle's voice echoed through the room and Bebe scrambled to sit up. "Look at you! You look so great!"

Bebe smiled and touched her head where they'd had to shave her hair for the surgery. She was certain Michelle was being too generous.

"I brought you this," Michelle handed her a cardboard box that smelled of chocolate and vanilla.

"Thank you."

Michelle shifted her weight. "I also brought a visitor. It's my father."

Bebe looked down at the box and ran her finger across the Espresso Walk logo. Greg Fitzgerald was here to see her? Would he be mad about what happened, and what she'd said? It wasn't very nice to have someone accuse him of adultery.

She met Michelle's eye. "Is he angry with me?"

Michelle laughed. "Of course not. He wants to meet you, and he found something at his office that he thought you might like. But if you're not up to it, I can leave it for you. He won't be offended."

Bebe looked at Harry, who gave an encouraging nod.

"I'm happy to wait outside," he said.

She grasped his hand. "Stay." She turned to Michelle. "I'd love to meet your father." She should at least apologise to him.

Michelle disappeared and returned with Greg.

"It's lovely to meet you," Greg said. "I'm sorry to hear about the surgery and the treatment, but Michelle has told me you're doing much better."

Bebe nodded. "The doctors are very positive."

He smiled. "That's wonderful."

She knitted her fingers together and took a deep breath. "I'm so sorry about…"

He held up his hand and she paused. "Don't. It's all forgotten."

"I was so silly. I got this idea in my head and then there were a few coincidences and I…"

"Coincidences?" he asked.

Bebe blushed. "I get a rash sometimes from parsley."

"So do we!" Michelle said.

Greg shook his head. "I don't."

"What!" Michelle snorted. "What do you mean?"

He shrugged. "I just hate the stuff and Jennifer used to put it on everything in such huge quantities. It really ruined her pasta sauces, so I told a little white lie in order to get her to cool her heels."

"But I get an itchy throat." Michelle brought a hand to her throat.

"Maybe you are allergic to it, but I just don't like it," Greg said.

Michelle furrowed her brow. "Maybe I just don't like it either."

"And the blood type. Michelle and I share a blood type." She looked up at her friend. "O Negative."

"Michelle has the same blood type as her mother. I'm A negative."

Bebe pressed fingers to her nose. "I'm sorry."

"I know it must have been hard never to have known your father," he said.

"It was." She glanced up at Michelle. She was lucky. Greg was so fatherly in his navy jumper missing a button at the collar, and his round face—the sort of comforting, old-fashioned, steady figure she'd never had in her life.

He cleared his throat and removed a wooden picture frame from a paper bag that had been under his arm. "This is for you. I thought you might like this." He held it out to her.

She took it and inspected the photograph that lay inside the frame.

He leaned forward and tapped his finger against the glass. "That's Arne. I found this on the hallway wall at work. We're not good at throwing anything out at that office, but I'm pleased we didn't. I thought it should be yours."

Bebe traced her finger over the glass, looking at her father's smiling face. "Thank you," she whispered, blinking back tears.

"He was a good man, Bebe. He had a great sense of humour, he was a kind soul, and he and your mother were a wonderful couple," Greg said. "I'm so sorry that you never got to meet him, but I'm certain he'd be very proud of you."

Tears streamed down Bebe's face as she studied the photograph of her father. Arne. She'd come home for answers. While they looked a little different to what she had anticipated, she finally understood her past and could look to the future.

CHAPTER 47

Michelle grunted as she heaved a large box of empty milk cartons and cardboard packaging into the recycling bin out the back of Espresso Walk. She dusted off her apron and pulled the door handle, but it didn't open. She jiggled the handle, but to no avail. It was locked.

She felt in her pocket for the keys, but they weren't there. She tried the other, followed by the pocket in her apron.

Where were her keys? She brought a palm to her forehead. She'd left them on the bench after she'd locked the front door. Great. She was stranded outside without her keys, handbag or phone.

Pulling the door again for good measure, she then rested her head against it.

This was first time she had been entrusted to close up all by herself and she'd ended up locking herself out. Tessa would think she was an idiot. Probably because she was an idiot. Who on earth did things like this other than her?

Okay. She took a deep breath. It wasn't time to beat herself up. Plenty of time for that later. She had to think. She needed to get back inside to get her things so she could drive home. Or did she? If she could find a way to call her parents she could get a lift home, and then a lift back tomorrow when Harry opened up. At least the premises were secure for the night.

A wave of panic spread over her. She clasped a hand to her mouth. She couldn't go home. She'd left the coffee machine on a rinse cycle. She couldn't leave that overnight. What if the bucket overfilled with water and flooded everywhere?

Not to mention the register hadn't been tallied and there was garbage to take out from the kitchen. That would stink by the morning if it wasn't removed.

Think. She had Harry's number, and Gabriel's and Tessa's, but they were stored in her phone inside. She glanced around. The pharmacy was still open, and she was certain they would let her make a quick phone call, but whom could she ring? She looked at her watch. She could try Double Shot if the pharmacy let her look it up in the directory, in case Tessa was there, but they would have closed by now. She was certain she'd be unable to Google the private mobile numbers of her colleagues.

She took a deep breath. There had to be an answer.

And just like that, there was.

Leon.

If anyone knew how to get in a locked building, it was him.

But did she dare contact him after his last dismissal of her?

But that was personal. This was business. His business. He was like a trained burglar. He could get her into Espresso Walk, retrieve her keys and her bag, and then she could lock up properly.

She was more than happy to pay if the lock needed to be replaced. It was the least she could do given her stupidity.

She'd been putting in such hard work at the café, she didn't want Tessa to think she had been careless.

Pulling her arms around herself to protect against the early evening chill, a little voice told her that she could call any locksmith.

But she knew Leon. She trusted him. It was a shame he didn't seem to trust her, but that was her own fault.

She explained her situation to the pharmacist and he loaned her his phone. She punched in Leon's number.

"Eastern Locksmiths. Leon speaking." He sounded professional and helpful—the knight in shining armour who rescued flustered people who had locked themselves out of buildings.

"Leon, please don't hang up. It's Michelle and I need your help. I've been locked out of work." The words came out in a rush.

The line was silent.

"Leon? Are you there?" she repeated.

"You're locked out of work?" His voice sounded tense.

"I am. And I've left the coffee machine rinsing. And all my stuff is inside. I need to get in."

He cleared his throat. "Okay. I'm on my way." The line went dead. No goodbye, no niceties. He was only doing this because it was his trade. That was it—purely a business transaction.

That was enough to save her work-wise, but it wasn't enough to save her from heartache.

She waited out the front of Espresso Walk. More shops had closed, and the local office workers had, largely, gone home. Even the pharmacy dimmed its lights and prepared to close.

Finally, a set of headlights appeared and Leon's car pulled up. He turned off the engine and emerged from the cabin. "Hey."

"Hey," she said with a small smile.

He stepped onto the footpath, the streetlights illuminating him.

Her heart lurched. He looked so incredibly gorgeous that the pain of not being able to wrap her arms around him or kiss him was almost physical. She'd appreciated how comfortable she'd felt with him over the past few months, but never how excited she'd been to see him. She'd pegged him as some safe option, and he was safe, comforting, and reassuring, but he was so much more than simply that.

There was spark. Definite spark. And it was still there. For her at least.

"This is your place?" he asked, taking a step towards her.

She'd been too busy gazing at him lovingly, and was startled by his question. What did he mean? "Leon, I work here."

He shrugged. "Do you have any proof that you are entitled to enter these premises?"

She stared at him. Why was he talking like a lawyer? She scoffed. "You know I work here."

"You did. How do I know you *still* work here?"

She looked at the café and then back to him. What on earth was wrong with him? "Why would I pretend to work here?"

He folded his arms. "Look, I'm a professional. I don't think it's unreasonable to ask to verify that I'm not helping someone break into premises they have no lawful right to enter."

She gestured at her apron. "I'm wearing the uniform. Leon, I don't know what to say. If I can borrow your phone, I may be able to find Tessa's social media account and message her, or Harry's and ask, but"—she looked down—"I was hoping you'd be able to help me out. I know I probably don't deserve it."

There was a pause and his shoulders relaxed. "Which door?"

"The back, please. It's only the lock. The front door is bolted from the inside as I had to do that first."

They walked around the back alley and she showed him the door.

He removed some small tools from a box and within thirty seconds, the door swung open.

"Thank you," she said. "Wait a minute. I need to turn this coffee machine off." She ran through to the café and flicked a couple of switches just as the water bucket was inches from overfilling and spilling onto the floor.

"Phew! That was close." She picked up the bucket and found Leon's arms reaching out to take it from her. Their eyes locked and her stomach flipped. "Thanks," she murmured and looked away. It was hard meeting his perfect cornflour blue eyes and knowing they probably wouldn't gaze at her in the same way they once had.

"It's heavy," he said, placing it on the counter.

"Yeah." What had happened to their friendly and easy conversation? *Yeah.* That was the best she could come up with like a grumpy, monosyllabic teenager. "I really appreciate this," she said, leaning back against the counter. "I screwed up in not taking my keys with me."

He shrugged. "If stuff like that didn't happen, I wouldn't have a job."

Was he angling for payment? Exactly how much of a business transaction was this? "I'm happy to pay you."

"That's not what I meant. You don't owe me anything."

She gripped the side of the bench and looked down at her sensible black work shoes before looking up to him. "I do, actually. I owe you an apology. I should have told you I was seeing Ashton that night."

"It's in the past."

"But I also need to thank you."

He tilted his head. "Why?"

"When I returned home, I wanted nothing more than to leave here, and get back together with Ashton. But as I got to know you, I saw how badly he treated me compared to how things were with you. It became so clear that he wasn't good for me."

Leon shifted, but said nothing.

"I should have told you about meeting up with him. I told him that night that I wanted you."

There was silence.

"I'm sorry."

He sighed. "I'm sorry too. I got jealous. After you told me about him that night at my place, I looked him up and he's everything I'm not."

"You're better than him," she said fiercely.

He rubbed his neck. "I'm not rich and worldly—"

"You're so much more than that."

"I wondered if you were settling for the primary school outcast, and then in came the cool kid again to sweep you off your feet." He paused. "I adored you from the moment I saw you as a kid—you know that, right? I spent my entire childhood with a crush on Michelle Fitzgerald."

"No!" Her mouth fell open. "I didn't know that."

"I never thought you'd look at me, and that day I ran into you here, I couldn't believe it. It was like a dream come true." He frowned. "But when Ashton turned up, I felt I couldn't compete. It was like primary school over again and you were going to run off with the kids who stole my lunch."

Tears prickled at the back of her eyes. "I'm so sorry."

"I wondered if you weren't over him."

"No. I don't even know what I ever saw in him. I was looking for something when I travelled, something different than my family, but you know what? I was blinded to what was in front of me. You showed me that it's what happens in real life that matters, not what's filtered and put on social media for everyone to comment on."

"I did?"

She nodded. "Yes. I don't need the approval of random strangers. I want to be loved by my family and friends for who I am. I want to build a life, a real one. Here." She waved her hand around the café.

"How's the job going?"

She smiled. "I love it. I've been working with Gabriel, mostly on pastry work. Tessa was impressed and she's going to send me on a couple of courses. If I like it, I might do my apprenticeship with Gabriel. He's an amazing chef. He used to run a restaurant in Italy."

Leon looked at her thoughtfully. "That's great, really great. I'm happy for you."

"It's hard work, but it's worth it." Michelle drew in a breath. This was foolhardy. And while she'd grown, she'd not changed that much. She was still impulsive, and this could blow up in her face like so many other things in her life, but this?

It was worth the risk. Leon was worth the risk. "If you will give me another chance, I promise you that I will never hide anything from you. I'll never make you feel second best as you are my first choice."

He stepped forward. "Really?"

"Truly."

He cupped her chin, and the feeling of his hands on her skin again made her weak at the knees. "I've missed your spark in my life," he whispered. "I've missed the fireworks."

She smiled. "I've missed everything we had—the friendship and the spark."

"I've missed you beating me at Skee-ball," he admitted.

She laughed. "I've even missed your St Kilda scarf."

"I've missed the way you look wearing one of my work shirts wielding a hammer."

"I've missed cuddling up to you on your sofa." She brought her arms around his neck.

He raised an eyebrow. "I've missed your cooking."

"Can I cook you something for dinner to say thank you for rescuing me tonight?"

His eyes widened. "Now you're talking. You can show me all the fancy stuff you're working on here. They didn't give you the recipe for that pecan pie, by any chance?"

She nodded, slowly.

"I have missed that, but nothing I've missed as much as you."

She leaned up and their lips met, butterflies racing through her stomach as she felt her body against his. There wasn't anything about him that she hadn't missed, and as he drew her further in, she'd give anything to make sure that she never missed anything with him again.

For so long she'd thought that kissing him again would feel like home, but it felt even better than that—it felt like she was starting her life again.

ONE YEAR LATER

*T*he yellow cab made its way slowly uptown in the morning traffic. Michelle couldn't sit still. Even after flying for so many hours, the adrenaline was pumping. It simply hadn't been enough to follow Bebe on social media and chat via Skype. She needed to see her.

"Wow."

That was Leon's fifth 'wow' since they hailed a cab at JFK airport. She grasped his hand. "Pretty amazing, isn't it?"

He squeezed her hand back. "It's chaotic."

"I love it," she sighed. The energy was invigorating, she could almost feel the city pulsating with life and excitement as the cab weaved through the streets, each one filled with historical landmarks and buildings she'd only seen in movies.

"Are you looking forward to tomorrow?" Leon asked.

She nodded. "I'm so excited. I can't believe it. Oh! I think this is the street!" They watched from the window as the cab turned and pulled up outside an apartment building with a green awning. "This is it."

They buzzed the apartment and the sound of excited shrieking greeted them, crackling through the intercom. As they walked up the stairs, they were greeted by Bebe, her hair short in an elfin style and wearing an A-line denim dress and sneakers. She hugged them both, and brought them inside the small, but airy and light apartment, that was filled with paintings and sketches in frames on the walls and a drum kit in the corner.

"This is so cute," Michelle breathed.

Harry put his arm around Bebe, who looked at him happily and twisted a pretty amethyst ring on her finger. "It's a great location. Easy for Bebe for L'Or and near the subway."

"I love it." Michelle beamed at Bebe. She looked so well, not just in her cute dress and elegant hair cut, but her friend's smile was relaxed, and there was a certain peacefulness to her. Life here was suiting her. She glanced at the ring on Bebe's finger. Life with Harry was clearly suiting her too.

"Can I get you a coffee?" Bebe asked. "It's not Espresso Walk standard, but the cafetière is passable. And I bought some doughnuts too."

"I'd love some," Michelle said.

"I'll give you a hand," Leon offered.

"How are you going with work?" Harry asked as Leon and Bebe disappeared into the kitchen.

Everything about the apartment was miniature, but it was comfortable, welcoming and in typical Bebe style, impossibly chic thanks to the art, vintage lamp and large knitted blanket slung over the back of their sofa.

"Good. The apprenticeship is amazing. I'm learning so much from Gabriel and Tessa."

"It's a great opportunity."

"They were sad to see you leave." He was missed by everyone, especially Tessa who had relied on him to expertly manage Espresso Walk. "Tessa asked if I could smuggle you back in my suitcase."

He chuckled. "I miss them, but this is pretty good too. I have a sweet job at a place in midtown."

She glanced around and lowered her voice. "How's Bebe? I don't like to push on the email and Skype, but is she okay?"

"She's great." He said proudly. "She's following the plan and getting check-ups. Petra arranged this top doc here who charges more for one appointment than this place costs in rent, but he's been nothing but pleased with her results and scans."

"I'm glad. She seems well, and things between you, well they couldn't be better I'm guessing?"

He glanced towards the kitchen. "Every day with her feels like magic. Especially here." He waved at the window. "It's pretty cool. We're always at some art gallery or play or little jazz club. It's never dull."

"Are you playing?" She gestured towards the drum kit.

"A lot more than I did at home. I found a band to play with. They're a little serious about 'making it big'." He made air quotes around the last phrase, before giving a shrug. "But hey, it's fun and gives me plenty to do while Bebe is working hard in class. They keep her busy so I like to get out from under her feet where I can."

"It sounds like she's loving it." Michelle had thoroughly enjoyed her online catch-ups with Bebe and had heard glowing reviews about the L'Or Master Class.

"It's hard work, and she needs to take it easy at times and give herself time to attend medical appointments, but she loves it. She'll land at a big design house, I know it. She's already had a few chats with the sorts of places that I can barely pronounce let alone afford any of their clothes."

"Maybe she'll be able to score us some freebies."

She glanced up at Leon as he walked out from the kitchen with Bebe, holding two coffee cups. He handed her one, and squeezed her knee as he sat down. A surge of energy hurtled through her. They were here. On this adventure together.

"Bebe said you were going to a few other places after this?" Harry asked.

Michelle nodded. "Down to Miami, then Argentina, then back to Los Angeles and home." They had worked long hours the last few months to save cash for the trip. It had been hard work, but so much fun to look at travel blogs together and plot out their flights. They had a huge map in Leon's living room where they'd charted their course and their savings. There had been a certain amount of pride in paying for everything on her own, though her father had slipped her some US dollars in an envelope as they left the airport, in case they 'needed it'. She was determined not to need it after they had budgeted so carefully, but she was lucky to have it as a safety net.

She'd never known that planning a trip, or indeed, life with Leon could be so warmly fulfilling as they established their routine, and jobs back home.

She'd rallied against the suburban life like her parents had for so long, thinking that her future was somewhere far away from what she'd known.

But what use was glamour when you didn't have friends? Real friends. And family. The people who were there to catch her when she fell and loved her no matter what. The most important safety net of all.

She and Leon would never be globe trotters, but with him by her side and the life they could build together, the world was hers.

They bundled into a yellow cab that Harry had expertly

whistled down. Bebe grasped the bunch of tulips in her hand as she sat in the middle between Harry and Michelle.

"Are you ready?" Harry whispered to her.

"Ready," she whispered back.

"No second thoughts?"

Her heart sped up. There were none to be had. She didn't want to delay this moment. "None whatsoever."

"You look beautiful," he said. "I'm so lucky."

"And you look sharp." She adjusted the silver tie pin she'd found at a market. It sat perfectly against his navy skinny tie. "Hang on. Isn't it bad luck to see the bride before the wedding?"

He rolled his eyes. "Bad luck? Pfft. Bring it on, we can handle it. We can handle anything. I think we have already."

"We have." She smiled.

"This is the most exciting thing I have ever done," Michelle declared. She smiled at Bebe, who grinned back, and clutched her hand.

"Are you sure we couldn't have taken another cab?" Leon asked from the front seat of the car.

"No!" Michelle said. "This is fun! This is so squad goals!" She tapped Leon on the shoulder and handed him her phone. "Take a selfie of us, you've got the best view and the longest arms."

"I thought you were off your social media accounts," Harry said. "And last time I checked, your profile picture was a North Melbourne football scarf."

"Oh, this isn't for social media." Michelle grinned. "Just for me."

"Say 'wedding'!" Leon said, holding the phone up and they all grinned.

Bebe glanced at Michelle. She may not have been her sister, but she felt as real as what Bebe imagined one would as they had messaged, Skyped and emailed constantly since Bebe and Harry had left for New York six months earlier.

"Look at you two! How cute you are!" Michelle cooed to Harry and Bebe when Leon handed her back the phone. "You are the most beautiful bride ever, Bebe. You made yourself the perfect dress too."

Bebe looked down at her dress. It was a white lace shift with an elaborate 1960s amethyst brooch pinned at the waist that she'd found at a vintage store downtown.

"Can you send me a copy of the photo, please? I promised Cole." Bebe had designed her gown with Cole's careful input via teleconferences and was looking forward to seeing him when he visited in a few months.

She glanced across at Harry in his retro-inspired suit and smiled. He gave her a wink and squeezed her hand. She'd gone to Melbourne thinking that she may have found the truth out about her father. She did, but she also found Harry and new friends like Michelle and Cole. It hadn't been the easiest time in her life between her incessant worries about her parentage and then the tumour, but it had led her to the right people, the right moments and the right places.

Arriving at Central Park, they tumbled out of the cab and found her mother waiting, along with the celebrant.

"You look beautiful." Her mother kissed her on the cheek and took her hand. "I have something for you." She removed a small silver ring from her clutch bag and handed it to Bebe. "Your father gave me this before he died. We spoke loosely of marriage, but we couldn't afford a proper engagement ring. This was his, and he gave it to me before he passed away."

It was the ring. One of the items in the box that Bebe had puzzled over for so many years.

"I want you to have it."

"Are you sure?" Bebe asked.

"I'm sure."

Bebe slipped it onto her thumb. It was too big for her other fingers, but it sat perfectly. She'd never known her father, and never would, but the pieces she'd been able to put together painted the picture of a man who she admired and loved in her own way. Having the ring he'd worn and given her mother as a symbol of the life they intended to share, but never got to, nestled on her finger made her feel more connected to him than ever. "Thank you," she whispered to her mother.

She clasped her mother's arm and they walked towards the celebrant, where Harry was waiting, along with Leon and Michelle.

Harry held out his hand, and giving her mother's arm a squeeze, she stepped forward to take Harry's.

"I love you," he whispered to her.

"I love you too."

She glanced back, and smiled at her mother. It would still always be *you and me, me and you*, yet with Harry, she felt she had a kindred leaf spirit to blow along sidewalks be they in Melbourne or New York or anywhere else.

As long as they were together, it would feel like home.

THE END

THE THINGS WE ALWAYS WANTED

CAFÉ CHRONICLES BOOK 0.5

How far do we go for love when worlds collide?

Clare Harrison has always felt invisible to everyone other than her grandmother. While she has everything she wants in her career, something is missing: someone to love and a family of her own.

Pete Fitzgerald has family. Too much. The Fitzgeralds are loud, intrusive and always trying to set him up with the daughters of family friends. As he completes his PhD and contemplates moving back to his hometown, he's determined to meet 'the one' and hopes she can cope with his overbearing family.

When Clare and Pete meet, they are instantly drawn to one another. They want the same things in life, but as Pete's family unwittingly intrudes on his relationship and Clare's worries for her grandmother's health mount, their worlds begin to seem further apart than either of them thought.

Can they juggle the needs of their families to give them everything they always wanted, or are there too many differences to overcome?

The Things We Always Wanted is a romantic prequel novella to the Café Chronicles series by award-winning author, Megan Mayfair.

THE THINGS WE LEAVE UNSAID

CAFÉ CHRONICLES BOOK 1

Is it the things we don't say that haunt us the most?

Clare is anxious to start a family with adoring husband, Pete. When she takes on the seemingly simple task of obtaining her late mother's birth certificate, she finds herself in a family history search that will challenge everything she thought she knew about her life.

Scarred by her parents' ill-fated marriage, Tessa lives by three rules – dating unavailable men, building her café into a food empire, and avoiding her father. However, when her carefully planned life is thrown into chaos, Tessa is forced to decide which of these rules she's willing to break.

As Clare and Tessa's paths cross and their friendship grows, can they both finally unlock their family secrets in order to realise their futures?

The Things We Leave Unsaid is the first novel in the Café Chronicles series by award-winning author, Megan Mayfair.

THE THINGS WE PROMISED OURSELVES

CAFÉ CHRONICLES BOOK 3

Should we hold on to the promises we make ourselves?

Lottie De Luca lives to run, but since a terrifying attack while training, she's lost her passion and her way. Her career as a real estate agent is suffering, and she's disconnected from her friends. Will a chance meeting with an off-duty police officer help re-start her life?

Jess Goldsmith is a woman on the run after calling off her wedding to her childhood sweetheart, Hamish. Leasing an apartment from Lottie, she finds her a supportive friend as she deals with the fall-out of her disastrous engagement. When a terrible accident occurs, Jess fears her past mistakes have come back to haunt her.

As Lottie and Jess's friendship grows, both are forced to decide between loyalty, friendship and lasting love. Will they be able to keep the promises they made each other, let alone the ones they made to themselves?

The Things We Promised Ourselves is the third novel in the Café Chronicles series by award-winning author, Megan Mayfair.

ABOUT THE AUTHOR

Megan Mayfair writes fiction with a dash of intrigue, a sprinkling of humour and a spoonful of romance. And a lot of heart.

Her book, Tangled Vines, won the Romance Writers of Australia Romantic Book of the Year (Ruby) Award in 2019 in the romantic elements category, and she has been a finalist in the Australian Romance Readers Association Awards in categories including Favourite Australian Romance Writer.

She lives in Melbourne with her husband and three young children, and works in public relations. When not writing fiction, or press releases, she enjoys drinking coffee and spending time with her family.

facebook.com/meganmayfairwrites
twitter.com/MayfairMegan
instagram.com/meganmayfairwrites
pinterest.com/meganmayfairwrites
bookbub.com/profile/megan-mayfair

ALSO BY MEGAN MAYFAIR

The Café Chronicles

The Things We Always Wanted (Café Chronicles 0.5)
The Things We Leave Unsaid (Café Chronicles 1)
The Things We Never Knew (Café Chronicles 2)
The Things We Promised Ourselves (Café Chronicles 3)

The Tangled Vines Saga

A Matter of Heart (Tangled Vines Saga 0.5) *(Available as a free download)*
Tangled Vines (Tangled Vines Saga 1)
The Problem with Perfect (Tangled Vines Saga 2)
A Spoonful of Sugar (Tangled Vines Saga 3)

Anthologies

Christmas on Hope Street

To learn about upcoming releases, visit www.meganmayfair.com or sign up to receive her newsletter at www.meganmayfair.com/subscribe. Subscribers will receive a free copy of her novelette, A Matter of Heart, to download.

Milton Keynes UK
Ingram Content Group UK Ltd.
UKHW030238030224
437175UK00001B/25